Praise for *Blind Ambitions*

"This novel does have a vitality and energy that makes it hard to put down. Files packs her flashy and irreverent tale with Hollywood shoptalk and doesn't skimp on Technicolor local detail."
—*Publishers Weekly*

"Served up Lolita Files–style, as only she can do it, *Blind Ambitions* brings to life an entire new cast of hilarious, intriguing, and sometimes tragic characters in fresh situations—with west coast flava!"
—Eric Jerome Dickey, *The New York Times* bestselling author of *Liar's Game*

"A fast, entertaining read that is sexy and suspenseful."
—Karen Stoner, *Chicago Tribune*

"Workin' the pen like only Lolita Files can, she writes with an excellence and flair unsurpassed—often emulated, but never quite duplicated. Her talent is on a plateau unaccompanied."
—Olivia Ridgell, *Chicago Defender*

"With three sharply drawn, strong, and spirited women at its center, *Blind Ambitions* unfolds, a blockbuster plot pulsing with intrigue. . . . Propelled by flesh-and-blood characters, plus plenty of warmth, fire, humor, and insight, *Blind Ambitions* is sure to thrill Lolita Files's legions of fans and win new readers."
—Jaqueta Cox, *Miami Times*

ALSO BY LOLITA FILES

Scenes from a Sistah

Getting to the Good Part

BLIND AMBITIONS

LOLITA FILES

SCRIBNER PAPERBACK FICTION
Published by Simon & Schuster
NEW YORK LONDON TORONTO SYDNEY SINGAPORE

SCRIBNER PAPERBACK FICTION
Simon & Schuster, Inc.
Rockefeller Center
1230 Avenue of the Americas
New York, NY 10020

First Scribner Paperback Fiction edition 2001

For information regarding special discounts for bulk purchases, please contact Simon & Schuster Special Sales at 1-800-456-6798 or *business@simonandschuster.com*

Designed by Bonni Leon-Berman

Manufactured in the United States of America

10 9 8 7 6 5 4 3 2 1

The Library of Congress has cataloged the
Simon & Schuster edition as follows:
Files, Lolita.
Blind ambitions / Lolita Files.
p. cm.
1. Hollywood (Los Angeles, Calif.)—Fiction. 2. Motion picture industry—Fiction. 3. Women—Fiction. I. Title.

PS3556.I4257 B58 2000
813'.54—dc21 00-024796

ISBN 0-684-87144-0
0-684-87145-9 (Pbk)

This book is dedicated to the crown jewel of my life, my mother,

Lillie B. Files.

And to the loving memories of my father,

Arthur James Files, Sr.,

who was my biggest fan and inspired me in so many ways,

and

Carolyn Y. Brackett,

who touched so many with her love and her life.

CONTENTS

PROLOGUE

"Why you sittin' way over there? Slide over here a little closer to me."

Nervous, the girl cautiously scooted across the seat. They were at a dark corner of a neighborhood park. She had been patiently—no, anxiously—waiting for this date for a very long time. At last, it had come.

When they got to the park, they had gotten out of the car, taken what must have been the shortest walk in history, and, somehow—the girl still couldn't quite figure this one out—were now sitting in the back seat of the car.

Tonight, they were going to see a movie. A movie her cousin suggested they go see. Something strange with Jack Nicholson and a little boy screaming about "Red Rum." The girl liked Jack Nicholson. Ever since she snuck into the theater and saw him in Carnal Knowledge*, he had been one of her favorites.*

As soon as she slid over, a barrage of Tommy's hot, breathy kisses rained upon her neck. She squirmed and giggled, but he quickly covered her mouth with his own, and she quietly gave in.

It was her second tongue kiss, ever. Her body felt like it was on fire.

"Mmmmph," she mumbled, trying desperately to wrestle her mouth away. "We better stop."

She was shaking, but she wasn't sure if it was from the cold night air, or the excitement of the moment. The boy pulled her closer to him and found her lips again, his tongue searching hotly as if her mouth belonged to him.

"Tommy, stop," she insisted. "I'm not even supposed to be out . . ."

"Shhhhh," he whispered. "You're always talking about how strict it is at your house, so I figured you'd be happy to be out for a minute. With me. But, hey, I can take you back, if that's what you want."

The boy straightened up, adjusted his clothes, and opened the car door, as if he was going to get out.

"No!" the girl cried, reaching out for him.

The boy, staring straight ahead, smiled slyly.

"That's what I thought. Then stop whining and act like you want to be with me."

He turned to her and wrapped his strong, muscular arms around her, this time even tighter than before. He had her fastened so tight, it was as if she were in a cocoon. She was barely able to move. He worked his way down her neck and began to kiss the tops of her breasts. She babbled nervously.

"Nobody knows I'm gone. I'm supposed to be in bed asleep."

"Then that makes this even better," he replied.

They were sitting in the back of his old, dusty El Dorado. The seat was well-worn and worked out, its dull pleather having long since seen better days, way before Tommy assumed ownership. Every time he moved, the cushions creaked and groaned. It was like an alarm going off in her head. Still, it wasn't quite loud enough to silence the one going off in the core of her body.

She weakly pushed at him.

"Put your arms around my neck," he demanded.

"Why?" she asked, her voice small and trembling.

"Because I want you to," he whispered.

It was her first time with him like this. After days of his flirting in the hallway at school, a chicken-scratched note he'd had his sister give her, and the kiss, her first tongue kiss, that day he walked her halfway to her house, she was finally out on a date with him.

She was heady with excitement and lust. The lust part was new. While she'd hugged on her pillow many a night, wrapping her body around it, pretending it was him, that had only been fantasy.

This was real. This heat, this kind of passion, was stronger than any pillow could ever evoke.

Tommy Dennis. She'd had a crush on him for three years. But Tommy was popular, and one year older than her. Even though she was quite pretty, Tommy seemed way too far out of reach for her to even dream about.

Tommy was beautiful. Everybody at school thought so. His eyes were what had always fascinated her. They were deep and hypnotic. She'd seen him with lots of different girls. All of them as beautiful as him, in one way or another. But he had told her that she was the most beautiful. And tonight, she believed him.

Tonight, she was the one with him. Tonight, none of those other girls mattered.

Until last week, she'd never even known he wanted her, or that she could have him. Not like this.

"Put your arms around my neck," he insisted again.

Unable to resist his demands, or her body's, she did. She nervously moved her fingers up to his hair. Tommy rubbed his strong thighs against hers, pressing her downward, deep into the cushions of the car. The seat croaked, creaked, and groaned, and something sharp and gnarled was stabbing the girl in the small of her back, but her adrenaline was too high at that moment to care about anything other than her own mounting passion. The sounds of her and Tommy's combined heated breathing overwhelmed the cacophony of the seats, and all discomfort became infused into a synchronous mesh of pleasure and pain.

"Stop it, Tommy," she mumbled. "I can't do it with you. I've never done it before."

"I wish I could, baby girl. But you got me so hot. I've been wanting to be with you like this all year."

"Nuh-uh!" she replied with surprise, leaning back a little to look into his face.

"Uh-huh," he moaned, sliding the thin straps of her summer dress over her delicately shaped shoulders. "And I know you know I'm going away to the Army in three more weeks. I want to spend as much time with you as I can. I need something to dream about during all those long lonely nights in boot camp."

The girl, suddenly angry, tried to push him away. She pulled the straps of her dress back up over her shoulders.

"So you just wanna do it with me, then leave and go away to the Army? Get off me!"

Tommy pressed her back down against the seat and kissed her neck, mouth, forehead, and shoulders. She began to calm a little. He raised up on his arm above her, his dark eyes staring deeply into hers.

"Baby girl, do you know how pretty you are? Do you know how many guys are jealous of me for even getting the chance to be with you? I'm not trying to do it with you and leave. Are you crazy? How could anybody leave a woman like you?"

In the darkness and the unusually chilly night air, the girl peered back into his eyes, looking for the lie. Even though he had called her "baby girl," he had also called her a woman. She'd never been called a woman before. Now, even in the awkwardness of the back seat and with the uncertainty of his words, it made her want him all the more. Tommy leaned down and kissed her softly on the lips, running his tongue along the outline of her mouth. She smiled and wrapped her arms around him tighter.

This time, he slid the dress down until it was around the middle of her waist. The cool air washed over her torso, making her already engorged nipples harden to the point of hurting. Tommy hovered over her hungrily. The girl's breasts were now free for the first time ever in front of a man. Embarrassed, she looked away from Tommy's wide-eyed gaze and stared into the cracked grayness of the roof of the El Dorado.

Tommy delicately kissed the swell of her bosom, and she felt as if she were going to faint. When his mouth covered her nipples, her eyes closed tightly, and something wild, big, and wet seemed to well up inside of her. She found herself wrapping her legs around him, just like she'd been doing all those nights, in bed with her pillow.

She felt one of his hands free itself for a moment, and then she heard a zipper. When he pulled her panties down and slipped himself inside of her, she barely made a sound. She squeezed her eyes together even tighter, and held on to him, just like she'd seen the lady do in the bathtub scene in Superfly.

She pretended she was covered with bubbles, in a bathtub just like that, and was experienced enough to do it like the woman in the movie.

Tommy thrust rapidly above her. He wasn't gently kissing her neck anymore. Now he just pounded his body against hers, whispering into the darkness for her to "do it, do it, do it, do it," his tongue darting in and out of her ear fast and furiously, until her ear was wet in a way that wasn't sexy at all.

This didn't feel like she imagined it would. It wasn't the gentle regulated fluffiness she had come to know with her pillow. Tommy's tenderness had now turned rough. She wondered if he even knew it was her lying there beneath him.

"Tommy," she whispered, softly kissing the underside of his neck.

Tommy pounded on.

As he pounded, the sharp gnarly thing that was stabbing her on the seat jabbed her squarely in the back.

"Ow!" she cried, her eyes opening wide.

Tommy didn't even notice. He just kept humping away.

She couldn't bear to watch him moving like that above her.

She squeezed her eyes shut again, and tried to raise herself back to the level of excitement she'd been in before, just before he'd slipped inside of her.

"Tommy," she moaned, moving her body beneath him. "Tommy, Tommy, Tommy . . ."

"That's right, baby girl," he grunted. "Do it like that! Talk to me! Do it, do it, do it!"

In her fantasy, she became the lady in the Superfly *flick. She splashed on, thrashing her body beneath him, covered with the bubbles of a dream.*

She tried to make herself explode the way she had done so many times with her pillow. She moved against him, feeling her body responding to her mind. Tommy's wet tongue moved in and out of her ear. The pitch of her body grew feverish, and she felt her passion escalating rapidly towards a point of release.

Tommy thrust fiercely above her, grunted loudly, and collapsed. He was covered with sweat, and the back of the car felt hot, fogged and sticky.

Pinned beneath him, she was no longer able to move. Everything in her middle just knotted up into an unfulfilled promise. She wasn't smiling like the lady in Superfly. *She wasn't splashing around happily in a tub of bubbles and dreams.*

She was just hot and uncomfortable in the back of a musty car.

"Tommy," she whispered, trying her best to hold on to her dream.

"What?" he grunted, completely spent.

"I love you, Tommy," she dared to whisper. "I've loved you for a long time."

"What?!" he snapped. "Girl, don't be foolish! How can you love me? You don't even know me like that! You know I've been going with Peggy for more than two years now!"

He sat up, tucked his shirt in, and zipped his pants.

The girl lay there, stunned, her panties around her ankles, her dress around her waist, the dream somewhere balled up on the floor of the car. She didn't even know who Peggy was.

"But we just did it," she whimpered. "I just let you do it to me."

"Do you know how many girls have let me do it? What's so big about that? You're just a kid. I'm getting married when I come back from boot camp."

"But I thought you were gonna think about me while you were away."

"I am," he said. "But I know you're not crazy enough to think you're the only person I'll be thinking about. Come on. That was me playing the game. You know the game."

"No I don't," she whispered. "This was my first time."

"Oh. Well . . . sorry. Now you know. Watch out for guys like me. We like to get around. But I'm about to slow down. I'm getting married. So I've gotta have my fun while I've still got the chance. It's not like I'm gonna cheat on Peggy. What kinda guy do you think I am?"

Tommy opened the door and got out of the car. He stretched in the night air, slammed the door shut, then opened the door to the driver's seat and got behind the wheel. He turned around and looked at her.

"Fix your clothes and come on. We gotta go."

She lay there on the seat for a few seconds, her head spinning.

"But what about the movie?"

"You know damn well I wasn't taking you to no movie. Like you really wanted to go. Who likes that guy anyway? Jack Nicholas."

"It's Nicholson," she replied softly.

"Whatever," he said. "I ain't never even heard of him."

He cranked up the car.

She adjusted her clothes.

"I have," she mumbled.

• • •

A month later, Tommy probably still didn't know who Jack Nicholson was. And the girl didn't know who Peggy was either. Perhaps it was someone from another school.

It didn't matter. The girl had found out that Tommy and Peggy were definitely engaged.

And what else she found out was that Tommy Dennis was gone. He had zipped away, off to the Army, leaving nothing behind but a bad memory, and a tiny scar in the small of her back from where the cracked pleather in the back seat of his raggedy El Dorado had nicked her.

Oh yeah.

And something that made her period stop.

Part One

Second Winds

IT'S NOW OR NEIMAN'S

Desi fumbled with the keys at the front door of her house in Culver City, barely able to balance the bags of groceries she held in her arms. The wind was coming at a slant, right in her direction (of course), causing her to be pelted relentlessly by hot drops of smog-infested water that seemed to fly at her with a sense of purpose.

They said it never rained in southern California.

Well, whoever *they* were, they lied.

Today the rain was coming down with a vengeance, spewing upon her out of the heavens with a fierceness that seemed deliberate in its intent. It was September 20. Officially the last day of summer.

How appropriate, she thought. Everything today was apparently the last. The last of the summer. The last of her luxuries.

The last damn straw.

That is, if things didn't change. And soon.

She normally kept her thick hair blow-dried straight, but the rain caused it to revert back into its natural, loose-bodied curl. Now her dark brown shoulder-length hair was sticking to her face and neck, a clammy mess that didn't help the muggy feeling she'd been awash in all afternoon as she drove around in the post-lunchtime traffic and sun. She'd avoided the freeways, but La Cienega had been jammed, and so was Sepulveda. Even as she made her way on Slauson, cars were backed up. People were moving at an absolute crawl.

Despite the rain, she'd been driving with the windows down, and her body was hot to the core. There was nothing she could do about it. She couldn't turn on the air conditioner in the car. No way could she afford to burn up her gas like that. These days, she had to make the dollars stretch as far as she possibly could.

As she stood at her front door, her bulky brown purse slipped off her left shoulder, which, in turn, caused her to lose her balance with the grocery bags, which were already weak because they were made out of paper and soaked all the way through. Desi always chose paper over plastic. At least it was biodegradable, recyclable, something. She'd been in California a long time now, and subscribed fully to the idea of living a clean life and leaving behind a clean world.

She stumbled, trying to recover her balance, but the bags gave way altogether. The lush, tender, rose and yellow late-summer peaches rolled loosely onto the porch, the fuzz picking up dirt like fresh Velcro. Already fragile, only hours away from being classified as overripe, they bruised instantly.

The peaches were followed by the big green bell pepper she'd spent far too many minutes picking out. The jicama, cucumber, plum tomatoes, and fresh cilantro all hit the porch with a smack, and the fresh-baked loaf of sourdough bread, a treat for herself, fell top down in the muddy puddle that had gathered beneath her feet. The bread had been wrapped in paper. As the driving rain pelted it further, it became a nasty mess.

A box of Gardenburgers bounced on its corner, rolled down the front steps, and landed flat on the sidewalk, the rain smattering an angry tune against it. At that exact moment, a frog decided to leap over and claim the box as its home. It perched itself square in the center.

Desi just stared at it, the crowning insult on a miserable day.

She pulled her purse back up on her shoulder, slipped the key in the door, kicked it open, and then began the harried task of gathering up the scattered food. Two of the peaches were damaged beyond consumption. She collected everything else in her arms as best she could and tossed them inside the front door.

Desi gave a quick glance over her shoulder. She decided to let the Gardenburgers be.

She closed the front door, kicked off her shoes, and walked into her living room.

Desi collapsed in her burnished leather armchair, the one facing the front door, and surveyed the wet groceries on the floor in the foyer.

Well, there was nothing that could be done about it. She'd have to make do with the food. She wasn't about to go out and waste more money, especially when she didn't have much to use, let alone waste. There wasn't much left, other than her savings, and that wasn't a whole lot. Just a couple thousand dollars. She hadn't yet begun to dip into it. She swore to herself she never would.

Desi hadn't started on her credit cards yet either. That was definitely the no-no zone. She'd had an ugly episode with her credit cards when she first arrived in LA. She had stupidly lived off of them for the first few months, confident that she'd immediately get well-paying work in the industry. Everybody back home was always telling her how beautiful she was, how she looked like a movie star, so it was no worry for her at all.

She used her credit cards for the cheap motel she stayed in when she first arrived, she used them for groceries, gas, car repairs, headshots, clothes, acting classes, everything, with a fervor and mindlessness that she hoped to never see again.

The cheap motel turned out to be not so cheap after all. While the weekly rate wasn't bad, there was a charge every time she picked up the phone to make a call, local or long distance. The charges for the calls quickly mounted, until the phone expense was greater than the actual motel rate.

Desi also quickly learned that LA was full of women, black

women, who looked like movie stars. Women out of work. It was a well-known fact that Hollywood had little place for actors of color. Not in general. Desi figured she'd be an exception, blow up overnight and make megabucks, and then be able to effect change and open doors for other people of color. That was her *first* Hollywood lesson: She was no exception. And these days, other than a Denzel here, a Will Smith there, and an Eriq LaSalle on television, there were very few exceptions. There certainly weren't any black women out there commanding eight-figure salaries, and those making seven could be counted on one hand. Whoopi. Angela. Whitney. That was about it.

On the Latina front, Jennifer Lopez was able to command big bucks. These days, however, as her hair got blonder and blonder, she looked not so much Hispanic as she did a white girl with a tan. Which made it easier for Hollywood to accept her and place her in roles. Pretty soon they'd be pretending she was white. Something that was much harder for them to do with a black woman.

Desi canvassed everything to find acting work. She read *Backstage West*, *Variety*, *Hollywood Reporter*, and any other trade magazine or rag she could get her hands on. At one point she had three agents that she operated between, none of whom helped her book anything. She mailed out unsolicited headshots to casting agents, but received no responses. At night, she hung out at restaurants and clubs known for their celebrity clientele, in the hopes of being discovered. She found out about auditions on her own and showed up, stunned at the staggering number of beautiful black women who were all trying out for the same roles. Not one callback ever came. Her desperate pursuits always turned out the same.

Nothing. Not one single gig.

In the process, Desi the ingenue, newly disillusioned, spirits sagging, and without any offers for industry work, accrued, in her first two months in LA, over fifteen-thousand-dollars' worth of debt, with no income to offset it. Long before she got any real work, the creditors were hovering and harassing her around the clock. It had been a horrible experience. She swore to herself that it would never happen again.

Things were tight now, but it wasn't as bad as that situation had been. There were no creditors hovering. She didn't panic every time the phone rang. At least, not because she was afraid there'd be a creditor on the other end.

She'd been anticipating the phone ringing, and, even though it might bring good news, she also knew the good news wasn't necessarily good news for her future.

It had been a while since she'd done any industry work that paid her well. She did a film the year before, but the budget was small and she was only paid twenty thousand dollars. She was very aggressive about working, but the roles were scarce. The last part she had auditioned for went to Nia Long. Since then, there hadn't even been any auditions worthwhile enough for her to go to.

The last good-paying work she'd done was a commercial. She had taken it against her better judgment, but it had turned out to be a major blessing for her. She made over sixty thousand dollars from that commercial. It was a national spot for Burger Boss that paid her ten thousand dollars up front and delivered amazing residuals. Those residuals kept her going for a full year.

It was the first and only commercial she'd ever done, and it had been a major letdown for her to do it. She considered herself too big for commercials. At least, the kind of commercial that one had been, where she was one of three attractive black women who grinned and giggled in the background, not the featured actor in the spot. Her face, she believed, was far too recognizable and popular for her to even consider doing the commercial. But she needed the money, so she took the gig.

All her industry friends and acquaintances had been shocked. But work was work. It paid the bills. What made it such a good deal was that the Burger Boss people had done a major blitz in an attempt to seriously compete with McDonald's, Burger King, and Wendy's, so the ad received extensive play on all the networks, not just UPN, WB, and BET and during so-called "urban programming."

Her agent told her to expect the residual checks every thirteen weeks or so, but, to her pleasant surprise, they arrived every month. During one unusual streak, checks arrived every week for five weeks straight. The monthly residual checks averaged forty-one hundred dollars a month for about thirty runs per month of the ad spot. That was more than enough for her to pay her bills, keep herself in the gym, stay out on the circuit doing the parties and premieres, and send money back home. That monthly check was sweet. It gave her a chance to get comfortable. And a little complacent. She didn't even think about auditions, foolishly believing that, with all the films she'd done in the past, work would come to her. To her alarm and disappointment, it never did.

The ad had stopped running more than six months ago. Burger Boss's campaign to compete with the Big Three didn't exactly pan out, so they cut back on their national ads. Her ad was completely taken out of rotation. And the checks dried up, seemingly overnight.

She considered another commercial, but she knew that was like the kiss of death. If she did another spot that was not a national campaign for a major product, like shampoo or makeup, or for a major car company, then she'd be pigeonholed for sure. Her agent advised against it. Besides, her agent told her, the Burger Boss thing had been the exception. Most commercials didn't pay that well, and didn't deliver anywhere near the residuals she'd grown accustomed to receiving. At best, she could expect a check for five hundred dollars a month. That is, if the commercial got a decent rotation.

Desi turned up her nose at the thought of five hundred dollars a month. That would do nothing for her. But, as a result of refusing commercials, she was now faced with the prospect of having to get a real job in the real world. Something that would bring in enough dough to allow her to keep her face in the industry, and, at the same time, take care of the responsibilities she had at hand.

But getting a nonindustry job posed a major catch-22: it was cool to be a waiter, waitress, or service person when you weren't a recognizable face. People expected that of actors-in-waiting. But if you were famous or semi-famous and then took a job outside of the industry? Forget it. You could kiss your career in the entertainment business goodbye.

She'd been rejected from ten nonindustry jobs already. Every interview she had, while complimentary, turned out to be a no. Most of the people were pleasant, some even fawning, but they said no nonetheless. Every one had instantly recognized her. Some even quoted her films to her, as if she wasn't aware of her own body of work. All of them mentioned the Burger Boss gig.

In a town like LA, where everyone was focused on who was who and who did what, she learned that it was hard for her to not be recognized. None of the people who interviewed her believed that she was giving up the limelight. They were all afraid that her presence would be just a temporary thing. While her presence might mean a momentary increase in revenue, they knew that pretty soon they'd be faced with the hiring process again. None of them wanted that.

Some wondered why she was leaving the industry. Was she on drugs? Did she have some kind of habit that had ruined her career? She answered so many personal and humiliating questions that she almost quit the job search thing altogether. That, however, was not an option, so she gritted her teeth and forged on from one interview to the next.

Desi had applied for a job as a personal shopper for Neiman Marcus. It was her last chance. If she didn't get it, she'd have to make a drastic life change.

The job paid very well. If she got it, it would mean that she would be able to stay in Los Angeles. But what was the point of being in LA if she was no longer able to pursue her dream? That was her whole reason for being there in the first place. Taking a nonindustry job would kill her chances at that. No doubt about it. Just ask Gary Coleman. He hadn't had too many offers since he'd started working as a security guard at the Fox Hills Mall. Star or not, once you took a job outside the industry to pay the bills, and the industry found out about it, the powers that be just didn't take you seriously anymore.

She sighed, thoroughly frustrated.

If she didn't find work soon, she had made up her mind to go back home, back to Jensen, Alabama. There was no way she could stay in LA, be as well-known as she was, and be broke. She couldn't take a job that was too common and ordinary, because then she'd risk ridicule, and she was too proud for that. At the same time, even though the last thing she wanted to do was go back home after all these years, she was afraid of what it would mean if she got the job at Neiman's.

Some of the very women she competed with for roles shopped there. Not only might she run into them, she might, ironically, end up being the one they arrogantly requested to help them select their attire. Once word got around that she was working outside the industry as a personal shopper, even though on its own it was considered a prestigious job, her career would be over. No one would ever hire her as an actress again.

She'd had three interviews already. The store manager, the manager of the designer clothing department, and the district manager were all impressed by her sense of style, and they reveled in the fact that she had a recognizable face. Desi figured they would offer her the position. It was just a matter of waiting for the phone to ring.

She prayed that it wouldn't. At least, not right away. She needed more time to think about what all this meant, to examine the repercussions again. She wasn't ready for a ringing phone.

If it rang, answering it would mean more than just the chance to earn a decent living.

A ringing phone with a job offer from Neiman's, right now, would be a death knell.

The beginning of the end.

Desi sat in the leather armchair, limp, staring at the food scattered all around the foyer. She was hot, she was sticky, and she was so, so tired. Tired of the day. Tired of the situation. Tired of her crazy never-could-catch-a-break life.

Money, it seemed, was always an issue. When was her life ever going to change? She'd seen her peers, women like Lela Rochon, Vivica Fox, and Vanessa Williams, all claim their place. They were constantly getting work.

What was the difference between her and them? She was just as pretty, just as smart, and thought she had a pretty good agent. And, like Vanessa, Desi could sing. No . . . she could *sang*, as they said in church. She had legions of people back in Alabama to prove it. There'd been many an eye that had welled up just hearing her notes ricochet off the walls of Mt. Nebo Baptist Church. Every now and then she sang at West Angeles, the church she attended in town, just to keep her lungs on point. West Angeles was very popular, and she'd caused more than a handful of well-known celebrities to catch the spirit there as well. She was once offered a recording contract with a major label by a record exec who happened to be in church during one of her solos. The man had tears in his eyes when he approached her. She flatly turned him down.

Desi didn't want a record deal.

She wanted to be a movie star.

And no amount of fame as a singer was going to take her off that course. She wanted to be known as an actor first, and she was unwilling to compromise that in any way.

Even if it meant an uphill struggle, which it had, all the way.

Desi sighed heavily and rubbed her temples. She didn't feel like gathering up the food in the foyer, but she figured she'd better get about the task of doing it. It wasn't like she had the luxury of just letting it sit there to go to waste.

Just as she pressed her hands against the arms of the chair to raise herself up, the phone rang.

Desi's breath stopped cold. She stared at the phone as it jingled on the table beside her. She hadn't even checked yet to see if she had any messages. Perhaps Neiman's had already called. There was a caller ID box next to the phone, but she refused to let her eyes affix themselves to it. She didn't want to see the inevitable, even though she knew she would have to contend with it soon enough.

The phone kept ringing. Desi sat frozen in the chair, afraid to remove the cordless receiver from its cradle. If it was Neiman's, then that would change everything. Whether they said yes or no, that call would affect the rest of her life.

Her heart beat heavily against her skin. The blood in her temples rushed and pounded with a thunderous fury. Beside her, the phone rang again and again.

She sighed.

"*Please, Lord Jesus, let me be doing the right thing*," she whispered as she reached for the phone.

As Desi brought the phone up to her ear, her eyes filled with tears.

FEAST OR FASHION

Hello?"

There was a pause at the other end. Desi could hear slight breathing, but the person wouldn't say anything.

"Hello?"

"Um . . . yes . . . hello," a deep, resonant male voice haltingly responded. "I'm trying to reach . . . Desi Sheridan."

"This is Desi Sheridan. May I ask who's calling?"

"Is this Desi Sheridan I'm speaking to now?" the voice asked, almost sounding surprised.

"Yes it is," she said politely, wiping away a tear that was tracing a path down her left cheek. "Who's calling?"

"Um, yes, Miss Sheridan, my name is Randall. Randall James. My partner, Steve Karst, and I own a company called—"

"I'm sorry," she cut in. "Whatever it is you're selling, I'm definitely not interested."

She clicked off the phone and placed it back in its cradle, heaving a huge sigh of relief that it had not been the people from Neiman's on the other end of the line. She rubbed her eyes, trying to remove all traces of tears that might still be lingering. She was grateful for the reprieve. At least it gave her a little more time to think.

Something about this whole Neiman's thing was filling her

with way too much dread. She'd heard Oprah say something once that really stuck with her. Something about doubt. That if you had it, it was your body's way of telling you not to do something. A warning from God. It was just a matter of whether a person chose to listen or not.

The phone rang again.

Desi looked down at the phone as if it were a rattling snake. She still avoided the caller ID. She was so fearful of being offered the Neiman's job, yet so fearful of not taking it, that she didn't know what to do. She felt that if the words NEIMAN MARCUS appeared on her caller ID, it would immediately seal her fate.

She counted to ten. The phone rang three more times during the time that she was counting. She took in a deep breath, and picked up the phone again.

Before she could say hello, a voice was already speaking.

"*Miss Sheridan, please, don't hang up again!*" the deep voice implored. "This is *not* a telemarketing call! I'm not some crazy solicitor. I'm actually calling you about a project my partner and I are developing for network television."

"Who is this?" Desi asked suspiciously. "And why aren't you calling my agent? His name is Ken Ashton. You can reach him at 310-555-1811. All my work comes through him. He checks out what's legit and what's not. So I advise you to give him a ring."

She was about to click the phone off again when she heard him yell,

"*Wait!*"

Desi paused, and brought the phone back up to her ear.

"Look, whatever your name is, how did you get my number in the first place? How do I know you aren't some stalker? That's not very original out here, you know. You won't be the first."

"I'm not a stalker, Miss Sheridan. My name is Randall James. My partner, Steve, and I own a production company called Vast Horizons. We're developing a new series for network television, and we happen to believe you'd be ideal to play the part of one of the main characters. To be perfectly honest, the character was actually written with you in mind."

"How did you get my number?" Desi snapped. "I'm unlisted, and my agent doesn't give it out without my permission."

"You're good friends with Sharon Lane, right?" the man asked.

"Yes. As a matter of fact, I am."

"Well, Sharon and I go way back. We grew up in the same neighborhood in the Bronx. She gave me your number. She thought it'd be alright."

Sharon Lane was an African-American producer who had worked on a number of major films. She knew everybody. She was also one of Desi's best friends.

They met eight years before, when Desi was twenty-six, during the filming of *Living Foul.* It was Desi's first real acting role on film. It was also her first time working with the controversial African-American director Jackson Bennett, who, since then, she had worked with twice.

(Including a film he did that she headlined, *Flatbush Flava.* That was the one that was supposed to make her a star. He had personally told her so. It had a decent studio budget, lots of celebrity cameos, a solid cast, and a pretty good promotional campaign. Lenny Kravitz did the sound track.

It was dead on arrival. The critics panned it and the public didn't show. The only real thing of note about the film was that the sound track sold ten million copies. It was phenomenal, and it helped make Lenny Kravitz, who was already a mega rock star, damn near granite.

Desi hadn't headlined a film in the four years since. She was also skittish of Jackson, who continued to get studio budgets and kept making controversial black films year after year. He called periodically, offering roles here and there—never anything of consequence. Most of the parts paid nothing, and weren't even real ensemble work. She usually stayed away. She even wondered if, for her, Jackson Bennett wasn't the equivalent of career kryptonite.)

Desi's role in *Living Foul* had been small, but she spent extra time on the set out of sheer excitement and enthusiasm. There she met Sharon, who was the production manager. The two spoke casually a few times at first. Then, as Sharon noticed Desi hanging around, she enlisted her to run errands when Desi wasn't in front of the camera. The two quickly became friends, as Desi was practically Sharon's unofficial second assistant. Their friendship continued long after the film was wrapped.

They had been hanging ever since.

They had done the town and gotten high together at least a dozen times in the past year alone. Not that Desi was one to get high very often. But Sharon was good people, and always cool to be around.

They would usually chill at Sharon's place, listen to some nice reggae and East Coast hip-hop, grill some seafood, and have a smoke as they talked about who was doing what and what jobs might be coming around. Sharon was the only person on the West Coast Desi knew who was into East Coast music the way she was. She loved hanging out with her.

They had taken vacations together to Jamaica, St. Barts, London, Aruba, St. Marten, and Costa Rica. They'd been to Amsterdam twice. The two of them hit New York on a regular basis, just for the hell of it.

Desi hadn't traveled anywhere of late. These days, she couldn't afford it.

Sharon had hooked Desi up with work before. But right now, even Sharon was having a hard time. It had been a while since she'd had a full-time position. Over the past year, she divided her time between freelance jobs here and there, being in love, and lounging around. She was in a fairly new relationship, only six months old, so she spent more time than not involved with the being in love and the lounging.

"How do I know you're not lying?" Desi asked the man on the phone.

"Sharon told me you'd say that. She's at home right now. Do you have three-way?"

"Yes."

"Okay. Click over and dial her on the other line. I'll wait. You can call her and confirm."

Desi, without ceremony, immediately clicked over and dialed Sharon's number.

"Hello?" Sharon chirped. Her already-perky voice had an unnatural lift, like she was on helium.

"Did you give my number to some guy named Randall James?" Desi asked.

Sharon drew a short, quick breath. Desi could tell she was getting high at that very moment. Not that she was incoherent. Sharon just loved to get high. It didn't affect anything she did in any negative way. Desi didn't know how Sharon managed it, but getting high seemed to enhance her ability to be the consummate professional. She was living proof of why marijuana should be legalized.

"Yep," Sharon said, exhaling. "Listen to what he has to say. This could be a major thing for you."

"How do you know him?" Desi asked. "He said you grew up together."

"We did. But, beyond that, Randall is no joke. He works for Massey-Weldon. He's written for some of their best shows. He's won, like, three Emmys or something. In this town, that's a big deal for a black man."

Sharon took another quick breath, then spoke again in a strained voice with her mouth full of what Desi guessed must be smoke.

"Last year, he and his partner won an Emmy for *Westwood*."

"He writes for that show?" Desi asked, impressed.

Sharon exhaled slowly. Desi could almost smell the fumes coming through the line.

"Yep," Sharon finally responded.

"Wow. I love that show. The writing is terrific."

"Good," Sharon said. "So talk to him. He just started his own production company, and, if I didn't misunderstand him, which I don't think I did, he has a role for you that might give you the break you've been looking for."

"Is it a sure thing?"

"Come on now, girl. Is there such a thing in this town? At least it's worth listening to him. It's not like he doesn't have any clout or an impressive track record. I wouldn't give your number to just anybody. I've got more sense than that, I think. High or not."

Desi chuckled. Her first chuckle in a long, long time.

"Okay. Well, I've got him on the other line, so let me go. I'll call you back later and tell you what he says."

"Don't call me back tonight," Sharon said quickly. "I've got company coming over. And, if I've got anything to do with it, I'm going to be under deep cover for the rest of the night, if you know what I mean."

"I know what you mean. Well, thanks. I think."

"You're welcome, I think," Sharon replied, then hung up the phone.

Desi clicked back over.

"Hello?" she said.

"I'm here. Did you get her?"

"I got her."

"Did she confirm that I'm authentic?"

"Yes, she did."

"Good. For the record, Miss Sheridan, I wouldn't be calling you now if I didn't think this was something that you could truly benefit from. I've been following your work for a very long time, and I know that if we pair you up with this show, it's a guaranteed formula for success."

"If you've been following my work for such a long time, then how come we've never met before? This industry's not that big. Sooner or later, most black people meet each other. That is, I'm assuming you're black. Sharon called you a brother."

"Last time I checked. And we have met before."

"When?" Desi asked, surprised.

"At a birthday party for Will Smith. Last year. You were there with Sharon. I came over and introduced myself to you when you walked over to one of the food tables."

Desi searched her mind for the moment and his face.

"I'm sorry. I remember being at the party. I just don't remember much of what went on there. I go to so many industry parties, I can't even keep count."

"The goal is to go to the ones that matter the most," he replied with authority. "Try not to spread yourself so thin."

Was this guy trying to school her? she wondered. *Just because he had a few Emmys to his name? Let a cop pull his black behind over at night in Beverly Hills. See what those Emmys mean then.*

"Whatever," she replied stiffly. "Tell me about the show."

The tension in her voice was obvious. Randall noted the change and his mistake. He quickly adjusted his tone.

"I'd like to, but I'd prefer to do it face-to-face. I want to show you a copy of the pilot script, tell you the concept, our vision for how it should go, the whole nine. I want to give you the full celebrity pitch."

Desi instinctively frowned. Despite his attempt to kiss up to her, in no way did she want to go back into that afternoon's smoggy, sticky, uncomfortable weather, driving with her air conditioner off.

"It's raining out. I just came back in. In all honesty, Randall, I'm not up to going out again."

"I didn't mean today," he said. "My schedule is pretty tight as it is. How about if we meet tomorrow? It's a much easier day for me."

The thought of going out into the heat at all didn't sit well with her, even though it was for something that might, as Sharon and he implied, be life-changing for her.

"Can you make it later in the day?" she asked.

"Sure. Would you mind a business dinner?"

She hesitated, then thought about the prospect of a free, possibly elegant meal. As callow as that sounded, her finances had reduced her to seizing opportunities like this.

"Dinner is fine."

"What about Spago's?" he said.

"Ew. Spago's is much too trite and touristy."

Even though, theoretically, she was a beggar, she surprised herself that she had the nerve to be choosy.

"I really don't care for Spago's either," Randall replied. "I just said it because I thought it was the appropriate thing to say."

"You don't get out for dinner much, do you?"

"No, I don't. I do more takeout than anything these days. I've got too much going on right now to know what's hip and what's not."

"Well, for the record," Desi said, "the *in* spot for me is Crustacean in Beverly Hills. And you can never go wrong taking me to Georgia's or M & M's."

"M & M's?!" Randall laughed outright. "Damn! No disrespect, but it sounds like you're a cheap, 'round-the-way kinda date. I would have never figured you to be an M & M's or Roscoe's kind of girl."

"I didn't *say* Roscoe's."

Her tone again immediately put him in check. Because he didn't know her, he couldn't tell if she was being playful or merely tolerant. He'd already made one faux pas with his comment about her attending so many industry parties. Since he didn't know what expression was accompanying her current tone, he figured he'd better stop being too lighthearted with her too quickly.

"Well, um, M & M's, Roscoe's, what's the difference?"

"Trust me," Desi answered flatly, "it's huge. And if you'd really done your homework on me like you claim you have, you'd know that I'm from the South, and M & M's is down-home-style cooking, so that's right up my alley."

"Is that where you want to go?" Randall asked, now completely put in check.

"No. How about The Cheesecake Factory?"

"That's one of my favorite places," he said, feeling back on track. "I can't believe you just took me through this whole soul food exercise to wind up at The Cheesecake Factory."

"You're the one who brought up Roscoe's."

"You're right," he admitted. Desi thought she could hear a smile in his voice as he spoke. "Alright, Miss Sheridan, which Cheesecake Factory do you want to go to?"

"The one in the Marina."

"Yes. I know where it is. How about if I meet you there at, say, seven tomorrow?"

"Can you make it eight?" she asked, for no reason other than to not seem too easy.

"Eight is fine." Randall was all business again. "And, Miss Sheridan, I'm really looking forward to meeting you again. I think you'll really be interested in what I have to say."

"We'll see," Desi said.

I hope was what she meant.

"Well, I'll see you tomorrow at eight sharp."

"Goodbye, Randall," she said, and abruptly clicked off the phone.

She placed the receiver back in its cradle and slumped limply in the chair.

"Wow" was all she could muster.

She sat there, staring at the food in the foyer, wondering what kind of role this man could possibly be calling to offer, and why Sharon seemed so positive about it as well. She hoped it was something worth her while. There had been far too many gigs that seemed to have promise but just didn't pan out.

Some of them had even been referred to her by Sharon, so the fact that Randall came through her was not necessarily a guarantee.

As she sat there, the phone rang again.

She looked down at the caller ID box.

NEIMAN MARCUS showed up in large black letters.

Desi stared at the phone. It rang once. It rang again. She let it ring and ring and ring. Her answering service was set to pick up after six rings, not the standard four. Four was too quick. Sometimes it took her at least five rings to locate the cordless phone.

She wasn't quite ready to talk to Neiman's.

After five rings, the phone was quiet.

"I guess they didn't want to leave a message," she said aloud.

She stared at the phone, wondering if it would ring again. She stared at it for a long time. For what seemed like an eternity.

It didn't ring.

"Good. I'd rather talk to Randall first before I talk to them anyway. At least, this way, I have options. If things work out, I may not have to take the job after all."

She pushed herself up from the chair and made her way to the foyer to gather up the scattered food.

As she knelt down to pick up the jicama, she made the conscious decision to find her Bible that night. It had been far too long since she had prayed.

Her grandma said the Lord was always listening.

Desi hoped He wasn't too busy. She hated coming to Him when she was desperate, instead of on a regular basis.

Better now than never, she decided.

Now was the perfect time.

With her future teetering on the brink of fulfillment or failure, she knew it was time to hand things over to a higher authority.

When Desi touched the jicama, she realized that she was already on her knees. She didn't need to wait until later to pray. She could do it right now, right there in the foyer.

Her eyes closed, still clutching the jicama, she sent a quick request up to the heavens.

"Heavenly Father, please let me have just a minute of Your time. I'm sorry I've been gone for so long, but I know You know my heart, and can feel it's in the right place."

She paused, searching for the proper words. Her grandma told her to always be specific in prayer, and believe with all her heart that He would provide.

"He might not give you what you want," she used to say, "but He'll always give you what you need."

Desi mulled things over, choosing the exact words to convey what she was asking.

"Dear Lord, I've been out here for eight years, and I've been trying so hard to fulfill what my spirit compels me to do."

She nervously squeezed the jicama.

"I know You wouldn't have let me come this far if this wasn't where I was supposed to be. I don't want to go back to Jensen, but if that's what you want, Thy will be done."

She rocked gently, no longer measuring the words.

"If it's not what you want, though, please, please, please send me some sort of sign. Let me know these eight years haven't been in vain. Let something happen that shows me, without a doubt, that this is what I am supposed to be doing. I ask these blessings in Jesus' name. Amen."

Desi opened her eyes, feeling an immediate sense of relief from the act of prayer alone. She resolved to do it more often. For now, she'd leave the rest up to Him.

She got up from the floor and began gathering up the rest of the food.

DESTINATION MOON

"Yo . . . *yo . . . yo . . . yo . . . yo!*"

The high-pitched, drawn-out words were accompanied by two ultraviolet beams of light that twinkled from bloodshot eyes peering around the cracked door.

"Good God, girl! How long you been smokin'?"

Sharon giggled as she opened the door completely and let the man in.

"It's not a *quantity* thang, Glen. It's all about a state of *being*."

Glen smacked her on the butt as she closed the door behind him. She peeped him up and down as he walked into the foyer.

He was an even six feet, with smooth, ultra-dark skin and close-cropped hair. His back was to her. Sharon could see the firm outline of his triceps through the finely woven fabric of his dark gray Gucci suit. Even in executive attire, he had the stature and bearing of an African prince.

"*'It's all about a state of being,'*" he teased, mimicking her voice as he turned towards her. "Well, I hope your state of being includes being ready for *me*, and that it didn't take no sinsi to get you there."

She slipped into his arms. He leaned down and kissed her.

"Naw, baby," she said, licking her lips, "it's not even like that. The weed is for me. It's like sipping on a fine wine. Purely an enhancement. Straight-up righteousness."

She kissed him again, long and hard.

"Mmmmm," he moaned. "I think I just got a contact high."

Sharon giggled, nestled her hand in his, and led him into the living room of her cozy Westwood town house. The room, an earthy blend of dark and light browns, was illuminated by the glow of candles and was softly tinged with the scent of myrrh.

Not a hint of weed was in the air. The only giveaway was the exquisitely carved bong and the lighter sitting atop the wide, short-legged mahogany coffee table. There were two wineglasses and an open bottle of cabernet on the table beside the bong. The bottle was half empty. One of the wineglasses was half full.

"Looks like that bong's not the only thing you're hitting," Glen commented, examining the cabernet. "Is this the first bottle of the night?"

"Yeah. I've only had two glasses."

Sharon had her arm around his waist.

"And the one you're working on now is your third, right?" His left brow was raised rhetorically.

"Yeah. So? I got thirsty. My mouth was getting dry."

Glen set the bottle down and sank back into the overstuffed cream-colored couch.

Above his head hung a magnificent tapestry of Robert Nesta Marley that Sharon had picked up in Jamaica. It was a mixture of fiery reds and radiant yellows that seemed to generate warmth and send it out into the room.

Glen positioned himself so that he was comfortable, kicked off his expensive black leather shoes, and loosened his silk tie. Sharon, lounging in a short dashiki dress purchased in West Africa, sat on the floor beside him, slipping her bare feet under the coffee table and scooting close to the edge. She dug her toes into the tight loops of the neutral Berber carpeting and leaned her head back against Glen's knees.

Bob Marley's *Babylon By Bus* CD was playing. "Exodus" was rocking from the speakers of her surround-sound system. The music was up just loud enough to set the mood.

"We must be feeling mighty yardie tonight," he commented.

"*Movement of Jah people,*" she sang, bobbing her head.

Glen, amused, casually placed his hand in her thick tangle of rust-colored locks.

"It's funny . . . I spent my whole life avoiding ghetto girls and street skanks, in search of a sensible, refined woman. And so I meet you, Miss Strong Black Mover and Shaker. You had a suit on and everything. Look at you now. You smoke more weed than Wu-Tang, and can cuss a hoodrat under the table. How'd I let you trick me like this?"

"I'm good, baby," Sharon crooned. "I thought you knew. I'm a shape-shifter." She made a waving motion with her arms and her torso. "Don't blink, or I'll turn into a crack hoe on your ass."

Glen burst into laughter. He bent down and kissed the top of her head.

"*Mmmm,*" he moaned, his fingers burrowing deep towards her scalp. "Your hair smells good. What's that, almond oil?"

Sharon nodded, enjoying the feel of his mouth and fingers as they played about her head.

She had been growing her locks for the past six years. They were strong and regal, like tight pieces of Egyptian rope, and three or four of them had cowry shells attached to their ends. The locks fell a few inches below her shoulders and framed her brown face beautifully, giving her an exotic-yet-natural look. She was very proud of her locks, and consistently corrected people when they referred to them as "dreads."

"There's nothing *dreaded* about my hair," she always replied. "Does seeing my head make you scared?"

While laughing was the instinctive thing to do at such a comment, seeing Sharon's face as she delivered it squashed any thought of taking her or her nondreaded locks lightly.

She slipped her hand beneath Glen's pant leg and caressed his calf. He leaned back against the couch, lost in a reverie of peace.

"How is it that you make me so happy?" he asked with a euphoric sigh. "You're like a tonic, baby. You take away all my ills. Don't ever change that . . . please."

Sharon, caught off guard by his words, felt something warm bubble up in her heart.

She gave his calf a gentle squeeze.

"How was your day?" she asked, taking a sip of wine.

"Long, hectic, unappreciated. What else is new?"

"I appreciate you, baby," Sharon cooed, once again bobbing her head to the music. She lifted his pant leg and kissed his calf.

"You appreciate me now because you're high," Glen responded, "but if you were sitting across the table from me in a conference room, or were on the phone negotiating one of my clients' contracts, believe me, it'd be a totally different story."

"Of course it would," she replied, "but that's not what we're doing right now, is it? Right now, I'm about to take a gulp of wine and then suck your calf. Bet you'll feel appreciated then."

Glen leaned his head back, laughing. Sharon took a quick swig, then started on his leg.

"Stir It Up" billowed gently from the speakers.

"Sometimes, I swear," he said, "you'd never know that you were the older one."

Sharon halted, mid-suck, her hand still around his calf. She raised her head.

"Glen, why does age always have to come up in our conversations? I thought it wasn't an issue."

"It's not. It only comes up in the sense that you just never seem to grow up. You're way older than I am and . . ."

"I'm not *way* older than you. It's only twelve years. It's not like I'm eighty and farting dust. Jesus, I'm only thirty-eight."

Sharon released his leg and took another swallow of wine.

"And if I'm so damn old," she snapped, "what the hell were you doing coming on to me in the first place?"

"You look like a kid," he replied, his laughter fading into a good-natured chuckle. He leaned his head back against the cushion behind him. "You look younger than me. And I told you, your age doesn't bother me one bit. So what if you could technically be my mother, if you'd had me at twelve?" Glen was trying hard not to laugh. "It was your mind that drew me. And that suit. And those sexy locks."

Sharon gripped her glass of wine, a little too tightly, and stared forward into space, scowling. The music couldn't even change her mood.

"You sure know how to kill a high," she muttered.

Glen lifted his head. His hand, still resting in her hair, gently massaged her scalp.

"Baby, I was just playing."

"Well, don't *play* with me," she replied, brushing his hand away. "Just because your day was fucked up, it doesn't mean you have to fuck up mine."

"My days are always fucked up. You're just sensitive about your age."

"Funny, I never was until I met you."

She poured another glass of wine for herself.

"Can I have some of that?" Glen asked.

Sharon set the bottle on the table and lit the bong.

"Pour it yourself, you bourgie bastard."

As she took a long pull from the bong, Glen leaned down, lifted her locks, and gently kissed the nape of her neck. Sharon closed her eyes, savoring the sensation of his kiss and the infusion of the pungent smoke as it passed through her mouth and exited her nose. Glen kissed the side of her neck, then nibbled her left earlobe. Sharon raised the bong back up to her lips, but Glen took it from her hands and put it back on the table.

"You don't need that," he whispered. "I've got something that will make you fly."

He turned her face around to his and covered her mouth with his own.

Sharon closed her eyes again and placed her arms around his

neck. She kissed him hungrily, searching his mouth for all kinds of solutions. For some reason, she just couldn't find any.

She pulled away.

"What's wrong, baby?" Glen asked. "I told you I was just messing with you before."

"I don't know," she sighed. "I've got so much on my mind. Work, you, me, my life."

"Here we go . . ." he groaned, sitting up.

Sharon glared at him, her eyes narrowed.

"What do you mean, *'here we go'?* I have a right to be concerned. I've been in this town a long time. You were still in high school when I came here."

"*Now* who's bringing up age?"

"Yeah, I'm bringing up age, because it's not fair! I've been in this town for ten years. I've worked with everybody. And I still have yet to be really put on. But you, straight out of law school, you come out here, and you're repping major movie stars and have nothing but A-list clients. How fair is *that?!*"

"Perhaps you should have become a lawyer," he joked.

"Glen, I don't find a damn thing funny."

She glared at him, her face rigid.

"Is it to the point where you're jealous of other people's success?" he asked, adjusting his tone.

"No," she said with a frown. "You know I'm not about that. I don't resent other people because they're getting breaks. More power to 'em. I'm just tired of not having any."

"That's not necessarily true, Sharon," Glen commented. "You've had lots of breaks, and you're very well-respected. Look at how many high-powered Hollywood jobs you've held."

"But where did they get me? None of them have proved to really put me over."

She toyed with the bong, listening to Bob singing about the concrete jungle. She leaned her head down on the table.

"Glen, do you know how many actors, directors, writers,

crew people, and other producers I've helped launch the careers of? And they've all promised to return the favor in a big way. Has it happened yet? Huh? This town is so full of shit."

"So leave it," he said, his tone matter-of-fact.

Sharon lifted her head and sighed.

"I can't. Not until I make it. I've put in too much time to leave."

"Well, now. *That* makes sense."

Sharon looked up at him. As she suspected, Glen wore a smirk.

"Go on, Glen. Laugh at my career. You probably laugh at me when you're out there cavorting with all your hot little nubile clients."

Glen stroked the back of her neck.

"You're hot and nubile, baby. And you're kinda agile, too. That move you put on me two nights ago? *Man!* I don't know. You sure you're not in Cirque du Soleil or something?"

Sharon couldn't resist smiling.

"Cirque du SoBlack," she quipped.

They both laughed.

"Show me my feet," he commanded, his tone soft but firm.

Sharon, suddenly coy, pulled her left foot from beneath the table. She turned slightly and raised it towards him. Her small foot, a size six, was delicate and shapely. Her toenails were painted a deep chestnut brown. There was a tiny silver ring with the word *love* engraved on it encircling her fourth toe.

Glen kissed the arch of her foot.

"*Mmmm . . .*" he moaned, "I love my feet. These are *my* feet. Don't you forget it, either. I just let you borrow them during the day to walk on. But these bad boys? These are *mine!*"

Sharon blushed and giggled, all at once.

"Who's the silly one now?"

"You just better not let nothing happen to my feet," he mumbled, his lips still pecking gently at her arch.

She watched him, suddenly feeling weak, swooning on the inside. Their eyes met and stayed locked for an eternal five seconds. Glen leaned down again and pulled her face close to his.

"Stop being so insecure about everything," he said reassuringly. "Let's deal with you and me one day at a time. As for your career, nobody can take from you what the universe already has laid out."

"So what does that mean?" she whispered.

"It means you're destined to succeed, baby. Nobody can take that away except the Big Man himself. You just have to be ready for your success when it happens. Not taking a quick drag off a bong and missing the moment when it comes your way."

Sharon opened her mouth to say something in protest, but Glen quickly covered it with his own, probing her mouth with deep determination.

He pushed the coffee table back with his foot, then slid off the couch onto her, pressing her back into the firmness of the carpet.

"You said you could make me fly," she moaned, leaning into him as he covered her body with caresses and kisses.

"I can," he whispered. "Where do you want to go?"

"Take me as far away as I can get," she replied, her voice thick.

"How about . . . New York?" he replied, tickling her neck with a flurry of licks.

"Not far enough."

"What about Jamaica?"

"Uh-uh. Bob's already taking care of that for me."

He slid down her belly and lifted her dashiki. He flicked his tongue into her navel. She arched helplessly towards him.

"Well, baby, how far do you want to fly?"

Sharon pressed his head downward, deep between her legs. When he opened his mouth and she felt the magic, she leaned her head back, closed her eyes, and moaned.

"That's right, baby," she cooed. "Keep flying, just like that. And don't you . . . unnh . . . stop . . . unnnh . . . until you take . . . me . . . to . . . the . . . moon."

SMILES TO GO BEFORE I REAP

Alright, Bettina . . . I'm outta here!"

A few people here and there were passing through the sumptuous lobby of the Massey-Weldon building on Avenue of the Stars in Century City, on their way home or back to their offices for late-night work.

Randall James, six three, dark brown, with a shiny, clean-shaven head and rich thick brows, looked fit and fine in a well-tailored dark blue suit as he stepped off the elevator. He strode past the elegant towering water fountain that spewed eternal. The owners of the company, the powerhouse husband-and-wife creative team of Wade Massey and Anna Weldon, made sure the fountain was never turned off. According to them, it was a symbol of how prolific their production house was. It was also a constant, not-so-subtle reminder to themselves and their employees that they remain that way.

Randall's heels resounded loudly as he made his way across the freshly polished caramel and cream Italian marble over to the reception desk.

"What are you so excited about?" Bettina asked, adjusting her headset. "I haven't seen you this fired up in, well—"

"A long time," Randall replied, cutting her off, sensing where she was going. "I've been excited since. You just haven't had the pleasure."

"And what a pleasure it was, Mr. Arrogant."

The phone rang. She raised her finger for him to wait while she took the call. She smiled innocently.

Bettina's smiles. They always seemed so innocent. Everything about her seemed innocent. And, when it came to Bettina Hayes, *seemed* was truly the operative word. The appearance of innocence had gotten her out of numerous situations, from failing to deliver important messages, to reprimands for arriving late to work and returning late from lunch. All she had to do was flash that naïve smile and bat her long-lashed, slightly slanted eyes, and people relented.

It was why Massey-Weldon, one of television's most powerful production companies, had tolerated her for so long. It seemed an honor to be bestowed with Bettina's smile. People worked for it, especially men. Once they got one, it didn't matter what she'd done wrong. That innocent smile made everything alright again.

Tall, delicate, and curvaceously lean, light brown with short, curly, jet-black hair, Bettina was fresh-faced and naturally pretty. She never wore makeup, but always radiated cover-girl beauty. She looked every bit of twenty-four.

Bettina was every bit of thirty-six.

Her strikingly natural beauty had afforded her the privilege of choosing from LA's most elite men, including high-profile celebrities—actors, athletes, agents, and all kinds of powerbrokers in between. Many of them included high-profile *married* celebrities. But she didn't care about that. She took her lovers as she could get them, hoping to gain opportunity and position along the way.

Bettina's sexual prowess was legendary, although none of her lovers ever really kissed and told. But there was a secret society of men who all knew that each had had her.

There was also a not-so-secret society of wives and girlfriends that she'd had confrontations with about their men. Catfights, phone feuds, death threats—one woman even stuck a potato in the tailpipe of Bettina's silver Mercedes SLK, a gift from an older lover, an entertainment attorney who had been promising her (forever, it seemed) that he would introduce her to some of his producer clients who he knew could help get her career going. The potato situation destroyed her engine, but the husband of the woman who put it there, a star player for the LA Lakers, bought Bettina another car. A candy-apple red Viper.

She'd been driving it ever since.

Because of her conflicts with women, Bettina was a loner. She didn't have any girlfriends. Had never had one in her entire life. She'd never really got along with women to begin with, including her own sisters, who were much older.

Her problems with women began early. On her very first day of kindergarten at a refined, highbrow (so her parents thought) Montessori school, four-year-old Francine punched button-cute Bettina square in the face.

Knocked her flat down to the ground. All the other little girls stood around laughing. They didn't care for Bettina anyway. She was a little too cute for their tastes. Too many boys apparently thought so.

"Jamie's *my* boyfriend," squat little Francine announced, her fist still balled up. "Stay away from him or I'ma *kick* your ass."

Bettina was undaunted. It was the first day of school, after all, and boys were open for the picking. Nobody had claimed anybody yet, as far as she was concerned. Besides, Jamie had kissed *her,* and, because she liked it so much, she let him do it again.

She kicked the portly little girl in the stomach. Hard.

Bettina's mother had dressed her up like a doll for her first day of school. The pretty, dainty little girl with the radiant smile was the center of Marva and Hadley Hayes's world, an unexpected baby that had come fifteen years after their last child. They had three other girls, ages nineteen, twenty, and twenty-two. Now in their second wind of parenthood, Bettina was their joy.

So Marva dressed up her daughter to make sure that she would be just as adored in school as she was at home. A frilly, handmade, special-ordered pink dress. Frilly little white socks with pink ruffles around the top. And the shoes. Those lethal-toed patent-leather black things that were the nightmare of every man who'd ever held a child.

Bettina kicked Francine with those shoes. Kicked her in the epicenter of her fatness. Francine's face balled up into a horrified cocktail of pain and surprise. She fell onto her back and Bettina pounced on her. She pounded the little girl in the face. Within seconds, all the other little girls leapt onto Bettina. When the Montessori teachers finally managed to pull them off, dainty little Bettina was speckled with bruises. The frilly little handmade, special-ordered pink dress hung from her in tatters. The socks were filthy. Her top lip was busted, and her hair was full of dirt.

But the little hard-toed shoes were still intact. And the other girls weren't without their share of scratches, bites, nicks, cuts, bruises, and missing clumps of hair.

Little Jamie, the catalyst for the schoolyard skirmish, was thoroughly excited by the melee and the sight of the dirty, bedraggled, beaten-down girl standing there, somehow managing to look as sexy and confident as a four-year-old with a shredded dress and a busted lip could. He broke up with Francine immediately, walked over to Bettina, and took her hand.

"Wanna be my girlfriend?" he asked, his front teeth so large he could barely close his mouth.

"No," Bettina replied flatly. "You like fat girls who fight. I'm a lady. I'm too good for you."

He offered her a piece of candy.

Bettina looked at it, then looked at him. It was chocolate. She liked chocolate. She reached out with her dirty little hand and took it.

"*Now* will you be my girlfriend?" he asked.

"Will you bring me chocolate every day?"

He nodded. Bettina smiled, and, to him, even though she was dirty and the teachers were now escorting her away, the brilliance of her teeth and the innocent curve of her lips made her seem refreshingly pure.

He brought her chocolate every day. That is, until she didn't want them anymore. From him, anyway. Jamie was soon replaced by Oliver, Lenny, Karen (he was Muslim), Damon, and a succession of others.

Over the course of the kindergarten year, Bettina systematically took the boyfriends of all the girls who'd jumped her.

Each of them happily came, bearing the gifts of her choosing.

Since then, she couldn't care less if the girls didn't like her.

Just as long as the boys always did.

Bettina learned early how competitive women were for men. It made her that much more determined to always be able to have her pick. Taken or not.

Her looks had helped her get every job she'd ever had. She'd been lucky enough to always be interviewed by men for the jobs she applied for, and she knew how to work her charm. Men loved giving her gifts and taking care of her, at least for a little while. No one ever knew who the men were, exactly. There were always suspicions, rumblings, but never any concrete evidence. Nothing other than a new car here, and a new wardrobe there. Weekend getaways. Nooners. A sudden change of residence and phone number.

Trappings.

Bettina was never seen with her men in any publicly conspicuous way. But it was generally acknowledged that *some*where in the background, some*body* was there. For how long, it was never known.

They came and went so quickly, sometimes even Bettina wasn't exactly sure.

And while her good looks had gotten her many gifts, into many beds, and through many doors, she was still single, and, careerwise, not exactly where she wanted to be. She'd hoped that at least one of her liaisons would bear business fruit to her benefit. Pillow promises had been made. But pillow promises,

Bettina found, were hard to confirm once night faded into dawn.

One thing she knew for certain: working as a receptionist for five years at Massey-Weldon was not going to cut it. Wade Massey had promised her two years earlier that she wouldn't be at the front desk for much longer. But that was during a whirlwind week of wining, dining, and late-night grinding at the Park Hyatt in Century City. Anna Weldon had been away on a location shoot in Toronto. The star of one of their most successful shows was threatening to walk out, and Anna went to do a little hand-holding. While she was away, Wade held a lot more than Bettina's hand. Once she'd gotten him into bed and worked him over, he did everything but promise to have her baby.

A week later, after Anna's return, Wade was brief and elusive. Bettina hadn't been able to pin him down, one way or another, since. Meredith Reynolds, the vice president of Entertainment and Development, stuck pretty close to him these days. She'd been sticking close to him for years, but, of late, she was like Velcro. A wedge that came between him and everything at the office, including, sometimes, his own wife.

Bettina hated Meredith. Meredith was the reason, she believed, that she'd been stuck at the front desk for so long. She wasn't sure, but she thought Meredith suspected what had happened between her and Wade. When opportunities became available in Development, Meredith always passed Bettina over. In most instances, she didn't even look her way. Bettina had stolen enough men to know that the vibe Meredith was giving off to her had nothing to do with work.

It was strictly a cat thing.

Meredith had pissed around her territory, and she, claws bared, dared Bettina to step into it.

But she wasn't fretting about Wade Massey anymore. Or Meredith Reynolds. Bigger plans loomed on the horizon. And, from the looks of things, a window was finally about to open.

Randall stood in front of her now, full of nervous energy.

"So, Mr. Big Shot," she asked, "why are you so giddy?"

He leaned in closer towards her, resting his arms on the reception counter.

"That crucial business dinner I told you about is tonight."

"Ohhhh . . . ," she began excitedly, "the one with—"

"Yes," he replied quickly, trying to run interference with her overeager mouth. "Now lower your voice before you draw attention. Steve and I are already on edge about this whole thing as it is."

"Oh. Sorry," she whispered.

The phone rang again. Randall waited for her to get the call. She quickly dispatched it to the proper party.

"So D-day is still on, right?" she asked.

"Yes, ma'am! Any minute now, we're outta here. Carlos will be on board first. He's giving his notice a couple of weeks after we leave. Then you're up next."

"So you're really serious about letting me produce?"

"Slow down, Magic Mama, slow down. Work with the team and write a few shows first. Then we'll see what you can do."

He called her "Magic Mama" because of her powerful smile. In sweeter days, few though they were, he claimed her smile worked magic on him. Bettina blushed sweetly at his familiarity.

"Did you read my *Frasier* spec script yet?" she asked.

"I've already read the other material you gave me."

Another call came in. She took it and sent it on its way.

"Why haven't you read the script for *Frasier?*" she continued.

"No reason," he said. "Don't worry, I will. I'm trying to get a complete gauge of your talent."

"I thought you already had one," she said in a soft, sexy tone.

"As a *writer,* Magic Mama. I already told you, I want you on the team. You're tenacious as I don't know what, and you've been around this business long enough to know the game. Hell, if people can come to this town with six dollars and become producers inside of a year, there's no reason *you're* not ready."

"Tell me about it," Bettina sighed.

"Well, half the time, it's just about getting a break and knowing somebody. You've been the receptionist here forever. Your chance is long overdue."

The phone rang. She hurriedly answered it. There was no one on the other end. She resumed her conversation.

"I'm glad you see it that way, Randall," she said. "I'm tired of being ignored around here while white kids fresh off the street are given all types of opportunities."

"Well, it's not just about being black, although that's not something that works in your favor. It's about being able to show and prove once you get your chance."

"Well, I've already shown and proved with you, I thought." She batted her eyes at him.

Randall sighed, then frowned.

"Listen, Bettina, stop going there already, won't you? That's under the bridge."

"I know, Randall. I just like to play with you."

"Well, stop playing like that," he replied, his tone serious. "It isn't and won't be appropriate for business, under any circumstances."

"Yeah, yeah, Randall. It was just jokes. *Sheeeesh.*"

"And, by the way, next time write a spec script for a dramatic show. *ER*, or something like *The Practice*. It gives producers an opportunity to see just how dynamic you are. If I had a dollar for all the writers trying to break into the business who had a *Frasier* spec script . . ."

"Yeah, I know, but comedy is so popular. It seems like it's easier to get hired if you can crack a funny on the page. I figured if I can write a funny episode of a high-brow comedy, then I'm a magic mama for real."

"That's apparently what you and ten thousand new writers are all banking on as you sit back and draft your *Frasier* spec scripts," he said, his tone less harsh. "Look, I gotta get outta here." He moved away from the reception area.

"Wait!" Bettina whispered loudly. "Does Meredith know yet?"

More people were beginning to pass through the lobby area. A few were lingering here and there, having end-of-the-day conversations. The phones were no longer ringing as much.

"Of course not," he replied, leaning in towards her again. "She's got no idea. Steve and I have it all figured out. All we have to do is walk. There's nothing she can do about it."

He chuckled at the thought, furtively glancing about the reception area to see if any of the passersby might have heard.

"Now how are you going to pull *that* off?" Bettina asked, bewildered. "That bitch is determined to keep you two under her thumb forever."

"Well, now," Randall replied, patting her hand playfully, "we're just going to have to fuck with her thumb, aren't we?"

He gave her a wink as he walked away. The heat from his touch made Bettina warm in a familiar way.

Randall glanced back.

"Wish me luck," he mouthed.

Bettina smiled, giving him the hundred-watt treatment.

The phone rang again.

Randall took off as she answered it, knowing that, even though Bettina's smile carried more suggestive weight than he had use for, he'd just been given all the luck in the world.

HAVE YOUR CAKE AND MEET HIM, TOO

Desi walked towards the entrance of the restaurant as the valet driver pulled off with her car. She was nervous. Very nervous. One way or another, after the dinner tonight, her whole life was about to change.

"Table for one?" the hostess, a pretty, blonde, athletically anorexic actress-in-waiting type, asked.

"Actually, I'm meeting someone here. His name is Randall James."

"Yes," the hostess said with a smile, not even bothering to check the list she had in front of her. "Right this way, please."

She led Desi to the dining area outdoors. Most of the tables were filled with chattering people. A cool breeze washed over her from the marina. Desi wondered if it had been such a good suggestion to meet at a place like this to conduct business. It seemed a little too casual, almost kind of romantic. The hostess guided her towards the front. Desi spotted a tall, bald, handsome black man who began to rise as she neared his table. He was smiling broadly.

She was quite sure she had never seen him before.

"Here you are," the hostess said, waving her hand towards

the empty chair across from Randall. "Your waiter will be with you shortly."

"Thank you," Desi replied politely. She turned her attention to Randall, who was standing there with his palm outstretched.

"Wow . . . Miss Sheridan." He beamed. "A pleasure to finally meet you. Again. You look . . . fantastic."

Desi shook his hand, then reached for her chair. Before she could even touch it, he stepped over and pulled it out.

"Please. Allow me."

"Thank you."

She'd thought about it and thought about it the night before. She wasn't going to talk a lot tonight. She wasn't going to get too excited. This town had let her down ten times too many. Every time she got her hopes up about something, it never panned out, not the way she wanted it to. This time, she'd let him lead the conversation, and she would only say as much as she deemed necessary. What was most important was that she not appear too hungry or desperate, and that she maintain control. That way, she could clearly gauge how serious he was, and how significant this project could be for her career.

The word for the night is terse, she'd told herself on the drive over. *Act elusive. Act like a star.*

She definitely looked the part. She wore a simply-cut mid-calf-length peasant dress. It was soft teal with red flowers and had an open back with crisscross straps. Her shoes were red leather high-heeled sandals with straps that wrapped around twice and were tied a few inches above the backs of her ankles. A number of heads had turned when she walked in. There were many smiles of recognition. Desi knew the outfit had been a good choice.

Since her hair had gotten wet from the rain the day before, she had decided not to blow-dry it into its usual straightness. The thick naturally curly look worked well with the dress. The highlights of her dark brown hair brought out the richness of her dark brown eyes. She decided to let her mane be.

Why not try something different, she figured. After all, she had nothing to lose.

"I *love* your hair!" Randall exclaimed as he sat back down across from her. "I don't think I've ever seen it like that before."

"You say that like you know all my looks," she replied, then caught herself. Damn. She'd said too much. Already, she was messing up her own plan.

The setting, she thought, with darkness creeping across the sky and the relaxing breeze cooling the surface of her warm skin, was definitely too laid-back and romantic for her to be conducting business. She was treating this man like a suitor, something she didn't have time for right now. Hence the sarcasm. She tried to channel her mind back into a business state.

"Thank you," she quickly added. "I decided to try something new."

"Well, it's perfect," he said with admiration. "Just perfect. It's exactly what we're looking for."

Desi measured her thoughts before she made her next statement.

Make it about business, she reminded herself. *And make it to the point.*

"Now that I'm here, I don't want to hold you up too long. So why not just cut to the chase. What's this project you wanted to talk to me about?"

There, she thought. *Kind of blunt, but not too bad.*

"Wow. You don't mince any words."

"Not in this business," she said.

At that moment, their waiter arrived. Also blond, also athletic, he didn't look like the actor type. He seemed a little more surfer dude.

"Are you guys, like, ready to order?" he chirped.

Definitely a surfer dude.

Randall glanced over at Desi.

"Do you mind if we discuss business over a meal? I was hoping that, since this *is* a business *dinner,* we would at least get to have the dinner part to go along with it. I'm starving. I haven't eaten all day."

Desi thought she saw a playful gleam in his eye.

Instinctively, she sighed.

"Can I at least have a menu, then?"

"Dang!" the surfer dude chuckled as he handed her one. "I thought I gave you a menu! Like, where's *my* mind?"

Obviously at sea, she thought.

The waiter stood there with his pad and pen. Waiting.

"Can I have about five minutes?" Desi asked, uncomfortable with his hovering.

The waiter chuckled again.

"Oh! Sure! Dang! Of course! I'll be back in a few!"

He darted away.

"Seems a little slow on the uptake, doesn't he?" Randall said with a smile.

"*Some*thing's wrong with him," she replied as she opened the menu and began to peruse it.

Desi loved The Cheesecake Factory. Loved practically everything about it. Except for one annoying factor: the menu. It had too many choices, and, being the true Libran that she was, while she could make critical decisions without hesitation, when it came to making decisions about things like movies or meals, when there were too many options to choose from, she was always stymied and overwhelmed.

She flipped to the first page, appetizers, and was just about to scan the list, when the waiter suddenly reappeared.

"You guys ready?" he said, beaming, pen and pad in hand.

"Goodness," Desi said, flustered. "I *just* opened the menu. I asked you to give me five minutes. Is that going to be a problem?"

"Oh! Dang! No! Cool! Five minutes? That's nothing! Take your time! I'll go get you guys some water!"

He dashed away again.

Randall was softly chuckling and shaking his head. Desi glanced at him over her menu.

"He's something else," Randall said, studying his menu.

"I told you, he's got problems," she replied, flipping through her menu as well.

"Here you go!" the surfer dude said, placing the glasses of water in front of them.

Randall and Desi both looked up simultaneously. No way was he back. He had *just* left. It wasn't even twenty seconds.

"Ready to order now?" He grinned. His pen was poised.

Desi huffed and slammed her menu shut against the table.

"Just give me the Jamaican Black Pepper Shrimp," she said, disgusted. "With a glass of Paradise Tropical Iced Tea."

She picked up the menu and practically threw it at him.

The surfer dude, oblivious to her annoyance, was scribbling away, but managed to catch the menu, a vacant smile on his face.

"And you, sir? What'll you be having?"

Randall, also irritated, leaned in towards Desi.

"Are you sure that's what you want? Don't just order something if it's not what you really want to get." He looked up at the waiter. "She asked for five minutes. Don't you have any concept of time?"

The surfer dude's brows rose and his head drew back into his neck.

"Don't worry about it, Randall," Desi said. "I always get the same thing when I come here, so it's no big deal. I just thought for once I'd try something different, but perhaps I'd better stick with what I know."

"You sure?" he asked again, truly concerned.

"Positive," she replied, impressed with his sincerity. She felt herself beginning to relax a little.

He handed his menu to the waiter.

"Alright, I'll have the same thing, too. With a frozen Iced Mango." He looked over at Desi again. "You sure you don't want an appetizer or anything?"

"No," she said, openly smiling. "I'm fine."

Don't I know it, Randall thought. *So I know you've got to know it, too.*

The waiter scribbled away.

"Is that it?"

"Yes," they both responded at the same time. Their eyes met, and they both laughed.

The waiter laughed, too.

Desi and Randall both stopped laughing and frowned at him. He caught the hint and abruptly walked away.

Randall laughed again.

"I hope he's as quick with our food as he was quick to press for our order."

Desi shook her head, smiling.

"I don't know where they got him from. That was a first. The waitstaff here is usually cool, not kooky like this guy."

Randall raised his glass of water.

"Well, here's to a productive meeting, and the opportunity to discuss business with such a beautiful dinner guest."

Desi raised her glass, and he clinked his against hers.

"Thank you," she said, "I think. Unless you got me here under the pretenses of business, and this is really a cheap attempt at a date . . ."

"No, ma'am!" Randall reassured her. "This is definitely about business. I think, after you hear everything I have to say, you're going to know that for sure."

Desi took a sip of her water and leaned back in her chair, ready.

"Then, Mr. James, let's hear it. I want my full celebrity pitch, just like you promised."

By the time the Jamaican Black Pepper Shrimp dishes arrived, Randall and Desi were in the thick of conversation.

There was a slick brochure for Vast Horizons on the table. Desi had already gone through it and learned of Randall's extensive impressive credentials: double degrees from NYU, one in business and the other for film school. (She'd already asked him why he was working in television and not film. He had film projects already lined up for the production company, he said. His dream had always been to positively change the way African-Americans were portrayed, not just on the big screen, but on the small one as well.)

Right after college, he came out to LA and, through a friend from NYU, immediately booked a job as a production assistant on John Singleton's *Boyz N the Hood.* That job led to other projects and connections, and a chance to show off some spec scripts he'd written. This resulted in a position as a writer at NBC. After a two-year stint writing for three shows, all of which were ultimately canceled, Randall ended up at Massey-Weldon. He was referred by Donald Seltzer, one of television's top producers and powerbrokers.

He met Donald, a native New Yorker (which was an instant connection for them both), at a *Seinfeld* cast party. Someone had pointed Donald out to him, and he went over and introduced himself. They talked. Donald was impressed. So was Randall by Donald's approachable and candid demeanor, a rarity in Hollywood at any level. He told Randall to give him a call. Randall did, and actually got him on the phone. They did lunch at Donald's office.

From that day forward, Donald had been a mentor and industry godfather to him. He offered wisdom, advice, and encouragement. He even schooled him on the realities of the business when it came to people of color. Randall respected his opinion because, even though Donald was white, he had done his share to get shows about people of color on the air.

Three Emmys later, Randall had no question about the value of Donald's friendship, expertise, and the contribution the man had made to his burgeoning career.

At Massey-Weldon, Randall was paired up with a hotshot GQ-handsome, blond-haired, blue-eyed writer named Steve Karst.

They seemed as different as night and day. Steve was a golden boy from a well-heeled family in Beverly Hills. Randall expected him to be whitebread, but he was nothing of the sort. Hard-working and self-sufficient, Steve loved and loathed the industry. He loved it for the art form and opportunities for creative expression, but he hated it for its prejudices and warped presentation of cultural images.

Their first project together was to write for a show called *Creep,* a sitcom about an unlucky man who alienated everyone he met. Neither Randall nor Steve liked the premise but, since both were still relative newcomers and determined to make their mark, did their best to come up with quality scripts. After four well-written but poorly viewed episodes, *Creep* was canceled. Randall and Steve, however, learned that, as writers, they had incredible chemistry.

Massey-Weldon also noticed. The two were immediately moved over to write for *Stickies,* Massey-Weldon's top-rated sitcom. One season later, the James/Karst combo came up with a kick-ass episode that all of America was discussing the day after it aired.

The episode, entitled "Spongecoke," was an instant classic. The wife of the main character, desperate for sex but temporarily short on birth control prevention, poured some cola onto a kitchen sponge and used it for what she thought was a quick solution. Once in place, the sponge went haywire. The bulk of the show was devoted to her discomfort, then attempts at its removal—first by her husband, then her best girlfriend, and, ultimately, the hospital.

Deemed too irreverent at first by the producers, the actors loved the script and were able to pull it off with just enough raciness to not be censored. It brought Randall and Steve their first Emmy, and their partnership was officially sealed.

Since then, they'd won two more Emmys for episodes of *Westwood,* a dramatic series based on LA's hip community. Randall was concerned because there weren't any characters of color represented, but he faced resistance from Meredith Reynolds, his boss, every time he insisted something be done. He had lost count of how many meetings he'd been in where he found himself shouting and pounding tables, trying to get someone to listen.

After one such working session where he'd complained loudly about wanting to write an African-American character into the show, he was pulled aside and privately reminded by Meredith that he didn't have as much clout as he obviously believed he did. Just because he'd won some Emmys didn't mean he was irreplaceable.

"Randall, you can't keep going off like that in meetings. It makes you stand out, and not in a way that's favorable to your career."

"So what?!" he asked angrily. "Am I supposed to not say anything while I'm surrounded by institutional racism on a daily basis? This is *bull*shit!"

Meredith pursed her lips together, annoyed.

"You don't seem to understand," she replied. "There aren't many African-Americans behind the scenes in television. Only a handful. But there's plenty of them on the outside, just itching to get in."

Randall was silent.

"They would be happy to be here," she stated, "just to have the chance to work."

She locked gazes with him, hoping he understood the full gist of her words.

It was a threat. Not even a veiled one. Either pipe down or ship out.

"Look, Randall," Meredith sighed, "I'm not saying that what you want doesn't make sense. But it's best to do it slowly. Right now, people like you and Paris Barclay are winning Emmys. Use that power the right way. Don't just set it off like a bomb in people's faces. Timing is everything."

"Paris Barclay is getting to develop his own shows," Randall countered. "He has the chance to make a difference."

"But you're not him. Your time will come."

"My time is here. You and everyone else refuse to see it."

Meredith was unrelenting.

"America can't instantly accept black faces into their homes," she commented, honestly believing her own words. "It has to be done gradually, and be a true reflection of how things really are in the world."

Randall had wondered which world she lived in, where black people weren't walking around functioning as regular members of society on a daily basis. Maybe her world was like the New York on HBO's *Sex and the City,* where, amazingly, the characters never seemed to run into or associate with black people. Randall realized that the only person of color coming into safe, secure Meredith's Hollywood Hills home was probably her maid. She had no idea or concern that the world around her was changing, and that the so-called minorities were now becoming the American majority.

"What about people like Yvette Lee Bowser, Susan Fales-Hill, and Tim Reid? They've been executive-producing shows and carving the way for a while now. They're making changes."

"But not enough for America to notice," she answered. "Like it or not, Randall, the face of television is white. I'm not saying it's fair. I'm just saying that's the way it is. The best we can do is color that face in a little at a time. But you can't just spring it on viewers all at once."

Meredith, he ultimately realized, was off her rocker, just like most of the white producers and studio heads in their lofty ivory towers. They had no idea what was going on in the world around them, and still insisted on whitewashing everything on the air. African-Americans had been happily welcomed into the homes of a variety of viewers ever since *The Cosby Show* successfully depicted the diversity of the culture. Randall and Steve knew it was time for them to leave Massey-Weldon.

They also knew that, whether Meredith believed it or not, they *did* have enough clout to make a difference.

The final straw was when he and Steve pitched a dramatic series to Meredith that they knew would help change the face of prime-time television. It wasn't an all-black series, but an LA-based drama that involved a variety of cultures connecting through a common setting.

Ambitions was the story of five people. The central character, a sexy, sophisticated African-American woman in her thirties, was the owner of a popular upscale restaurant that catered to a high-powered clientele. Just ending a long-term relationship, she was cautiously putting herself back on the market and coming to grips with what it meant to be a successful single black woman looking for a partner. Her best friend, also African-American, was just beginning her second marriage amidst a maelstrom of controversy with her children and extended family. The conflict was over her choice of a husband, a prominent white plastic surgeon with a successful practice in Beverly Hills. The other two characters, a twenty-five-year-old white singer and a Chicano percussionist, both of whom played in the band at the restaurant, were slowly becoming romantically involved.

Meredith's expression as she listened had been stone.

"It won't work," she announced, once they finished their pitch. "The demographics are too crazy. Who's your audience? Teens? Twentysomethings? Thirtysomethings? What? Is it *Dynasty 2000? Melrose Place Revisited?* I can't tell what this is. And it's entirely too much color. This is not what I meant when I said do it gradually."

She rifled through their presentation packet, picking it apart.

"It reads like a daytime soap. Look at this. You've got Mexicans in here. Who wants to see a Mexican storyline? Mexicans aren't everywhere. They're really only found in California, Texas, New Mexico, and Arizona. The rest of the country won't get it."

Randall and Steve, amazed, glanced at each other as she prattled on.

"And the lead character is a black woman. That *definitely*

won't fly, not unless it's a comedy. You'd have to work it so the plastic surgeon was the central figure, but I doubt if that's a compelling enough storyline. Middle America will kill a show like this after the first few episodes. What's in it to make them commit? They simply won't be able to relate."

What got Randall was that Meredith was so comfortable with him that she didn't even bother to consider if he, as a black man, found her words offensive.

"I'm just telling you like it is," she continued. "That's the way of this industry. The public doesn't want to see dramatic shows about people of color and the white people who mingle with them. Not unless the show is primarily white. Maybe, just maybe, if this were a cop show, you might be able to pull it off. But not like this."

"How does this industry know?" Randall argued. "No one's ever given a drama with a black person in the lead enough of a chance to find out. This one will work precisely because it is so diverse. It has something for everyone. It's a real show about real people doing real things. Sure, some of them are wealthy, but some of them aren't. Because the demographics are so wide, that's *exactly* the reason it'll succeed."

"It's too risky," she said flatly, tossing the packet back across the desk at them. "Too much diversity scares people. I don't care what you might be seeing in all those Gap commercials or on videos on MTV. Those are just thirty-second spots and three or four minutes of singing. It might work in those formats, but not for prime-time programming."

Both men glared at her as she carelessly dismissed them.

"Bring me something with some teeth in it. Something young, hip, and fresh. Not too rainbow. Something where we can ease the color in a little at a time. Then we can talk."

Randall snatched up the packet, and he and Steve walked away.

"As a matter of fact," she called out, "leave that with me. I always like to keep a record of projects people come to me with."

Randall handed the packet to Steve to give to Meredith. He stood by the door and waited, the urge to strangle her almost overpowering. Steve tossed the packet onto her desk, and the two of them, disgusted, stormed from her office.

A week later, they were having another meeting. One that took several phone calls to make happen, but, with some strings pulled here and there, it was finally taking place. This time, the response was positive.

When they walked away, they had an official partner *and* financing for their production company. Dawson "Jet" Jonas, the legendary former running back for the Los Angeles Lords, had agreed to come on board. Since his retirement, Jet had amassed a half-billion-dollar empire of real estate and franchises, and was now ready to branch out into entertainment. He had run into Randall several times over the course of the past five years, and the two had a casual friendship.

The challenge had been talking Jet out of insisting the company be called Jet Jonas Entertainment. Randall and Steve assured him that their names would not be in the company title, either. After they explained to him their goals for Vast Horizons, along with their plans to reshape the face of television and film, Jet was excited. It fit perfectly with his own agenda for becoming a formidable, permanent part of the Hollywood landscape.

Jet agreed to use part of his real estate as collateral, and to flex his clout with banks to garner start-up capital in the amount of one hundred million dollars. All this in exchange for fifty percent of the company. They haggled with him, negotiating for a three-way, thirty-three-and-a-third partnership split. Sure he was bringing capital, Randall acknowledged, but they had talent and know-how. The conversation had gone back and forth until Jet finally agreed.

Now they knew they had their chance. The next step was pulling everything together, then permanently walking away from Massey-Weldon.

"So what makes you trust me enough to tell me all this?" Desi asked, forking a bite of shrimp. "How do you know I won't go back and casually run my mouth to someone who knows Meredith Reynolds? Can't you be sued by Massey-Weldon for some kind of contract breach?"

"For one," he calmly replied, "I told you all of this because I feel confident you won't misappropriate the information. Besides, Sharon told me you were trustworthy, and I know Sharon well enough to take her at her word."

He took a sip of his iced mango drink.

"Secondly, the show is definitely a go as far as we're concerned," he said. "We've had some conversations with a few network execs on the quiet. This town is notorious for stealing talent, so we only stand to benefit from the whole situation."

"I see," she mumbled, chewing a bite of plantain.

"No . . . ," Randall said with a smile, "it actually gets better."

"How's that?"

He pierced a shrimp, brought it to his mouth, and bit into it. He held up his finger for her to wait until he finished chewing. He cleared his throat of the spicy pepper and took another drink.

"Sorry."

"That's okay. Go on with what you were saying."

"Oh yeah. Well, the best part about winning that first Emmy three years ago was that Steve and I were able to negotiate the way we wanted. We signed five-year contracts, but we each have a clause about development projects. Mine says I have the option to develop my own shows within a reasonable time frame, a period not to exceed more than three years from the date the contract was executed. If those three years pass and I still have no projects in development, I have the right to leave and go elsewhere. Everything becomes null and void."

"Does Steve have the same clause in his contract?"

Randall nodded.

"Are your three years up?" Desi asked, sipping her tea.

"One month, three weeks, and two days ago." He grinned. "Someone at Massey-Weldon fucked up royally and let our development time frames slip through the cracks. I don't know if it occurred in Legal, or what, but Meredith hasn't caught it yet, and neither has anyone else. Everyone's been too busy. They haven't said anything, and neither have we."

"Wow. That works out great for you guys."

"It sure does. I still can't believe Massey-Weldon could let something as careless as this happen. Usually what they do is let you at least *start* a project. You know . . . get it on paper, act like it's being put in motion. Sure, they never let it get off the ground or take forever making it happen, but that still allows them to legally say that you have projects"—he made the gesture of quotation marks in the air with his fingers—" 'in development.' "

"Really?" Desi asked, shocked. "That's pretty sheisty. Why would they tell you *yes* when they really mean *no?*"

"Come on now, Desi," he chided, picking up a slice of plantain with his fingers, "surely you're not *that* naïve. You've been out here long enough to know how this industry works. You said you're from the South. You know that phrase 'You can catch more flies with sugar than salt'?"

He popped the plantain into his mouth.

"Yeah," she said, smiling. "My grandma used to say that all the time."

"Well," he replied, chewing, "it's the rule out here, except they never really have any intentions of giving you the sugar. Sure, they might let you smell it. They may even give you a granule or two. Television is just like film. It's run by the same people. They woo you, bait you with promises of profit and participation, and tell you how they're going to help you get your own shit started. The whole dog and pony show. How else are they going to get you, especially if you've got a little bit of a name behind you?"

"True," she agreed.

"They might give you a tasty signing bonus that placates you for a minute, but when it comes time for profits, they declare on the books that there were none, that everything's in the red, so there's nothing for you to participate in. Same thing with development deals. They give them to you so you'll feel like you got something out of it that benefits you more than them, but trust me, there's never going to be a contract written in Hollywood that benefits the talent more than it does the person offering the deal. *Ever.* The goal is to get fucked the least, because, no doubt about it, you're going to get fucked."

"Don't I know it," she replied.

"So what you do is get the most amount of money you can up front. Then you negotiate a fierce participation deal and royalty structure, and then you walk away with enough to be able to ultimately leave and build your own kingdom off the earnings you made."

Desi had stopped eating and was now sitting back in her chair, listening intently. This was turning into Hollywood 101, a lesson she thought she'd had eight years before. She apparently hadn't learned this part. It was probably why she was in the predicament she was in now.

Randall kept on, bursting with zeal. He was leaning in towards her, his hands gesturing wildly.

"See, Desi, Meredith was so busy squashing our ideas, she didn't even pay attention to the game. She could have approved *Ambitions*, knowing she never had any intentions of letting it get made. It would have placated us *and* protected the company. Sure, we would have been frustrated. We would have scratched our asses and our heads for a while, wondering if we were being given the shaft."

Desi laughed.

"You know what I'm saying?" he said with a grin. "But as long as she kept smiling and reassuring us, we would have hung out for a while, full of hope. The company would have had the benefit of us still writing for them and, once they trashed *Ambitions*, for whatever reasons given, could have let us start up development on something else. There's a million ways to kill a project in development. They can blame it on anything. Budget cuts, network resistance. *Whatever.* We would have believed them for a little while. Not too long, mind you, but for a minute. But they fucked up. Now Steve and I can just walk away."

"Wow," Desi exclaimed. "Will that get Meredith fired?"

"I doubt it. Wade puts much stock in her, among other things. He'll be pissed off, but probably not enough for it to freak her out. She'll catch the most heat from Anna. And the networks carrying the shows we write for. They're gonna set her ass aflame. Because of this mistake, at least two top-ten network shows will be in jeopardy."

"So you and Steve are the only ones leaving?"

"Yeah. Well, actually, we're taking the receptionist and a guy from Legal. Bettina's gonna write and, ultimately, we hope, produce. At least, that's the plan. And Carlos will handle all the contracts. He's sharp. Nothing slips by the man."

"Do you think they will try to offer you another contract and more money?" she asked.

He made a sputtering sound.

"*Of course!* Isn't that always how they do it? But it's too late. They had their chance. The people we've talked to at the networks are excited about the opportunity to do something cutting edge. They want to work with us. For some reason, getting back at Meredith and Massey-Weldon doesn't seem to bother them either."

"Really?" Desi asked. "I thought Massey-Weldon was revered in this town."

Randall sampled the black beans and rice that came with his shrimp.

"Mmm-hmm"—he nodded, trying to swallow so he could

speak—"they are. But they've got some skeletons in their closet that aren't too pretty. Wade Massey's screwed over his share of people. He steals writers like crazy, makes all kinds of pie-in-the-sky promises, then plays dumb after the fact. Anna Weldon's a sweetheart, but everyone knows that Meredith's a ladder-climbing, back-clawing bitch."

"You're just saying that because she doesn't want your show," Desi replied, digging into her food again.

Randall took another sip of his drink, shaking his head.

"No, Desi," he said between gulps, "I say that because that Aryan heffah is *truly* a bitch. Just ask Anna Weldon."

"Anna Weldon?" Desi asked, curious. "But doesn't Meredith work for her? She can't be a bitch to her own boss."

"She can if she's fucking her *other* boss." He smirked, piercing a piece of shrimp with his fork.

"Say *what?!*" Desi whispered, leaning in closer to him. "Are you serious?"

Her hand touched his in a familiar gesture. Randall's eyes did a quick shift to her hand on his. He was pleased that she seemed at ease around him.

"As a heart attack," he replied. "But, of course, that's neither here nor there. Anna acts like she doesn't know about it, although it seems the rest of the world does. How she can *not* know is beyond me."

Desi leaned back, removing her hand from Randall's. She took a sip of her tropical tea. She was getting off track, she realized, but Randall was so easy to talk to. He was giving her a good Hollywood schooling. Plus, she hadn't gotten a juicy piece of Hollywood gossip in a while. It was almost comforting to hear that other people's lives were as raggedy as hers.

"Anyway," Randall said, "all we have to do now is let the network execs we talked to know who the core cast members will be, then we're pretty sure we're going to get a green light from one of them for next fall's lineup."

"So what networks are we talking here? UPN? WB?"

"No way. I mean, no offense to them, because they've given a number of black shows the chance to make it, but upstart networks are notorious for dumping black shows once they get themselves fully up and running."

Desi nodded.

"That's true. Look at Fox. *Martin, Living Single, In Living Color*—all those shows helped put Fox on the map. Now it's all about *Ally McBeal.* Other than Lisa Nicole Carson, that show is about as lily-white as they come."

"I know," he said. "And I *like Ally McBeal.*"

"Me, too," she said sheepishly. "I watch it faithfully. Ain't that some mess? Hollywood has us so brainwashed, we're fully supporting shows that continually erase us from the face of the planet, when we should have our TVs turned off and be picketing them on a regular basis."

"Picketing won't do anything. All they'll do is close their blinds. It's hard to see from an ivory tower anyway."

They both laughed. A pitiful, that's-a-damn-shame kind of laugh, but a shared one nonetheless.

"I hope I don't seem bitter as I talk about this stuff to you," he said, his tone soft. "I'm not bitter. I've got way too much going on for that. It's just sad that this industry is the way it is."

"You don't sound bitter." She sighed. "I'm a black actress in Hollywood. While I don't know television, I've run up against some of the same obstacles you're talking about."

"I hear ya. Also, I apologize if I've been acting too casual with you." Randall's expression was earnest. "I came here expecting you to be this puffed-up Hollywood diva. I can't tell you how many black actresses I run into that are like that."

"Nope." She smiled. "Not me."

"That's good to hear," Randall replied.

Desi played with her food, twirling her fork around her plate. She suddenly looked up at him.

"Don't get me wrong, now," she said with a laugh. "I *can* be. For instance, if this meeting turns out to be a waste of my time, diva's gonna be the only thing you ever get from me again."

As she said it, she realized that if the meeting *did* turn out to be a bust, unless she decided to take the job at Neiman's, she'd be headed back to Alabama. If that happened, the odds of him seeing her again were almost nonexistent.

The thought made her visibly worried.

"What's wrong?" Randall asked, noticing her knitted brows.

"You still haven't told me what's in this for me. Are you offering me the lead? Is that what this is about?"

"I'm sorry. I thought I'd been saying that through this whole conversation."

He reached down into his satchel and pulled out a script.

"Here's the pilot," he said, showing it to her across the table. He flipped to the first page. "See that character?" He pointed to the name Raquel. "That's you, or, rather, who we *hope* to be you."

He flipped through some more pages. The character was in almost every scene.

"She's got a lot of screen time," Desi commented. "So the show would be built around me?"

"Actually, it's more of an ensemble format, with four other primary characters. But you would be the hub. The way we've got it written, your character, for the first two years, has the most critical storyline, and is the point from which all the other storylines radiate."

The first two years, Desi mused. Wow. That would mean she could stay in LA and, if the show was good enough, get her name back out there again.

"You've got it plotted out for the first two years?" she asked, casually taking the script from him.

"We've got it developed all the way through year five," he answered. "We allow for latitude and changes along the way, of course, but we have a general sketch of the flow of the characters and their overall development."

"If I like it, do I have to commit to five years?"

"We'd be happy if you'll just commit to one. You can set it up with the option to do more, depending on how you mesh with the role."

"I didn't know television worked like that. I thought actors were at the mercy of the network and the executive producer. If they decided all of a sudden that they want you out so they can restructure the show, then that was that."

"That *is* how it works, in many instances. But if the star is a hit with the audience and is the main reason they watch, then that star can call some of the shots as well. Much of it has to do with the contract you negotiate as an actor, and the contract we negotiate with the network. Most of it has to do with the ratings. The network has to be willing to guarantee enough episodes to allow the show a chance to establish itself."

"Then how can I be sure that I'll have job security? Suppose the executive producer suddenly decides he wants me out?"

"I'm the executive producer, along with Steve and Jet. We're willing to work out a contract that will give you a sense of security."

Desi rubbed her chin, her half-eaten food now completely pushed aside.

"But what if the viewing audience doesn't like my character? What if I don't turn out to be the ratings draw you expect?"

"I highly doubt that," Randall said, "but I'm sure you're open to working on character development. Aren't you?"

"Yes," she said, nodding.

"Well then, there you go."

She continued to flip through the script, noticing all the places Raquel appeared. It seemed too good to be true. There had to be a catch. Perhaps the writing sucked. Or the pay was low.

"Once you read it, you'll see that it's really well written,"

Randall remarked, as if reading her mind. "Steve and I are pretty proud of that script, and everyone who's read it has been impressed. Each of the networks we talked to has said that a show like this would get a really good budget."

She kept studying the script.

"What if, by some chance, you're not picked up by a network?" she asked.

Randall was just swallowing a bite of plantain.

"We will be," he said, gulping. "It's practically guaranteed. Vast Horizons is going to get this project on the air, one way or another. As it stands now, getting it on one of the major networks won't be a problem."

"What about if I want to do a film? Will this interfere with my film career?"

"We'll work it so that you can still do movies," he responded. "Television actors do it all the time."

Desi placed the script on the table in front of her and leaned back.

"Randall, do you know how many promises I've been made in this town? How many promises that have gone unfulfilled?"

He took a swallow of his now-melting iced mango drink, searching her face. She looked so young and beautiful, but her eyes had a weariness that seemed filled with disappointment. How had he never noticed that before? The eyes never lied, but she was good at making sure they did when she was onscreen.

"Desi, should you decide to come on board, regardless of whatever budget we get from a network, Vast Horizons will commit to paying your salary as negotiated. That's a promise we'll put in writing."

Her breath caught for a moment. She stared at him, waiting for a *but*. The silence hung between them. Randall ate a peppered shrimp.

"So you're telling me," she finally said, "just to have me as a part of the show, you guys are gonna pay me out of your company's pocket?"

He nodded, his mouth too full of shrimp to speak.

"Effective when?" she asked, trying not to sound too eager. Her pulse had accelerated so much that she could almost feel the blood coursing just beneath her skin.

Randall swallowed the shrimp, then made a hacking sound. "*Acckkk!*" he coughed, taking a quick sip of his drink. "Those little fuckers are *hot!* I think the pepper went down the wrong way!"

Desi was too serious and too excited to smile. All she wanted now was answers.

"Effective *when?*"

He cleared his throat of pepper and took another drink.

"We're willing to pay you a healthy, good-faith signing bonus upon execution of the contract. After that, your salary will be paid per episodes shot."

"I'd like participation," she said.

Randall smiled.

"Somehow, I knew you would. That can be worked out."

Desi scrunched up her face, still unable to take it all in. She stared at him, searching for some kind of trickery. Hollywood was full of trickery, and so were the men in it.

"Okay, Randall . . . let's cut the crap. Why me? Out of all the black actresses to choose from, why me?"

Randall scanned the area.

"Did you notice how we haven't seen our waiter since he brought out the food?"

"Yeah, yeah," she snapped. "Come on, now. Answer me."

He smiled.

"I don't know how much of our initial phone conversation you remember," he said, "but the character Raquel was written with you in mind."

She nodded.

"I remember you saying that. That still doesn't answer my question. Why me?"

Randall leaned closer to her, his eyes penetrating.

"Because I think you're a damn good actress. You were great in *Living Foul*, even though it was a small role. *Flatbush Flava* should have made you blow up, but I think Jackson Bennett's offended too many people to garner the respect he deserves. You took the brunt of the fallout that rightfully belonged to him."

Desi watched him closely.

"I've seen everything you've ever done, twenty-eight films total. I respect the fact that you're always working. You know what? I even saw that indie film that you probably thought only a handful of people caught. The one where you were a lounge singer. My God, you were terrific!"

He was referring to *Blue*, a small film she'd shot in London. She was really proud of the project, although it never went anywhere.

"Where did you see it?" she asked, blushing. Flattered.

"At the Toronto Film Festival five years ago."

"Oh my God, you were there?!" she exclaimed. "So was I!"

"I know." He smiled. "I passed by you several times on different days, but I didn't want to get in your space."

They glanced at each other for a moment, then, embarrassed, looked away. Desi slid her plate back in front of her and nervously picked up her fork. Randall grabbed his mango drink, now completely melted, and took a quiet sip.

He cleared his throat. She glanced up at him.

"Look, Desi," he began, "I don't want you to think I'm some crazed Hollywood stalker disguising myself as a TV writer-slash-exec by day. I don't use my career to pick up women."

She narrowed her eyes at him. He chuckled.

"Okay, okay. Maybe I've used it a couple—five times."

Desi giggled unexpectedly.

"But I'm not using it now. Like I said, I think you're an awesome actress. Period. The fact that you're beautiful and not a diva makes it even better. I'd be lying if I said I'm not and have never been attracted to you . . ."

She looked down at her plate, avoiding his eyes.

"But," he kept on, "that's just me stating my appreciation as a fan. We have a show we want to develop, and we want you in it. That's all that matters. Anything else is irrelevant. Anything else is gravy."

"So you don't have *any* other actresses you're considering for the role?" she asked, looking up.

"My short list had only one person on it. You."

"That's not very smart, is it? Suppose I say no? Then you're going to have to find someone suited to the role, or have to tailor it to them."

"This role was written for you, and I'm going to do everything in my power to get you to say yes. *Ambitions* is going to make you the star you deserve to be. Working on television doesn't have the stigma it once had. It won't interfere with your film career. If anything, it will only make you more marketable as an actress. As a star."

Desi toyed with the napkin on her lap. She sighed deeply, lifting her eyes up to his.

"Alright, Mr. James," she said, reaching into her purse. "Here's my card. It has the number of my agent, Ken Ashton, on it. Give him a call tomorrow. He's usually in just after ten. If it's okay with you, I'm going to take this script and read it tonight."

"Yes, definitely," he said. "Take it. It's yours."

"Thank you. If I like the way it reads, I say you talk figures and terms tomorrow with Ken. By the time you call him, he'll know my opinion of the script and whether I have any interest."

Randall took in a deep breath.

"Does that mean you're seriously considering it?" he asked, hopeful.

"It means you got my attention. Let's just see if you can keep it."

Randall smiled.

"I have no doubt, Desi, that I will. If it's alright with you, we'd like an answer, one way or another, pretty quickly. Not to rush you or anything, but we need to blaze full speed ahead to get this show ready for next year. We're about to be mid-swing of development season. People are out there pitching to the networks like crazy."

An answer pretty quickly. Those were just the words Desi wanted to hear.

"No problem," she said. "That's exactly how I like to work."

She stood, gathered her purse and the script, and extended her hand across the table.

"A pleasure meeting you, Randall," she said with a smile.

Randall stood abruptly, startled that the meeting was now, apparently, over. He'd hoped to linger with her a little longer over coffee, but perhaps, he realized, that was hoping for a little too much. Just yet. This was business, after all. First and foremost, he wanted her to commit to the show.

"Thank you for dinner," Desi said pleasantly, and walked away.

"I look forward to hearing from you soon," he called out.

Randall watched her as she made her way to the inside of the restaurant.

Good God, she's beautiful, he thought. *And talented. Please let her take this role.*

As he stood there, his eyes following her, he saw their waiter, surfer dude, approaching.

Randall, shaking his head, chuckled, opened his wallet, and threw a crisp fifty on the table.

The waiter rushed up to get it.

"Is that it? Would you like some coffee or anything?"

"No," Randall replied smugly. "My work here is done."

The waiter rifled through his pockets for the check.

"Do you want any change?" he asked, taking the fifty.

Randall, walking away, cut his eyes at the guy, amazed at his gall.

"Keep it," he replied. "You'll be needing it soon anyway."

"What do you mean?" asked the waiter, trying to catch up with him.

"I mean that you'll be out of a job. Your waiting skills suck."

Surfer dude laughed heartily as they entered the inside of the restaurant.

"No I won't," he said. "My uncle's the manager here. I've got more job security than anybody in this joint. Thanks for the tip!"

He raced off towards the bar.

Randall stopped, staring after the waiter, who was now gathering drinks from the bartender.

Disgusted, Randall made his way out of the restaurant and gave the parking attendant his ticket.

As he stood on the curb waiting for his truck, he glanced around him at all the seemingly happy white folks coming and going. They looked like they didn't have a care in the world. For some odd reason, he noted, almost all of them were blond.

White people, he thought. *Why does it seem like they always have it made?*

He caught a few furtive stares, as people entering the restaurant noted his big blackness topped off by a shiny bald head.

As he waited for his car, he thought he saw Desi driving away in a black 5 Series BMW. It looked as if she were letting her windows down.

"Nah," he muttered. "It can't be." Someone as well-recognized as she was wouldn't drive around with her windows wide open. Besides, it was too cool out.

The valet pulled up with Randall's dark blue Range Rover. The white attendant gave him and the truck a double take as he stepped out of the vehicle.

Randall chuckled as he stepped into his truck.

White people, he thought again, shaking his head as he pulled off.

TO SLEEP, PERCHANCE TO DREAM

The phone rang eight times. The machine never picked up.

Groggy, snatched from the cozy confines of an Amsterdam hash bar where she was having a good laugh and a good smoke with a fine faceless man sitting across the table from her, Sharon reached blindly towards the night table. She knocked the cordless phone out of its cradle, onto the floor. It hit the hardwood with a *clunk*.

"*Damn!*" she groaned, patting around for it in the darkness. Her eyes felt like trash. She leaned over the side of the bed and grabbed the phone from the floor.

"What the hell do you want?" she grunted. "And, I swear to God, it better be good."

"Girl, I know you're not asleep!" Desi shouted. "Wake up! It's only ten o'clock! What are you doing in bed so early? You've been sleeping a lot lately."

"Hey, hey . . . tone that down," Sharon whispered. "Damn. Can't you tell fucked-out when you hear it?"

Desi, feeling very happy and carefree, laughed.

If there was one thing she could say she envied about Sharon, it was her ability to get her sex on. Sharon made no bones about it. She loved being in love, and was always in it, one way or another. What she said she loved most about it was that it came with regular, hard-core sex.

She had a knack for finding lovers who gave her sex just the way she liked it. Desi often wondered if that was the thing that made her end up falling in love.

"The way to my heart is through my panties," Sharon once brazenly commented. "If you can make me come, you can make me go."

"I hope I didn't catch you in the act," Desi said in an apologetic tone. She hadn't expected Sharon to be in bed. She was a night owl who always seemed perky, no matter what time the call.

"If you had, I would have never answered the phone."

"Why didn't you just turn your machine on?"

"I forgot," Sharon grunted.

"I don't understand why you don't have voice mail on your phone to begin with," Desi replied. "You're the only person I know who still has a physical answering machine, and the one you have is old as dirt!"

"Whatever. What do you want?"

"And look at how you answered the phone!" Desi exclaimed, her voice still hyper. "Sharon, what if I was a major producer or somebody who was calling to offer you work? You can't just answer the phone like that!"

"I know every black son- *and* daughter-of-a-bitch working in this town," Sharon croaked, clearing her throat of phlegm, "and they all know me, so how I am won't be a surprise to anybody. If they want me for work, they want me for work. My reputation speaks for itself, so I don't give a damn about who is and who isn't impressed by how I answer the phone."

She cleared her throat again, making a sharp hacking sound.

Desi laughed.

"I guess you've got a point," she said. "But suppose it was somebody like Spielberg or Oliver Stone?"

"Right now, I'm not worried about what Oliver Stone thinks

about me. He's not exactly the poster child for perfect behavior. None of us are."

"Alright, alright," Desi quickly chimed, "but suppose it was Spielberg?"

"So. I already know him."

"You *do?!*" Desi asked, surprised. "How come you never told me that before?"

"*Please!*" Sharon scoffed, her voice still thick. "Like I got enough brain cells to spare to remember to tell you anything. It's a wonder I can even remember your name on a day-to-day basis."

Sharon, Desi knew, was joking. She was notorious for her memory. She never forgot anything, good or bad. For instance, people in the business who intentionally (or accidentally) snubbed her at functions, then, months or years later, approached her, wanting introductions to popular actors, celebrities, directors, other producers, or a part in a film she was working on. Most of them were oblivious to what they'd done, perhaps not knowing at the time how quietly powerful and connected she was in the film and television community. Some of them merely thought she forgot, their disdain being a generally accepted thing known as Hollywood attitude. Sharon usually gave them her ass to kiss.

"Ex*cuse* me?" was how she always responded. "I *know* you're not talking to *me*. Remember that time . . . ?"

At which point she would recount the transgression, then politely walk away.

A person only had one chance to do Sharon wrong. After that, the offending party, once amends were made, knew to show her respect. What it took to make peace with her was in direct relation to how badly she'd been offended. It could be anything. An invite to an intimate gathering. Premium seats at a New York Knicks game (including airfare to and from New York). Dinner at her favorite restaurant, the Polo Lounge at the Beverly Hills Hotel. Drinks at the Sky Bar. A bag of weed.

Sharon never told the offending party what he or she needed to do to make amends. She was completely unavailable once she pointed out the crime. All the person had to do was ask someone who knew her how to get back in her good graces. Since almost everyone, at one time or another, had rubbed Sharon the wrong way, figuring out how to win her back wasn't hard.

Usually, a formal invitation or tickets would arrive by courier. Mysterious packages wrapped in plain brown paper were delivered by limo. Flowers and gift baskets, accompanied by cards scrawled with varied versions of *I should have known* were conveyed. Sharon graciously accepted them all, and a newly forgiven acquaintanceship would begin.

People knew that, even though Sharon was currently freelancing, her life could change at any moment. She'd held high-ranking positions at some of the most powerful black production companies in town. She'd worked on projects with everyone from Ron Howard and Penny Marshall, to Bruce Willis and Laurence Fishburne. There was a bevy of stars in between that knew her and admired her work.

Word got around that she should not be slighted. No one ever knew when they'd be sitting in front of her, asking for a job.

When she wasn't holding a grudge, Sharon was a fun, upbeat person who loved living life to its fullest, generally well-liked by those who knew her.

As a friend, she was one of the best people to have around.

As an enemy, she was worse than acid rain.

Desi was glad Sharon was her friend, though she thought Sharon didn't fully realize just how talented, powerful, and connected she was.

"Okay," Desi said, still prodding Sharon with questions, "what about if it was Coppola calling you? Or one of the Weinsteins?"

Sharon groaned with frustration.

"I know the Weinsteins and they know me too, so I don't give a fuck. And if Coppola calls, that would mean he got my phone number from someone who already knows me, in which case he was warned that I'm unorthodox, but I'm good. So, either way, he'll know what to expect. You gotta go through somebody I know to get to me. That's just the way it is."

She yawned, a long, drawn-out sound that crescendoed in a squeal.

"Why am I even entertaining all these foolish questions?" she asked, annoyed. "I'm tired, I'm hungry, and I think I might even be horny again."

Desi heard a series of deep grumbling utterances in the background.

"It's Dez," Sharon said in response to the grumbles.

Again, the grumbling.

"Hell if I know," Sharon replied. "Dez, why *are* you calling me? I know it wasn't to play the what-if-so-and-so-calls-you game, 'cause, last time I checked, none of them so-and-so's have been calling me."

"This is important, Sharon," Desi replied, her voice ripe with nervous energy.

"So spit it out, then. I got company, and I'm about to hang up."

"Is it Glen?" Desi asked.

"Who else?"

"I'm being nosy, aren't I?"

"Yes you are," Sharon grunted. "So tell me what's up."

"Alright." Her phone beeped. "Sharon, hold on a second."

"Hurry up," she said.

Desi clicked over, then immediately clicked back.

"That was fast."

"It was a stupid hangup call. Anyway, I met with your friend Randall tonight, and he told me all about the show he wants me to be in. He really wants me for it, girl, and it sounds like it'll be something I can really sink my teeth into."

"Mmm-hmmm," Sharon said dryly. "And? It's not like I didn't tell you that already."

"I know, I know," Desi replied. "But come on. It's one thing to have somebody talk about how they're gonna put you on, and another having somebody ready to do it right now."

"Did he show you a contract?"

"No, but he talked about one. He's going to call Ken in the morning and find out if I like the pilot script enough to be interested in the role."

"Do you?" Sharon yawned.

"Are you *kidding?!*" Desi exclaimed. "I *love* it! It's *awe*some! The character he wants me to play has so much depth and potential. I feel like there's a lot I can do with the role."

"Did he write the pilot script?"

"Yes. He and his partner, Steve."

"And they're executive producing, right?" Sharon asked.

"I think so, along with Jet Jonas. Randall didn't say, but I assumed as much. Did you know Jet was putting up a hundred million dollars to help start their company?"

"Get out!" Sharon exclaimed, the jolt of Desi's words making her sit straight up. "Randall told me Jet was a partner, but I didn't know any of the details."

The line was quiet for a moment. Desi could hear the grumbling in the background again.

"Alright, hang on," Sharon muttered, "just give me a second. Yo, Dez, I just thought about something."

"What's that?"

"You need to find out if Randall and Steve are going to be writing for the show full-time, or if they're planning to hire other writers."

"Why would I ask that?"

"To protect yourself. I've known Randall long enough to trust that he's not going to attach his name to something that isn't quality work. But think about it: it's one thing to read a script written by people whose work you respect, and another to be signed for a show that's no longer being written by those people."

"Yeah," Desi replied softly, now concerned. "So what does that mean?"

"It means you just finished reading a phenomenal pilot script. Before you commit yourself to anything, you need to make sure the scripts that follow are going to be just as good."

Desi grew silent. She hadn't even thought about that.

"I mean, I don't think you seriously have anything to worry about," Sharon added, sensing Desi's change. "Look at David E. Kelley with *Ally McBeal, The Practice,* and *Chicago Hope.* He does it all. But it takes a minute to get to where he is. He's what's called a show runner."

"What's that?"

"A show runner is a person who executive produces and writes. It's just like the name sounds . . . they pretty much run the whole show. David E. Kelley EP's all three of his shows *and* writes full-time for *Ally* and *The Practice.* It *can* be done."

"You say that like you don't think Randall and his partner can do it," Desi said.

"Well, I don't mean it like that," Sharon replied. "All I'm saying is that it takes a while to become a David E. Kelley. It doesn't just happen overnight. He started out as a story editor for *LA Law,* proved himself, then ended up taking over the show as EP when Steven Bochco left. He worked with Bochco on *Doogie Howser,* and then he did *Picket Fences,* and started getting all kinds of critical acclaim. Show runners are made, not born."

Desi was still worried.

"Are you saying Randall and Steve aren't show runners?"

"Well, as of right now, no, they're not. Show runners have the ear of the networks and can get projects put on just like that. They can shepherd projects in. Networks know that they can deliver. Mention the name Bochco, and see if anybody at a network walks the other way."

Desi was silent, poring over the meaning of Sharon's words.

"Right now Randall and Steve have some clout because

they're Emmy-winning writers. That's nothing to sneeze at, either. They're on their way. You're hooking up with them at a good time. Just make sure you find out if they are, in fact, going to be writing for the show full-time."

"I'll make sure Ken asks Randall about that," Desi said. "I can't believe I didn't. I remember him saying something about the receptionist at Massey-Weldon coming to work for them as a writer and producer."

"Really? The receptionist?"

"That's what he said. I should have asked more questions."

"You're used to dealing with film," Sharon replied. "Television's a whole 'nother ball game. You'll see."

Desi heard Sharon mumble something, then make a muffled, cooing sound. The phone dropped onto the floor. It clanged in Desi's ear, making her pull the receiver away. Sharon fumbled around until she found it again. She could hear Desi shouting as she brought the phone up to her ear.

"Sharon? *Sharon!* Are you there?!"

"*Woooooops!* Sorry."

"What happened? What are you doing?"

"Nothing." Sharon's voice had a cryptic edge. "I dropped the phone."

"Oh. Well, thanks for pointing that writing issue out to me."

"No problem," Sharon replied, preoccupied. There was a muffled noise on her end of the phone. "Look, Dez, I gotta go."

Desi heard tussling, then grumbling, and another muted coo.

"Okay. I just called because I wanted to share my excitement with you."

Sharon let out something deep and throaty that seemed as if it could have been a laugh. Or a moan.

"Believe me, baby," she grunted, "I'm excited all right."

Desi was now frustrated by Sharon's antics.

"Just confirm for me one more time, and then I'll let you go . . . Is this guy Randall *really* legit? No bullshit?"

She distinctly heard activity in the background. The deep grumbling had turned into deep moans mixed with short, muffled cooing.

"*Sharon!* Did you hear me? Is he really legit?!"

There were more tussling noises, then Sharon answered.

"He's legit. Just make sure you get everything in writing. I don't care who anybody is these days. Randall's a good friend, an old friend, but a contract's a contract. Get that shit in writing, and make sure you're paid up front. If he wants you, make him work for it."

"I will. You know, you didn't tell me how good-looking he is."

"You didn't ask."

"It's no big deal," Desi replied quickly. "I'm just saying. So you guys grew up together, huh? Was he somebody that you used to date?"

"No, Dez," Sharon answered, her voice flat. "He's fair game. Free and single, as far as I know."

"I'm not trying to go out with him!" Desi protested. "This is work. I've got bigger issues on my mind. I was just asking."

"Whatever," Sharon mumbled, resuming what she was doing in the background.

"He's going to be talking terms and figures with Ken tomorrow," Desi said, ignoring the obvious symphony of sex that was orchestrating.

"Get everything in writing" was all Sharon replied.

"Alright. Can I show you the contract once I get it? You'll probably know what I'm looking at better than I will."

"*Mmmmhmmmmmmmmmmmmmmmmmm . . .*"

Desi was quiet, pondering. Moans and coos billowed from the phone.

"Glen's an entertainment attorney, right?" she asked.

"*Mmmmhmmmm . . .* you should see how he's entertaining me now."

Desi laughed.

"You're crazy. Seriously though, do you think I could get him to take a look at the contract? At a discounted rate? If it works out, I could pay him more later."

"If you let me get back to business," Sharon groaned, "I might be able to get it done for free."

"Okay," Desi quickly replied.

She opened her mouth to say something else, but the phone went dead.

Sharon clicked off the phone and dropped it onto the floor. She rolled over, climbed on top of Glen, found his already-risen center, and, making a circular motion with her hips, slid down onto it.

He placed his hands on her waist, holding her in place as she rocked above him.

Sharon threw her head back, her locks falling deep into the arch of her spine.

"Was Desi calling about business?" Glen grunted, leaning up to kiss her breasts.

"*Unnnnnh,*" she moaned. "No. Yeah. Sorta. Once again, someone other than me is being put on."

She rocked faster, trying to lose herself in the sex.

"I'll put you on," he groaned, sliding his hands up her back. He sat up, pulling her into him. Sharon rocked harder, her eyes squeezed tight. A score of errant locks had fallen into her face. Glen, still holding her close, gently brushed them aside as he kissed her lips, her cheeks, and her forehead.

They rocked in unison.

Sharon began to moan loudly. He watched her face, seeing the intensity of pleasure neatly blended with career frustration. Her eyes were closed and she was biting her lip. He wanted to do something to make everything alright for her. He cupped her behind, and rocked against her harder.

"Don't worry, baby," he whispered reassuringly, "everything's gonna be just fine."

Sharon, furiously working her crotch against his, was so deep inside her sexual stupor, his words seemed as if they were coming from outer space. She opened her eyes, twisting her face as she looked at him. What the *hell* was he talking about?

"Your time is gonna come," Glen continued. "I can feel it."

"I know it is," she replied in a staccato moan. "If you hang on for a just a minute, it's about to come . . . right *nowwwww-wwwwwwwww!*"

Two hours later, the phone rang again.

This time, Sharon was too lost in her sleep to hear it.

She stirred slightly, caught up in the physics of another dream.

She was uptown on the Major Deegan, headed somewhere in the direction of her old neighborhood in the Bronx. Her cell phone was ringing. She could see the number of the person who was calling. The call was very important, from someone she'd been waiting to hear from all day.

As she maneuvered up the highway, she tried desperately to take the call. She was eating a fried perch sandwich from a fish joint on 125th Street. She had one hand on the wheel and the other on the sandwich. She stuffed the sandwich into her mouth as she picked up the cell phone to answer it. She punched a button on the cell phone's keypad, but it didn't stop ringing. She punched another button, and another, and another, but the blasted ringing just couldn't be stopped.

Frustrated, she beat the phone against the steering wheel, but the ringing continued.

Glen jumped abruptly when Sharon reached out and beat against his back. He grumbled something, rolled over towards her, and lapsed back into sleep.

Even he didn't notice the phone as it rang.

It was picked up on the twelfth ring. The answering machine, old and erratic, was set to pick up after ten.

"You have reached the office of Sharon Lane," the ancient tape sputtered. *"I'm either on the phone or away from the office. Please leave an abbreviated message, and I will return*

your call at my earliest convenience. Oh . . . don't forget to wait for the beep!"

The tape queued itself back up, followed by a strangled, pitiful squall not unlike that of a dying swan.

There was a pause.

"Jesus . . . was that it? Was that the beep I'm supposed to be waiting for? Girl, you really need to fix your shit! I know you've got enough money to do it!"

There was a chuckle, then the voice went on.

"Look, Sharon, it's me, Jackson. I know it's late, but this is important. Two things: I got this mega, mega film I just got a green light for. I'm talking big bucks! Remember my epic Bob Marley flick? The shit was hush-hush because I didn't wanna jinx it, but now it's on. I just found out about it today. Yo, shorty, I got a thirty-million-dollar budget. That's right, say word! You're my girl, so you know I want you to head up my producers' unit."

In her dream, Sharon still couldn't answer the cell phone. It had stopped ringing, but no sound was coming out. She beat it against the steering wheel again.

Sharon struck Glen, who was now facing her, in the chest. As a reflex, he kicked her hard in the shin. She groaned and rolled over, still tangling with her dream.

Jackson Bennett kept on.

"Besides this gig, there's something else coming up. My boy Jet Jonas and I were just talking, and he's got some serious things jumping off. He's about to give Magic Johnson some good competition. I just left him an hour ago over at the Sky Bar. We were having drinks, and he started telling me about everything he's got going on. He asked for my advice, so I kicked your name around. Hope you don't mind. He said Randall James has been doing the same. That's your boy, right? Well, I don't know if Randall's talked to you about it yet, but they got big plans going on up in their spot."

In her dream, Sharon was still driving on the Deegan and the fish sandwich was still in her mouth. She accidentally dropped the cell phone, abruptly hit the brakes, and was immediately rear-ended by a red Ford Expedition. The fish sandwich, in its entirety, flew down her throat. She lunged forward in her sleep, choking and gasping.

Glen, sensing her moving away, unconsciously reached out and pulled her back.

"*Yo, shorty,*" Jackson rambled, "*Jonas has money and clout, and you know that's all it takes in this town. All they need over there is the right people working wit' 'em, you know what I'm saying, and it's on. They already got distribution on lock and everything. I told Jet that you were his girl. I think you'd kick ass working with them. They got a hundred million dollars to start. Do you know how many projects you can do with that much dough? I'm not talking blockbuster flicks, but you could make some nice romantic comedies and dramatic pieces with that kinda loot.*"

Sharon, still sleeping, frightened by her dream, wiggled her butt closer to Glen. She nestled deep against him. He held her tightly.

"*So check it . . . I'm not gonna run the tape out on your raggedy-ass machine.*" Jackson laughed heartily at his own words. "*But, seriously, on the real, call me first thing in the morning at my office. We gotta get jumping on this film. And we gotta talk about this other business. I'm tryna hook you up, shorty. Sharon, there's a whole lotta money about to get flung around right now, and two big bushels of it, maybe more, are flying your way. Handle yourself accordingly!*"

There was a click, a dial tone, then the sound of the tape rewinding. Midway through rewind, the tape made a sick warbling sound, then jammed. Streams of backed-up tape spewed out of the machine.

Sharon sat up.

"What's wrong, baby?" Glen grumbled sleepily.

"I don't know," she answered, her throat thick. "I thought I heard something."

The room was quiet.

Glen rubbed her back.

"Lie down. It was probably a dream."

"Yeah," she croaked, her eyes barely open. "I guess."

She leaned back and cozied up inside his arms. She felt a throbbing sensation in her shin.

"Did you kick me?" she asked.

He chuckled groggily.

"Girl, just shut up and go back to sleep."

MIDLOGUE #1

"Whatever happened to my mama?"

The little girl had just run into the house, her breath coming quick. She stopped inside the living room.

They sighed and glanced at each other, unsure of what to say to the precocious eight-year-old. The man was standing next to a box.

"What do you think about this new Easy Bake oven?" he said. "It was supposed to be a surprise, but I guess you caught us."

The little girl ran up and stood before them, examining the gift.

"Can I cook with it for real?" she asked excitedly.

"Well, Alicia, that's the whole point," the woman sharply replied.

Her patience had grown thin with time. Whereas she used to be able to entertain hours of empty, innocent questions, her answers had now become clipped and curt. The man cut his eyes at her. His patience, over the years, had remained securely intact.

He knelt down beside the little girl.

"How would you like me to teach you a thing or two about cake baking?" he whispered.

He stroked Alicia's dark curly hair, which hung thickly in two plaits. Alicia grinned.

"Men don't bake cakes!" she giggled.

"Well, this man does!" he replied, tickling her middle.

She laughed harder, scooting away from him. He scooped her up in his arms and kissed her squarely on the forehead.

Alicia threw her arms around his neck and kissed him back.

"You think if I learn how to bake a cake, it'll make my mama come back?" she asked.

The woman sighed again and walked over to the sofa.

"Why do we even bother?" she muttered absently. "Year after year. This is such a thankless job."

He glanced back at her, his eyes pained.

"It's not a job," he returned. "This is a person. A beautiful person. And, with or without your help, I'm going to do my best to positively shape her life."

"When have I ever not helped?" she snapped.

"I don't know." He sighed. "I can't really say. It seems that somewhere along the line, though, you just stopped trying."

Little Alicia was planting a series of kisses all across his forehead. He squeezed her tightly.

"Well?" Alicia asked. "If I bake her a cake, do you think she'll come back?"

"Sweetie," he said in a soft voice, "why all the questions about your mother all of a sudden?"

"Because," Alicia replied, her tone upbeat, "Jenny said that I didn't have a mama, and I told her nuh-uh, my mama's coming back for me, just wait and see!"

Her face was very close to his. She moved it even closer, peering into his eyes for an affirmative answer.

"Your mama had to go away, honey," he said. "We told you that a long time ago. But we love you. We really do. And we're going to do the best we can to make sure that you have everything you need. Haven't we done that so far?"

The little girl ignored his response and continued to stare into his eyes, as if searching for something clearer, like the word yes, or no.

"So . . . is she coming back?" she asked.

The woman on the sofa sighed heavily in annoyance.

The man put Alicia down.

"I tell you what," he said happily, "why don't we break into this box, you and I, and let's see if we can make us a cake for dessert tonight!"

Little Alicia stood before him, waiting for her answer.

The man knelt down again and began to open the box, pulling apart the top flaps and reaching inside to pull out the contents.

The woman watched Alicia. She'd seen her get this way before. It seemed to happen in cycles, every two or three years, as the little girl's circle of friends began to grow. Children probed, asked questions, taunted and teased. Alicia always came back with the same old question. They were usually able to divert her to other things. When it happened of late, there was no getting the child off the subject.

The man sat the oven on the floor.

"Ooooh," he cooed. "Alicia, baby, we're gonna have lots of fun with this!"

Little Alicia stamped her foot.

"Is she coming back?" she whined.

The man pulled out a tiny pair of aluminum baking pans.

"Well, would you look at these!" he exclaimed. "Aren't they the cutest little things you ever did see? Almost as cute as my little button right here . . ."

He reached out to touch Alicia's nose.

Her eyes were red and misted over. She backed away.

"Is she coming back?" the little girl whimpered.

The man glanced over at the woman, helpless. She offered no sympathy. He looked again at little Alicia. Tears were now beginning to streak the full swell of her cheeks.

He reached out for her, his arms open wide. Alicia looked at him, her lips trembling. As his hands touched her small arms in an attempt to pull her in, she shrieked.

"I want my mama!" she cried, and fled from the room.

She raced down the hall, into her bedroom, and slammed the door.

The man was still kneeling on the floor, beside the Easy Bake oven and the open box. He glanced over at the woman.

Unfazed, she got up from the sofa and walked out of the house.

Part Two

Transitions

THIGHS WIDE SHUT

Bettina stared up at the white ceiling.

There was a curious pattern in the far right corner that had been holding her attention for almost half an hour. The more she looked at it, the surer she became. She opened her eyes and closed them, peering through the fading shadows of dawn, but the shape remained the same, growing clearer the more she examined it. She wondered if she was hallucinating—that maybe she wasn't seeing what she thought she was.

She looked at the thing again. From where she lay, she could clearly see its outstretched wings. And robe. The only thing missing was the halo. What in the world was an angel doing etched into the corner of her ceiling?

She glanced away for a few seconds, then let her eyes return. She could still see it. How long had it been there? Why hadn't she ever noticed it before?

Even though the bedroom windows of her Santa Monica condo were closed, the room had an early morning chill. She shifted her eyes over to the large silver-rimmed clock on the far right wall. It was six-thirty. She'd been awake for more than three hours, just lying in the darkness. What had awakened her, she couldn't remember. All she knew was that something was different.

The man beside her lay on his back, calmly sleeping. Bettina glanced down at him. Beneath the covers he was naked, and so was she. As she watched him, she realized that he might as well have been a stranger. She felt nothing for him, other than being annoyed that he was taking up more than half of her bed.

Devin Orrem was a portfolio manager. He was thirty-seven, tall, light skinned, and ruggedly handsome. Originally from Brooklyn, New York, he had a keen sense of wit and a flashy sense of style. There was a roughness smoldering beneath his surface that had piqued her curiosity.

Devin was wealthy and well-connected, and loved to lavish her with jewelry. He was also married with two kids. He'd spent the last ten nights at Bettina's place. They'd been playing house—cooking together, sexing it up, and talking about what was going on in their respective worlds. She never once saw him make a call to his wife. If he did, Bettina didn't care to know about it.

She and Devin had been bonding for the past few nights. He told her about a big deal he had pending that would net him a whopping quarter-million-dollar commission. She told him all about her plans to leave Massey-Weldon and go work for Randall and Steve at Vast Horizons.

Devin's wife believed he was away on business travel. Bettina wondered what kind of fool his wife, a well-known Beverly Hills Realtor, must be.

Wait a minute, she thought as she studied a glistening droplet of drool that was gathering in the corner of his sleeping mouth. His wife had claim to him and, according to California community property law, rights to half of whatever was his. His wife was no dummy. Bettina realized that *she* was the one who was the fool.

As she glanced from Devin, to the clock, back to the angel (which now appeared to be hovering in the corner of the ceiling), all she knew was that she wanted him gone. She squinted her eyes, studying the angel again.

Yeah. She definitely wanted Devin gone.

Her bed had seen way too many men. Men who didn't belong there. Men looking for a temporary hiding place from home. Men looking for good sex without accountability. Looking for what one guy once vulgarly referred to as "the ever-elusive tight black pussy."

"And it looks like you have it, baby," he'd said.

She had gone to bed with that man, as repugnant as she found his words. That was two years ago. She couldn't even remember his name. He was someone important, she thought. She met him at the Shark Bar. He drove a brand-new black Hummer and said he knew Spike Lee. Claimed they were good friends. He would introduce, if she desired.

Of course, no introduction ever came.

But he did, and was never seen or heard from again.

Bettina shuddered, remembering it all.

Devin made a gurgling sound in his sleep. Bettina's top lip quivered.

Everything was stacked in the favor of men, she realized, and nothing was stacked in hers. The tennis bracelet and diamond pendant Devin had given her were nice, but, when the dust settled, he was going home back to his wife, leaving Bettina alone with nothing but trinkets.

She couldn't celebrate holidays with trinkets. Trinkets couldn't hold her close at night. Trinkets couldn't father children, and they *certainly* weren't helping to advance her career. Devin's being well connected served her no purpose. He wasn't introducing her to anybody, despite countless promises that he would. He was too jealous to share her at all.

Something about the angel kept disturbing her. She wasn't sure if it was the outstretched wings, its undeniable shape, or the fact that she had never noticed it there before now. She blinked her eyes rapidly, then looked again. There it was, blatant and bold.

Bettina knew a hint when she saw it.

"Get up," she said loudly, shaking the man. "Devin. Get up."

Devin stirred slightly, then rolled away from her. She shook him again, this time harder.

"Devin! Get up!"

He arched his back, stretched, made a groaning sound, and turned in her direction. He reached out, trying to pull her close. She could feel his hardness pressing against her leg.

"Come here, baby," he whispered. "Gimme summa that good morning love."

Bettina's lip instinctively curled in disgust as he touched her.

"Stop it," she said. "Get up. You've got to go home."

He sleepily nuzzled against her breast, flicking his tongue across her nipple. She shoved him away.

"Devin, get out. I don't want to do this anymore."

Consciousness began to wash over him. He sat up, eyes blinking.

"What the hell are you talking about?" He frowned. "What happened? Did you have a bad dream?"

"I've apparently been having one for some time now. But I'm not asleep anymore. That's all that matters. Get dressed. Go home."

She threw the covers aside and slid out of the sprawling four-poster bed. She could sense the warm sensation of his eyes scanning her nakedness, and didn't like the feeling at all. She walked across the room and grabbed the rose-colored handwoven Japanese silk robe (a gift from Randall, of all people) from the back of the curved beige brocade chaise facing the bed. She slid into the robe and tied it securely around her body. She sat down.

The further away from him, she thought, *the better.*

Devin, stupefied, sat in the bed, staring at her.

She's about to give me drama, he feared. *This is the part where she tells me I'd better leave my wife, or else. Like I need this shit first thing in the goddamn morning.*

"Bettina . . . baby," he began, "let's not do this, okay? You know how I feel. All I need is a little time to get my shit together, and then I'm outta there. Then it's just you and me, baby."

Bettina laughed bitterly.

"What are you *talking* about? I don't *want* you! Why would I want a man who would leave his wife and kids, just like that? Once we got together, you'd do the same thing to me!"

"I'm *not* just leaving them . . . ," he stammered.

"Exactly," she quipped, cutting him off. "You're not leaving them at all, are you?"

Devin sighed, baffled. He dropped his chin to his chest.

Why are women so fucking unpredictable? he mused. *She just needs some dick, that's all. She woke up this morning all bent outta shape, and now all of a sudden I'm the bad guy. A good piece of dick will fix everything.*

He grew hard just thinking about it. He couldn't understand why women didn't just ask for dick when that was all they really wanted in the first place. They had to take you through all these *other* machinations, only to end up with a stiff one between their legs. He'd thought Bettina was different, but that was okay. If she wanted him to play macho man, he was more than happy to do it.

Devin threw back the covers. Bettina was relieved.

"Good," she sighed. "Now get dressed and get out."

When he stood from the bed, Bettina saw his erection rearing its fiery red head. Devin did his best Mandingo swing as he swaggered towards her.

"What the *fuck* is the matter with you?!" she screamed. "Get away from me! I told you, I want you to leave!"

"You don't really mean that, baby," he crooned, coming closer. "Now come here and let Daddy love you up. I'm gon' make everything better, just watch and see."

Bettina, angry and frustrated, sat back on the chaise, pulling her knees protectively up to her chest.

"Don't come near me, Devin," she threatened. "I'm serious. I'm not playing with you."

Devin came over anyway, his penis rock-hard. He leaned down, reaching for her. Bettina, now angry, frustrated, *and* keyed up, was kangaroo-ready. She kicked him, à la Francine and kindergarten Montessori, square in the middle of his tightly rippled stomach.

Devin, stunned and unsuspecting, fell back into the plushness of the bone Karastan. His erection was blazing. The kick excited him even more and sent what felt like an extra liter of blood to his already-overengorged tool. He'd always wanted to have a fight as a prelude to sex, and Bettina was just the kind of firecracker to give it to him.

He got on his knees and crawled towards her, his hardness stabbing him in the stomach with each move that he made.

Bettina couldn't believe he didn't get the message.

"*Get out of my house, Devin!*" she screamed. "Before I call the cops! After that, I'm calling your wife! She oughta arrive just after they get here. Then she can see what kind of husband she *really* has!"

Devin saw the fury in her eyes. It spurred him on. If he was lucky, she might even let him smack her around a little, not just on the ass, like he often did. Perhaps they could have a real fight and he could work her over good, Brooklyn-style.

"*Who's my bitch?*" he whispered. He knew Bettina liked it when he called her that. She usually dug her well-manicured nails deeper into his back and buttocks when he said it. Got him in trouble a few times with those nail digs. Pissed his wife off something lovely. She got over it. He'd blamed it on his eager new masseuse.

He kept crawling Bettina's way.

Bettina sprang from the chaise and ran over to the phone on the nightstand beside the bed. She picked it up and dialed 911.

Devin, still on his knees, followed her with his eyes.

"Yes," she said plainly, "I'd like to report a disturbance."

She's taking this fight shit much too far, he thought.

"Bettina," he said nervously, "put the phone down."

"There's an intruder in my home," she continued. "I need you to get someone over here as quickly as possible."

Sweat began to form on Devin's top lip. His erection, seemingly granite and invincible up to that moment, withered, as if it had been pricked with a pin. Confused, he sat back on the carpeting, the lush new pile chafing his butt.

"Bettina, what do you think you're doing?"

"No," she said, ignoring him, "I'm in my bedroom, but I can hear the person moving around inside my condo."

This bitch is actually calling the cops, he realized.

Devin pushed himself up from the floor and walked towards her. Bettina shot him a look that warned him to stay away. Unsure, he raised his palms and backed up.

"Yes, that's my address. How long? Okay, thank you."

She hung up the phone.

"The police are on their way. At the most, it'll take them five or ten minutes to get here. I advise you to get dressed and then get the fuck out."

Her face was grim. She sat on the side of the bed.

Devin was now concerned.

"Bettina, what's going on? Why would you call the cops on me? I haven't done anything to you."

"I asked you to leave," she said, "and you didn't. I asked you nicely. Asked you three or four times. Instead, you come at me with a rock-hard dick, like that's supposed to do something. Why couldn't you just go?"

Her face was firm, but her eyes were wet.

Devin, his nakedness now excessive, took a step towards her.

"Stop," she warned. "Please. For your own sake, put on your clothes and go."

He sighed heavily, shaking his head in frustration, and walked over to the closet where his suit was hanging. He picked up his boxers from the floor and stepped into them. He picked up a white tank top and pulled it over his head. He slid the mirror-covered door aside and reached for his gray pants.

"I don't get it," he muttered, his back to her. "What just happened?"

"Nothing, and everything," Bettina replied. "I don't want to see you anymore."

He slipped into his light blue dress shirt.

"That doesn't make sense," he continued, his fingers deftly closing the buttons. "What's this really about? It's not about me leaving my wife, is it?"

She shook her head.

"It's not about you at all. It's about me. I'm just tired of doing this. I'm tired of men like you passing through my world. Men I don't even love. Men who don't even love me."

Devin, putting his right arm into the sleeve of his jacket, stopped cold. He laughed angrily, suddenly realizing what was going on.

"So *that's* what this is about?" he sneered, turning towards her. "You think I don't love you? What, have you met somebody now that you think is for real? Is that it? Because I'm married, now I've got to go?"

Bettina tightened the sash on her robe.

"This isn't about anybody other than me. I want you out of my life. That's all there is to it."

Devin reached inside the closet for his shoes. His socks were tucked inside them. He angrily pulled the socks on. He was bursting with jealousy.

"Where did you meet him?" he demanded. "Huh? At work? At a party? I don't see how you were able to get anything started. I've been here every night for more than a week!"

He wasn't ready to let go of Bettina. He *definitely* couldn't take her being with another man. He'd rather see her dead first.

He stood in front of the closet, boiling inside. Despite everything he knew about her, he felt like she was his. She was so delicately beautiful, like a naïve little girl—the polar opposite of his tough-as-nails, take-no-shit wife. Bettina accommodated him and made him feel like a man. The thought of her making love to someone else made Devin want to rush over, choke her, and snap her beautifully graceful neck in two.

"So what was last night, huh?" he challenged. "A final hoorah? Bust a nut then bus me out?" He began pacing the floor like a cougar. "You think I'm gonna let someone like you use *me?* You obviously forget who you're dealing with, my dear!"

Someone like you, Bettina noted. Now what did he mean by *that?*

Stop kidding yourself, she silently acknowledged. *You know exactly what he means.*

"It's not like you haven't been using me," she softly replied. "Now go, before the cops get here."

"Let me tell you something, you little skank." Devin's eyes were full of fire as he slipped his feet into his black handmade Italian leather shoes. "I don't just give away expensive jewelry. Ask my wife. I haven't given her any in years. And I don't have casual affairs, either. You meant something to me, and that's probably more than you can say for all the other men you've been with."

Bettina looked away, not wanting to see or hear him anymore.

"How many of them would be willing to forgive your ugly reputation, huh?" Devin asked, now standing over her. "Not one time did I ever let that get in the way. I knew you were a freak. Everybody knows it. But I treated you like a person, not just a pair of legs with a hole between 'em."

Bettina felt her insides lurch as the bitter taste of bile and irony rose in her throat.

There. He'd said it. The very thing she'd wondered about herself was now brought forth into the light. A freak. She was a Hollywood whore. High-class, high-strung, yes—but nevertheless a well-known, oh-you've-had-her-too-did-she-suck-your-so-and-so whore.

All this time, she had fooled herself into believing that everything she'd done was for her career. That people didn't talk. No one, not really, knew any of her business or just how many men she'd been with.

But that was a lie. That's all black folks did in LA. Talk. Gossip, gossip, gossip about other people's business.

What became of her original goal? She had come out here to make it and be a big-time Hollywood writer and producer.

What had become of *her?*

There was no career to speak of. And she had been making it, all right. Just not the way she'd planned. She couldn't believe that, for all the five years she'd been here, she had nothing of substance to show for it. Just lots of toys and a condo she owned free and clear, compliments of lover number twenty-eight. (. . . Or was it lover number forty-two?) There'd been lots of sex and lots of trips and lots of angry wives and vicious girlfriends, two or three private detectives with photos of her in interesting positions along with a few tapes of racy phone conversations, and, *oh yeah,* a shitload of condoms flushed out into the Pacific. Enough to wrap all that water up into one big balloon.

She snickered pitifully, shaking her head.

She had actually done the math recently. Devin was lover number forty-five, which meant she'd averaged nine men a year since her arrival in LA, each affair with a life span of no more than a month and some days. Actually, some had overlapped. Amazing how generous a man could become in less than a month. Amazing how, with all their generosity, it hadn't changed her life one infinitesimal bit.

If it weren't for the new job she was going to have with Randall and Steve, there would be nothing at all. She found it funny that, of all the men she'd been with, the one with whom she'd had the shortest fling was still around in her life as a friend and had turned out to be the one to make a difference. All those others had been for naught. It had just been sex.

Gratuitous, pointless, means-to-no-ends sex.

Bettina felt like she was going to throw up.

"Don't think you're getting away with this," Devin hissed.

"I'll ruin your name in this town. That won't take much anyway. You're lucky I had anything to do with you in the first place."

"Get out," she replied, not looking his way. "The cops are probably already outside. If I were you, I'd go away peacefully. I can make a call to your wife that will screw you over worse than anything you could ever do to me."

Devin stood above her, filled with venom and rage.

She refused to look up at him.

"You're a fucking *bitch!*" he screamed.

Bettina said nothing.

Needing to do something, but unsure of what, Devin spat at her.

It landed on her cheek, a big thick glob of morning phlegm that began a slow descent down her face. Bettina quietly wiped it away.

Somewhat satisfied, he grabbed his briefcase from beside the bed and marched off angrily. Bettina sat perfectly still, listening as he made his way through the hall and across the living room. She heard him unlock the front door and open it. There was a pause, then he slammed it closed.

Relieved, Bettina heaved a cathartic sigh. She ran out into the living room and locked the front door, carefully securing the top bolt.

There were no cops coming. She had only pretended to call them so that Devin would leave.

She ran back into the bedroom and sat down on the side of the bed. A million emotions were racing through her. A million emotions were washing away. She checked the ceiling.

There it was, its wings broader than ever.

"Thank you," she sobbed, falling onto her knees. Her voice was choked with tears. "God, thank you, thank you, *thank you* for setting me free!"

Still on her knees, she leaned her face into her palms and let herself have a good cry. Her body shook uncontrollably as she let it purge of all she'd done in the past five years, and the years before that. When she finished, she knew.

"No more," she said out loud. "No more married men. No more men with girlfriends. No more casual sex. Dear God, as you are my witness, know that I am going to wait. From this day forward, until I meet the one You send me, these legs are closed for business."

She nodded with conviction as she spoke the affirmation, then looked up at the ceiling.

"I just pray You help me know him when he comes."

She smiled, feeling a certainty, a power within, that assured her she would.

"Thank you."

As she said the words, she felt clean inside, something she hadn't felt in years, despite how innocent and wholesome she appeared.

As if to make everything concrete, she rushed over to her nightstand, snatching open the drawer. It was like a novelty store inside. An assortment of flavored creams, colored jellies, motion lotions, fluorescent condoms, a six-pack of Rough Riders, and a pair of candy panties all stared up at her. Bettina reached in with both arms and tried to gather everything up. Then she had a better thought.

She opened her arms, letting the items fall back into the drawer, then raced to the kitchen, opened a cabinet, and grabbed a trash bag. She raced back to the bedroom, dropped to her knees at the nightstand, and began dumping the contents of the drawer, two at a time, into the plastic bag.

She got up and walked over to her dresser, dragging the bag along with her. She opened the second drawer on the far left. Inside were an array of toys, varying in shape, size, and specialty. She grabbed the small black vibrator—the one she used when the man of the moment wanted to see her pleasure herself—and threw it into the bag. The shiny silver handcuffs she'd bought at a funky bohemian shop on Melrose followed. Bettina shook her head, realizing how big a role she'd played in her own undoing.

There was a cat-o'-nine-tails and four red satin scarves that had been used time and time again to tie her up, tie her down.

Into the bag they went.

She pulled out the long-handled black back massager. Her personal private favorite. She didn't use it with anyone other than herself, and she wasn't using it on her back, that was for damn sure. That back massager was most effective at getting the job done.

Bettina felt a hollow pang, followed by a split second of hesitation, as she removed it from the drawer. It was like throwing away a close friend.

"You gotta go," she announced aloud. "There will be no more sex of any kind. Not even with myself."

That would be hardest, she knew. She had been pleasuring herself, half the time without even realizing it, since she was twelve. She'd felt the first explosion, accidentally, during a pop quiz in history class. She was squirming nervously in her seat, unsure of any of the answers because she hadn't done the week's reading assignment. The friction created a heat and caused a bundle of energy to build beneath her that made her squirm even harder. When the nervousness heightened into a pleasurable fear as the teacher collected the tests—hers blank except for her name and the date—she felt the starburst. It radiated throughout her body, making her rush abruptly from the class, down the hallway, and into the bathroom. Bettina had never felt anything like it. After she felt it, she knew she wanted to feel it again and again.

She threw the black back massager into the bag.

Three other vibrators followed, along with a set of ben-wa balls and a studded black choker and leather leash. As the items flew into the bag, she realized what Devin had meant when he'd called her a freak.

After the drawer was emptied, she closed it and moved to the next column of drawers, starting with the one at the top. That drawer, and the two below it, were filled with lingerie favorites from Victoria's Secret, Frederick's of Hollywood, and mail order items from Adam and Eve.

She loved her lingerie, but now, she knew, she loathed what they represented. With no second thoughts, she threw everything away.

I'll just have to buy all new stuff, she decided.

She would have to go shopping immediately, on a break from work, if possible. With everything thrown away, she would have to go naked underneath her clothes until she could get to the store.

She closed the dresser drawers, sat on the floor, and examined the overstuffed bag. A trash bag for a trashy life.

She got up, went into the living room, and unlocked the front door. She peered out. No sign of Devin. Hopefully, he was long gone. It was still quite early. None of her neighbors were milling about.

Bettina tiptoed down the hall with the bag. She opened the door to the trash chute and tossed it in.

She ran back into the safety of her condo and bolted the door.

Now, all she needed to do was take a shower.

She needed to wash away Devin and the night. She needed to wash away all the others that had been before.

Bettina walked into the bathroom, oblivious to the cold beige tile beneath her feet. She stepped inside the glass-encased shower and turned it on. Jets of scalding hot water sprayed her from four different directions. She gritted her teeth and let it burn, the ruthless water stripping away the outer surface of skin and making way for the new. She reached for the frilly thing that hung from a hook in front of her and squeezed a glob of cucumber melon shower gel onto it.

As Bettina lathered her body, the entire surface flushing red from the heat, she imagined years of madness, absence of conscience, and reckless living sliding away. The glass walls of the shower were thick with steam.

Bettina put away the frilly thing, squeezed a handful of Nexxus Pep'R'Mint herbal shampoo into her palm, and worked it into her hair. The pores of her scalp opened up, sending a tingling chill through her that partially countered the burning heat of the water. She reached for the Neutrogena bar and thoroughly scrubbed her face. Twice. She wanted to make sure all traces of Devin's spit were gone.

Quickly, bravely, she stuck her whole head into the steaming hot streams of water, the foam cascading from her hair, gently blending with the suds on her face and her body. She let it all rinse away as the hot water beat painfully against her. She endured it. As penance, she figured, it was the least she could do.

Bettina turned off the faucet and opened the door. She stepped out into the thick, steamy air, grabbing the plush tan towel hanging from a hook just outside the shower. She briskly worked the towel through her hair and over her face, then rubbed her body until there wasn't a drop of water to be found. Every inch of her skin felt alive.

She wrapped the towel around her body, secured it, and walked over to the sink. The mirror above it was covered with steam. She reached out with her right palm and wiped a spot clear.

Bettina saw a flushed red face staring back at her. Blood, inspired by the scalding water of the shower, was pulsating furiously beneath her light brown skin. She leaned closer, examining herself. Her hair was a tangle of black ringlets sticking to her head. Her nose, delicately upturned, was crimson. Her lips were so rosy, they looked as if they'd been punched or pinched.

Who needs Retin-A, she thought, *when a hot shower and a change of heart will do?*

She leaned back, turned on the faucet, grabbed her toothbrush, wet it, squeezed a line of toothpaste onto it, and vigorously brushed her teeth.

She spit into the sink, rinsed her mouth several times, and turned off the water.

"*Ahhhh!*" she breathed, exhaling a fresh gust of minty air. "Now I'm clean!"

She leaned in again towards her reflection and flashed herself a toothy smile.

"Hi. My name is Bettina. I don't think we've ever met before."

The face in the mirror grinned broadly in return.

"A pleasure," she said, beaming. "I think I'm going to enjoy getting to know you, my friend."

Bettina pulled the loosening towel tighter around her body. She walked back into the bedroom.

"I'm gonna burn these bedcovers and sell this bed," she announced.

She thought about it. She loved that bed. What she *could* do, she decided, was buy another just like it. As long as it wasn't this tainted one, what difference did it make?

She smiled, happy, relieved . . . *free*.

Bettina walked across the room and looked up, searching the corner for her angel. Even though daylight was sifting into the room, she found it harder now to see.

She walked closer to the corner where it had been.

All she saw was the white of the ceiling.

Every single trace of the angel was gone.

THEM BELLY FULL

"Good morning."

Desi had just put her teapot on the stove when the phone rang.

"Hey. Look . . . what does it mean when you dream about choking?"

"Who do I look like," Desi asked, "Dionne Warwick?"

She opened the cabinet and took out an oversized yellow cup. She closed the cabinet, took a peppermint teabag from a glass jar on the counter, dropped the teabag in the cup, then opened one of the drawers in the counter and pulled out a spoon.

"Come on, Dez, you're from the South," Sharon whined. "You should know about stuff like that. Southerners are big on numbers and interpretations."

"You're right. Hold on a second, let me go get my dream book," Desi said, closing the utensil drawer.

"Okay," Sharon replied, relieved.

Desi laughed, sitting down at the small table in her kitchen. She placed the cup and spoon on the table in front of her.

"Fool, I'm joking! I ain't got no dream book! I can't believe you even thought I did!"

"How the hell would I know?"

"Please. Besides, you're the one who's West Indian. Y'all invented all that hoodoo voodoo business to begin with."

"Voodoo is from Haiti. I come from Jamaica."

"Via the Bronx."

"Kiss my Bronx ass," Sharon replied. "I just need a simple answer. You gotta be able to tell me something. I dreamt last night that I got hit by a truck and swallowed a whole sandwich."

"What color was the truck?" Desi asked.

"Are you still playing with me?"

"No, it's just a simple question. What color was the truck?"

"Red," Sharon answered reluctantly.

Desi pondered a moment.

"Was it one of those minicab pickups or a tractor-trailer?"

"This is ridiculous," Sharon sputtered. "If I thought you were going to make fun of me, I would have never called you in the first place."

"Sharon," Desi insisted, "I'm not making fun of you. I just figured that if we talked it out, we could get to the root of what the dream was about."

Sharon considered her words. Maybe Desi had a point.

"Alright. It was a red Expedition."

"Wow. Did it hurt you?"

"I told you," Sharon exclaimed, "it made me swallow a sandwich whole!"

"Alright, alright," Desi said, "calm down." She leaned forward on the table, resting her head in her hands. "Now let's think about this. What kind of sandwich was it?"

Sharon paused, trying to remember.

"Uhhh . . . I think it was perch."

Desi's breath caught.

"What's wrong?" Sharon asked, bewildered. "Why'd you gasp like that?"

"Sharon . . . you dreamt about fish?"

"Yeah. And? So?"

"And you swallowed it *whole?*"

"Yeah, damn!" Sharon replied, frustrated. "What's the big deal?"

"Well," Desi said, "you don't have to be from the South to know that when you dream about fish it means somebody's pregnant."

"Somebody like *who?*" Sharon snapped.

"Honey, it ain't me. I'm having my visit right now, as we speak."

"Spare me already."

Desi absently scratched the nape of her neck, thinking.

"Listen . . . did you hit the truck, or did the truck hit you?"

"I hit brakes," Sharon said, "and the truck hit me from behind."

"So *you* stopped *it,*" Desi declared. "And it was red. That truck was your period, and it was stopped when you swallowed that fish sandwich whole!"

"Actually, the truck hit me first, *then* I swallowed the sandwich. But what difference does it make? I'm not pregnant."

"Are you sure?" Desi asked.

"Positive," Sharon responded.

"When was the last time you had your period?"

"Forget it, Dez. This conversation has gotten foolish. I gotta go."

"Sharon," Desi persisted, "you *have* been sleeping a lot lately."

"That's 'cause I've got so much free time on my hands!" Sharon screamed.

Desi grew quiet, allowing Sharon time to calm down. She silently counted to fifteen before she spoke again.

"Are you done yelling?"

"Sorry," Sharon said. "I had a rough sleep. And, to top it off, I woke up this morning and saw that the answering machine had chewed up the tape. That's probably why it didn't pick up when you called last night. I threw the whole thing in the garbage. I'm gonna get voice mail."

"Finally," Desi replied. "Welcome to the new millennium."

"Yeah . . . well."

Sharon let out a heavy sigh. Desi listened with concern. Something was definitely up.

"Sharon?"

"What?"

"When was the last time you saw your period?"

Sharon breathed heavily again.

"Sharon," Desi admonished, "talk to me. I'm your friend."

"It's been a minute. But I'm under a lot of stress. I've got a bunch of things on my mind."

"Have you been having unprotected sex with Glen?"

"Dez, you're not my mother."

"I'm not trying to be," Desi replied. "Have you?"

Sharon hesitated.

"A couple times," she confessed.

"Just a couple?"

"Alright, alright, maybe five or six. Ten, at the most."

"*Sharon!*" Desi exclaimed.

"*What?*" Sharon screamed back. "Stop yelling at me! I don't need a lecture right now!"

"Has Glen taken an AIDS test?"

"Yeah."

"Have you?"

"Yeah."

"Are you lying to me?" Desi asked. "Don't lie to me. It doesn't serve any purpose."

"I'm not lying," Sharon stated. "I told you, stop acting like my mother."

"I'm acting like a friend. What you're doing is very risky."

"Yeah, yeah . . . I know."

They were both silent again. There was a loud hissing noise coming from Desi's side of the phone.

"What's that?" Sharon asked.

"My teapot."

"Oh."

Desi got up, turned off the stove, slipped on an oven mitt, and picked up the teapot by the handle. She poured the hot water over her bag of peppermint tea. She held the phone to her ear with her left hand.

"I can't be pregnant," Sharon whispered. "I can't. You don't understand how this would ruin everything for me."

Desi listened, letting her talk.

"Glen would definitely be pissed. He doesn't want kids now."

"Did he tell you that?" Desi asked, placing the teapot back on the stove. She took off the mitt, sat down at the table again, opened the sugar bowl and took out two cubes. She dropped them into her tea.

"No, but he doesn't have to. I just know he doesn't. Dammit, Dez, he's twenty-six. He's in the thick of his career."

"So are you. Don't act like this is all your fault. Glen knew what the risk was when he stuck his naked dick in you."

Sharon gasped, then laughed.

"I can't believe you just said *dick*."

"Yeah," Desi said, stirring her tea, "I can't believe I said it either. It's the company I keep . . . hint, hint."

Sharon laughed again. This time, it was accompanied by a nervous quaver.

Desi took a sip of tea. Sharon, overcome with frustration, let loose with an anguished cry.

"*Aaaaaaaaaaaaarghhhhhhhhhhh!!!!!!!*" she screeched. "Dezzzzz!!! How could I let this happen?! This is *sooo* crazy! I should have more sense than this!"

"Sharon, just calm down. Besides, you don't know for sure if you're pregnant."

"Yes, I do. I get my period like clockwork. I always have. If it's a nanosecond late, I know something is up."

"How late is it?" Desi asked.

Sharon was silent.

"Sharon? How late is your period?"

"Three weeks," she answered, her voice barely audible.

"*Sharon!* And didn't you just have sex with him last night?"

"Three times."

"All unprotected?"

"All unprotected."

Desi sighed. She didn't know what else to say.

"Dez," Sharon pleaded, "don't sound like that. You don't understand what it feels like when I hold him and he holds me, and I feel him inside me, skin-to-skin."

"Does it feel like a death wish?" Desi responded. "Because that's what it sounds like the two of you have."

The comment pissed Sharon off.

"How dare you judge me," she snarled.

Desi realized her error. If Sharon was pregnant, the last thing she needed was Desi making things worse.

"I'm sorry, honey. Look, I'm not judging you. I just can't see how the two of you can be so reckless. This is LA, the original Den of Iniquity, right after Sodom and Gomorrah. I know you and Glen spend most of your free time together, but how can you be sure that you're the only one?"

"Because he says I am," Sharon remarked.

"And, of course, men don't lie."

"He has no need to. His word is bond."

"Absolutely," Desi said. "Why would Glen ever need to lie anyway? It's not like you're one of the most powerful, if underemployed, producers in Hollywood. You have no value. You certainly couldn't hook him up with new clients, introduce him to other powerful people, or anything like that, now, could you?"

Sharon felt a flash of fire fan within.

"So you think he's with me to use me? 'Cause if that's what you're suggesting, which it sounds like it is, you need to say so. It sounds like you've been thinking it for a while."

Desi raised the cup of tea to her lips, the steam causing her brow to reflexively knit. She sipped cautiously.

"You think he's using me, Dez?"

Sharon's voice took on a dangerous edge. Desi knew her well enough to know it meant proceed with care.

"Sharon, I've never even met Glen before. I know who he is by name, but I wouldn't know him if he ran up and bit me on the titty."

She waited for a laugh. Nothing came.

"Do you think he's using me, Dez?" Sharon persisted.

Her tone was firm and deliberate. The edge was razor sharp. Desi took another sip of tea, the mist from the surface now lingering against her forehead, jump-starting a sweat.

"I'm not saying that, Sharon," she replied. "I'm just saying . . . heck, what *am* I saying? Just don't undervalue yourself, that's all. He may be a high-powered attorney with high-powered clients, but you're still more connected. He's young and he's new to the game. There are people you can reach with just one phone call. People he might not ever get next to. Look at me . . . I didn't even know you knew Spielberg until last night. I would imagine Glen has an idea that you're the mother lode when it comes to that six-degrees thing. Half the time, with you, it's only one degree."

No sound, not even breathing, came from Sharon's end of the phone.

"I'm not saying he's using you. I know you're much too smart for that."

She could hear Sharon's breathing now. Desi waited for her to speak.

"Maybe I'm in love with him," Sharon whispered helplessly. "Did that ever occur to you, Dez? Huh? And maybe he's in love with me. That could have something to do with why all this is happening."

"If that's the case, the two of you can have protected sex and still be in love," Desi replied. "Then you wouldn't be worried about getting or being pregnant."

"Well now," Sharon replied flatly, "it's too late for that, isn't it?"

Desi shook her head, gently tracing her finger around the edge of the teacup.

"How did you get into a mess like this?" she asked absently.

"Desi Marie Sheridan, don't you *dare* talk to me like I'm a fucking idiot!" Sharon hissed.

"I'm not talking to you like that, Sharon," Desi said quickly, the mist on her forehead now a full-fledged sweat. "I just want you to be sure . . ."

"Fuck you, Dez," Sharon barked, cutting her off. "I called you as a friend. I already know what I need to do. I don't need a damn lecture from you about anything. And I damn sure don't need you to judge me."

"Sharon, I'm *not* lecturing you," Desi replied in a pleading voice. "I'm not judging you at all."

"Yeah, Dez, you *are* judging me. You come out here with your Southern ideals and your homespun Alabama ass-backwards advice, and where has it gotten you? You're no better off than me. I don't see you living the lifestyles of the rich and famous. And I damn sure don't see Mr. Right sportin' you around like you're the answer to his prayers."

Desi stared ahead at the butter yellow kitchen wall, wondering how the phone call had spiraled so out of control. Sharon was angry. Her rage was blazing through the line. She had never been angry with Desi before, not like this. They had cute little skirmishes that always ended in happy banter. She'd never felt the ire that she'd seen Sharon direct at others.

Desi figured the best thing for her to do was just let Sharon vent until her rage passed through.

"Can't we just talk about this rationally?" she asked.

"Just forget I ever called," Sharon replied.

There was the sudden sound of a dial tone in Desi's ear. She clicked the phone off, laid it on the table, closed her eyes, and took another sip of tea.

She sat still, letting the warmth of the liquid coarse over her tongue and caress it in a fluid stream. The steam from the surface of the tea passed through her nostrils, invigorating her lungs. She took in a deep breath as she swallowed.

She picked up the phone and dialed.

"What," the voice answered flatly.

"Look . . . I'm kinda broke right now," Desi said. "I ain't got no expendable cash to take you to the Polo Lounge, and I wouldn't know where to buy you some weed if I had the money to do it. You don't need to be smoking weed anyhow. You're pregnant."

Sharon was silent.

"Have you been smoking weed, too?" Desi asked, shocked.

"What do you think?"

Desi remembered that Sharon had been getting high when she called her two days earlier to confirm Randall James was who he said he was. Sharon was definitely still smoking weed. Desi figured she'd best keep her thoughts to herself.

"So what's it gonna be?" Sharon asked.

"Huh?"

"How are you going to make up for hurting my feelings?"

Desi smiled.

"Well, Sharon, I don't know. I told you—"

"Kiss my ass," Sharon replied.

"No, I mean, really—"

"No, Dez . . . I'm serious. Kiss my ass."

Desi didn't say anything, confused by Sharon's words.

"Start kissing right . . . *now!*"

Sharon sounded as if she had just started clocking a race.

Desi still said nothing.

"You seem a bit befuddled," Sharon said. "Let me help you out a little."

She began to make kissing noises into the phone. Desi giggled.

"I'm not laughing," Sharon declared, interrupting herself. "Get to smacking, you judgmental bitch."

Desi, still giggling, kissed the air in rapid succession.

"My ass still feels dry. Kiss harder."

Desi made loud, wet, smacking noises.

Sharon began to laugh. Desi broke down and joined her.

"I need to teach Glen that trick," Sharon muttered.

"Teach him how to use a condom first," Desi commented, unable to restrain herself.

"Just for that, gimme one more smack. And make it good."

Desi kissed the air. Loudly.

"Now shut the hell up," Sharon giggled, "before I ask you to do something worse."

The giggles faded into silence. Both women sat holding their respective phones, breathing quietly.

"What are we gonna do?" Desi whispered.

"What do you mean, *we?*"

"Now come on, Sharon. You know I've got your back."

"I know, Dez," Sharon replied softly, her voice thick. "I know you're here for me."

"We've gotta do something. Before you hung up on me, you said you already knew what you had to do. Did you mean . . ."

"I don't know what I meant," Sharon moaned. "I was just talking. You ought to know by now that I'm not the most rational bitch around. Listen . . . can we meet later today? I think it would help me to see you, not just talk to you on the phone."

"Sure. What time?"

"What time is good for you?" Sharon asked.

"Well, I'm expecting to hear back from Ken sometime soon about this thing with Randall."

"Oh yeah," Sharon said. "I almost forgot. Did you ask Ken to find out if Randall and his partner are going to be writing for the show full-time?"

"Yeah, I asked him."

"Good."

"I should be free later in the afternoon," Desi said. "How about we meet at Magic Johnson's Starbucks around three?"

"That'd be fine."

"In the meantime," Desi said, "try and calm yourself down."

"I'm calm," Sharon lied.

"Yeah, like a tidal wave."

They both laughed. Sharon's phone beeped.

"Hold on," she said, and clicked over. She was gone for three minutes. Long enough for Desi to finish most of her tea.

"Sorry about that," Sharon said, clicking back. She sounded excited. "Look, I gotta take this call. It's Jackson Bennett."

"What does *he* want?" Desi asked.

"You'll never believe it. He's still explaining it to me now. Let me go. I'll tell you everything this afternoon."

"Alright, I'll see you later."

"Peace!" Sharon said, and hung up.

Desi clicked the phone off and set it on the table.

"And I thought my world was raggedy," she said aloud. "Looks like we're all messed up. If it's not one thing, it's another."

She drank the last of her tea, wondering how Sharon was going to deal with her situation.

She also wondered what was going on with Jackson Bennett.

Desi got up from the table, tossed the teabag in the trash, and put the cup in the sink. She arched her back, stretching, then leaned forward and stretched some more. It'd probably be a while before Ken called.

She decided to take a mid-morning run.

BREACH BLONDE

"We quit," Randall and Steve announced after lunch.

Actually, it was after lunch*time*, but they hadn't had lunch yet. They figured they'd eat once the deed was done.

They were inside Meredith's office. Uninvited.

Her door was wide open, and her pitbull assistant Jeannie had been nowhere in sight, so the two unceremoniously waltzed in.

The view from Meredith's sprawling office on the tenth floor was breathtaking, literally, if not simply because of the sheer thick of the LA smog. It was a sweeping, panoramic glimpse of the house-dotted hills with a view of downtown in the distance to the right.

The design within was an interesting mesh of styles that went beyond eclectic, ranging from things neoclassical and impressionistic, to arts decoratifs, moderne, and nouveau.

Anyone who walked in knew Meredith Reynolds was an important woman who was apparently quite full of herself. Which was exactly what she wanted them to know.

Randall's and Steve's respective offices—while functional, relatively spacious, and tastefully decorated—could in no way compare to the combined elegance, artistic abandon, and flat-out hedonism that was represented in Meredith's expansive domain. An obvious perk of having the double advantage of being the VP of Entertainment and Development and the boss's kept woman.

A plush red velvet couch, with decadently curved mahogany arms and legs and sumptuous cushions that seemed to swallow whole all who perched there, sat angled across from her desk, facing the magnificent hazy view. An inviting black leather chaise, a lush combination of deco curves and nouveau lines, was just off to the side. There was a double-wide massage table, complete with all the accoutrements aromatherapy had to offer, gracing the area just outside the built-in, bone-colored marble shower and bath-cum-Jacuzzi.

A copy of Matisse's *Notre-Dame, une fin d'après-midi* was ornately framed in black on the wall just behind the couch. The wall contiguous wore an Ingres, his *Valpinçon Bather,* also framed in black. Meredith had seen it once in the Louvre, during a Parisian work junket-cum-holiday with Wade, and just *had* to have a copy framed for her office. Wade, ever willing to indulge her, obliged. Degas' *Portrait of a Dancer* hung a few feet away, in a direct opposing line with the black chaise. Meredith liked it most, she'd once commented, because "it matched the couch."

The delicately sculpted form of a woman in dancer's repose, an Erté, a *real* one (the accounting department had the forty-thousand-dollar receipt to prove it) adorned a glass coffee table. The base of said table was an interesting study in black wrought iron with a series of leaves wending their way through the table's limbs.

Lastly, but always of most interest to Randall, were the two zebra chairs made of real fur. They sat right in front of Meredith's desk.

Somewhere, Randall mused, two butt-naked zebras had been made pariahs of their tribe.

The office was an eyeful. The Diabolical Miss M., as Steve often called her, had, if nothing else, a splashy sense of LA flair.

Meredith was behind her big, expensive black lacquer desk, leaning back in her red leather chair. She was deeply engrossed in a thick document, which was raised close to her face. The chair was turned to the side, revealing her profile.

The thick sun-streaked blonde hair was blown straight and hung past her shoulders. The long, slender legs were crossed. Her tan, compliments of the prior weekend with Wade in Palm Springs, was fresh and flattering. It went well with her dark gray minisuit and simple black block heels.

Physically, Meredith was hot, Randall noted, which explained one of the reasons Wade was trying to hit it every chance he got. At thirty-six, she was only nine years younger than Anna Weldon, and she embodied a passion and hunger that kept her youthful and kept Wade obsessed.

Meredith's eyes were the only things that gave her away. Despite their bright blue hue, they were angry and dark, and seemed a thousand years old. If she looked at a person long enough, it almost burned.

Meredith's eyes revealed her desperation. She was determined to make it to the top, and she was not going to let anything, or anybody, get in her way.

Originally from Boston, she was born Hazel Atkins. Hazel had grown up in foster homes. She had no idea who her parents were, and not once in her life did she ever care to find out. Between the ages of seventeen and eighteen, she lived on the streets.

After spending two years working as a maid at a TraveLodge in Woburn, a gritty, blue-collar suburb of Boston, she took up with fifty-year-old salesman Emerson Cody. Emerson was leaving his wife and running away to start over. Hazel was sick of Boston and all of its suburbs, especially Woburn. She was desperate for something better. Emerson was her ticket out.

He was lying on the bed, watching television in his hotel room, when Hazel first met him. She stuck her key in the door and barged right in.

"I didn't hear you knock," said the pallid, short, pudgy, balding man. He was wearing only a white T-shirt and briefs.

"Should I come back?" she asked, unashamed.

"No. Go ahead and clean up."

Emerson watched her as she vacuumed the room. Her thick, dark brown hair was pulled back in a ponytail. He asked her general questions. She gave him general answers. They talked. At one point, Hazel was sitting beside him on the bed. Inside of an hour, she was down on her knees.

They drove to Los Angeles, California, in his sky blue Chevrolet Caprice. Twenty-year-old Hazel shacked up with him for four months in a little back house in Hawthorne. Emerson drank a lot and didn't work. When she asked too many questions, he beat her.

Emerson had a stash of money, three thousand dollars, that he'd brought with him from Boston. Hazel had seen it. He kept it stuffed inside a sock in the back of a drawer.

He made her take a waitressing job and, every night, demanded she hand over any tips she had made. Usually, the money went for booze. It was up to her to put enough aside to pay the bills and living expenses. When the tips seemed too slight, Emerson, in all his short, pale, pudgy baldness, beat the bewildered girl some more.

Hazel came in one night after work, her feet aching so badly she could hardly stand, and found Emerson passed out on the grimy couch. In his hand, he clutched an empty bottle of gin. Without hesitation, she gently pried the bottle free and smashed it across his head. Emerson regained consciousness momentarily, then hit the floor with a thud.

She walked into the bedroom, opened the drawer, and removed the sock filled with money. She took the keys to the sky blue Chevrolet Caprice, and Hazel Atkins was never seen again.

When she resurfaced five months later, she was living in Santa Monica as Meredith Reynolds, newly blonde and newly employed. She had a new birth certificate and driver's license, compliments of a shady but sexy fellow she'd met on Melrose. The car had been sold, and she was driving a red '67 Mustang. Her neighbor had a cousin who worked in television who desperately needed an assistant, someone loyal and committed, who was not afraid of work. Meredith thought she fit the bill.

When Meredith met Anna Weldon, they instantly clicked. Anna hired Meredith as her personal secretary at ABC. She moved up the ranks with Anna, and when Wade and Anna formed their own company, Meredith went with them, learning the business along the way.

Her affair with Wade began five years into his marriage to Anna. Wade quietly doted on her, taking her away on trips and supplementing her income. When it came time to select a vice president of Entertainment and Development, Meredith was the obvious choice. Not just because of Wade, but because she had gained the know-how the job required.

Fucking Wade on the regular, however, didn't hurt.

Now Meredith wanted more. For years, she'd been trying to get her own credit as the creator of a show. Wade promised that, once she brought a project that was worthy, he would give her that credit. Meredith was determined to get it. And the man. She wasn't going to stop until Massey-Weldon was Massey-Reynolds.

She flipped a page of the document she was reading, absently rubbing one leg against the other. Randall cleared his throat loudly to get her attention.

She lowered the papers and glanced over, finally noticing the two men standing in front of her desk.

"What do you want?" she growled. "Can't you see I'm in the middle of something?"

"Nothing major," Randall said smugly. "We're just letting you know that, effective right now, we're outta here."

Steve stood beside him with his hands folded.

Meredith was not amused.

She threw the document down on her desk.

"Look, you two, I don't have time for this," she said with a scowl. "If this is some strong-arm attempt to get me to fork over more money, forget it. The budgets are set for the fiscal year."

"We're not trying to strong-arm you, Meredith," Steve replied calmly, his voice firm and deep. "We just wanted to let you know so that you could make the necessary arrangements. Adios."

The two men turned to leave her office. Meredith was furious.

"*Wait a second!* You can't *do* this!" She was standing now, leaning with her palms pressed against the desk. She lowered her voice into an annoyed hiss. "We'll sue you for breach of contract. You've got two more years before we renegotiate. Now *get* back to work!"

They stopped just in front of the door. Steve laughed and Randall shook his head.

"Did you hear something?" Randall, amused, asked Steve.

"I'm not sure," Steve quipped, "but I *think* she said something about a breach. Sounds like she needs to read our contracts and check out who breached who, don'tcha think?"

"What are you *talking* about?" Meredith asked. "We haven't breached our contract with you!"

"Bye, bye, Meredith," Steve said, waving.

"Yeah," Randall added, "see ya later, girlfriend."

"What about our shows? You can't do this!"

"Uh . . . watch us," Randall said.

They smiled, high-fived themselves in front of her, then exited her office. Meredith could hear them laughing as they walked down the hall.

What breach? she wondered, plopping down in her chair. What on earth were the two of them talking about?

Frantic, she spun her chair around to the black lacquer credenza behind her. She snatched open a drawer and pulled out their files.

She opened Steve's, found his contract, and began to flip through it. Her eyes scanned the pages, looking for something, *anything*, that would clue her in. Her eyes sifted over the words, waiting for something blatant to jump out. When she flipped to page ten, she saw it.

"'Development of new projects,' blah, blah, blah," she mumbled, reading, using her finger to follow the words. "Da, da, da 'within a reasonable time frame, this period not to exceed more than three years from the date of execution of this instrument.'"

She flipped to the signature page. There it was, the date of execution. The current date was September 22. The document had been signed on July 31, 1997. Randall and Steve definitely didn't have any projects in development. She had dismissively turned all of their suggestions down, thinking she had plenty of time and that they weren't going anywhere. They were paid very well. She never gave them a second thought.

"*Shit! Shit! Shit!*" Meredith exclaimed.

She picked up the phone and dialed the reception desk.

"This is Bettina," the perky voice chimed.

"Bettina, have Randall and Steve come through the lobby just yet?"

"Randall James and Steve Karst?" Bettina asked sweetly, absently adjusting her headset.

"*Of course!*" Meredith snapped. "Who the hell else would I be asking about?"

"Well," Bettina began, "there's a Randall Faust in Accounting, and two Steves that work in Video Archives. Hold on, Meredith. I've got another line ringing."

Meredith huffed angrily as Bettina put her on hold. A few seconds passed.

They could be leaving the building, she worried. *I've got to stop them.*

"I'm sorry, Meredith. What was it you wanted?"

"Have you seen Randall and Steve?" Meredith snarled.

"No, I haven't," Bettina said, barely able to keep from laughing. "Oh, hold on, they're just stepping off the elevator now."

"Please instruct them to come to the phone," Meredith commanded.

Bettina's brows raised in amusement.

"I'll do my best," she replied, in a singsongy voice.

"Tell them it's important!" Meredith screeched.

Bettina put her on hold.

"Randall, Steve. Come here for a second."

The two were already heading her way.

"Check this out," she said, grinning, "I've got Meredith on the line. She wants to speak to you guys. She sounds *really* pissed. She told me to *instruct* you to come to the phone."

"*Psshhht!*" Randall sputtered, laughing. "That bitch is crazy. Fuck her."

"Tell her the same thing for me," Steve replied. "My days of taking orders from her are over!"

"Alright," Bettina said. "Hang on a minute while I do it. This is gonna be fun."

She cleared her throat, then pressed a button on the telephone console.

"*How dare you put me on hold for so long?!*" Meredith was screaming.

"I'm sorry, Meredith," Bettina replied pleasantly, grimacing at the loudness ringing in her ears. "I asked, but for some reason, Randall and Steve don't want to talk to you."

"Did you tell them I said it was important?"

"Yes, I did. Hang on, it's another line."

Bettina put her on hold again. Meredith was steaming.

Bettina returned.

"Sorry about that," she said.

"Bettina, what exactly did they say?"

"Well, um, Meredith . . . ," Bettina began, grinning at Randall and Steve, "this is kind of embarrassing."

"Enough of the bullshit," Meredith seethed, "just tell me what they said."

"Okay. Um, they said, and I quote"—Bettina cleared her voice—"'Fuck her, we don't take orders from that bitch anymore.'"

Meredith's face flushed scarlet. She was furious.

"I apologize," Bettina quickly added. "I'm only repeating what they said."

Meredith could almost see the mocking grin on Bettina's face.

Meredith slammed the phone down in her ear.

Bettina burst into laughter.

"That *bitch!*" She laughed. "You guys must have given her the good news."

"Sure did," Randall said. "Now we're outta here." He turned to Steve. "Wanna grab something to eat at Roscoe's?"

"Yeah, I'm starving!" Steve replied.

Bettina found it funny that golden boy Steve loved fried chicken as much as he did. It was his favorite meal.

"Don't you ever get sick of chicken?" she asked.

"Nope. Someone in my family's black, they're just not owning up to it."

"Why is that not a surprise?" Randall replied. Steve shoved him with his shoulder.

The three of them laughed.

"So, guys, how'd you pull it off?" Bettina asked, leaning forward. The phone rang again. "Wait, hold on a second." She punched a line. "Massey-Weldon." She frowned.

"I *hate* that! I get so many freaking hangup calls here, it's not even funny. Sometimes they just slam the phone down right in my ear."

"It's a major switchboard," Randall said. "You're bound to get hangups."

"Well, I get 'em by the truckload," she said. "Now come on," she said, turning her attention back to them. "How'd you guys do it?"

"One word," Steve replied. "*Breach.*"

Bettina's mouth opened in shock.

"Won't they sue you?" she exclaimed.

Randall snickered.

"*We're* not in breach, Magic Mama. *They* are. It's a short story. We'll tell it to you real soon. In the meantime, I want you to do me a favor."

"Sure. What is it?"

Randall leaned closer to her.

"I want you to make a couple of anonymous phone calls," he whispered, "just to get a buzz going."

"Okay," she said with a smile. "I'm game."

"Great." He slipped her a piece of paper with three phone numbers on it. There were the names of three well-known columnists and the magazines they wrote for. *TV Guide*, *Variety*, and *The Hollywood Reporter*.

"I want people to know about our leaving Massey-Weldon. Tell them we're starting our own production company and the rumor is that Jet Jonas is behind it. Casually hint at start-up capital of more than a hundred million. They'll do the rest."

"What if they want proof?" Bettina asked. "Who will I say I am?"

"Tell them you have a source inside Massey-Weldon. They'll call here to confirm if it's true. They'll probably call Jet at his offices, but he's prepared. We just want to stir up talk."

The phone rang again. Bettina answered it and took a message.

"Okay," she said, turning her attention back to the guys. "I can't do it from here, though."

"There's an empty office on the second floor," Steve interjected. "It's right around the corner from Bill Pearly in Legal."

"Good suggestion," Randall commented. "Bettina, can you get someone to cover the phones for you?"

"Yeah. Nina Swanson always helps me out. Don't worry, I'll get it done."

"Thanks," Randall said. "We really appreciate your help."

"Just make sure it's reflected in my new salary," she joked seriously.

"Don't worry," Steve reassured her. "We'll take care of you."

Randall gently tapped him on the back.

"Let's go, man, before Meredith gets the notion to personally come down here to talk to us."

"Good point," Steve agreed. "My stomach's starting to growl anyway." He turned his attention back to Bettina. "I'll guess we'll be seeing you pretty soon. I can't wait until you're working with us."

Their eyes met. His expression was warm and genuine.

"Thanks, Steve. I can't wait either."

"Well, we're out," Randall said, walking away.

Steve waved at her and walked off with Randall. Randall noted that, for once, Bettina wasn't her usual flirtatious self. He found it refreshing. Perhaps she was actually taking his advice.

Bettina watched them as they crossed the lobby. She could hear their conversation as they headed for the double doors leading out of the building. The two didn't care how loudly they spoke. All respect and regard for the hallowed halls of Massey-Weldon had apparently been jettisoned.

"Let's do the Roscoe's on Gower," Randall said.

"*No,*" Steve protested. "It's too little. The wait might be too long. I want my chicken *now* . . . I'm starved!"

"I'm tired of always going to the one on Pico. I feel like a regular. I get embarrassed pulling up there every other day."

"Maybe you're embarrassed at pulling up with your white, blue-eyed, chicken-eating friend."

Randall pushed open the door, smirking at Steve.

"Well?" Steve asked.

"Just shut up already," he sighed. "Let's go to the one on Pico."

Bettina laughed as she watched them. She punched a line and dialed Nina Swanson to see if she could cover the phones. She was also going to see if she could talk Nina into covering them long enough for her to run out and buy at least a panty and a bra. No one knew it, but Bettina was naked under her dark blue pantsuit.

She was excited about the new beginnings and what Randall and Steve's departure meant.

She couldn't wait until it was her turn to leave Massey-Weldon behind.

Meredith paced around her office in stockinged feet, her thoughts racing with lightning speed. Her shoes, kicked off in anger, were underneath her desk.

"How am I going to handle this?" she mused aloud. "Wade's gonna *kill* me! And Anna. Jesus Christ, Anna's gonna *flip!*"

She reached over and pressed a button on her phone.

"Jeannie, get me the Legal Department," she barked.

There was no response.

"Jeannie! *Jeannie!*"

Meredith rushed over to her office door and looked out.

"Where *is* she?" she sneered.

Her assistant was nowhere in sight.

"*Oooph!*" she huffed. "And you were so close to a raise."

She slammed her office door.

She plopped down on the red velvet couch, clutching her head. She somehow had to do damage control. Before it hit the media and panic spread on the sets of *Westwood* and *Stickies*.

Her phone rang. She jumped up, stormed over to her desk, and snatched up the receiver.

"This is Meredith," she answered sharply.

"Meredith Reynolds?" a husky voice asked.

"Yeah," she snapped, pissed at having to take her own calls. "This is not a good time for me."

"I won't keep you," the voice said cryptically. "This call is just to warn you. Two of your writers are about to leave."

"Too late," she scoffed, sitting on the edge of her desk. "They already have. Whoever the hell you are, your timing sucks. Goodbye."

"*Wait!* So Bettina left?"

"Bettina?" she questioned. "What's she got to do with anything?"

"She's in on it. They have a new company. Their first TV show is all set to go. Something called *Ambitions*. A guy in your company named Carlos, an attorney, is going with them, and so is the receptionist, Bettina. If she hasn't left yet, she's planning to. I just wanted to let you know."

"Who *are* you?" she demanded.

"Consider me a friend."

"I don't have friends."

"You do now. Fire Bettina while you still have the chance."

She heard a click, and then a dial tone in her ear. Livid, she slammed the phone down, then decided to call Bettina. Before she could pick up the phone, it rang again.

"*WHAT?!*" she yelled into the receiver.

There was a pause. When the voice spoke, it was curt and grim.

"You've got sixty seconds to get to my office. And I want some answers. Get up here . . . *NOW!*"

The phone went dead.

Wade had never yelled at Meredith before. As she got up from the edge of the desk to put on her shoes, she decided it was best to tell him exactly what had happened.

After that, she had another plan.

She opened the drawer in the credenza where she kept proposals for new shows. Her long red nails sifted past hanging file after hanging file until she came across the one labeled NO-GO'S. It was a thick folder, the first of three. Meredith struggled to pull it out. She sat the folder on her desk, searching through its contents. Ten documents deep, she found it.

The proposal for *Ambitions*.

Meredith smiled.

Randall and Steve may have gotten the first laugh, but, if she had anything to do with it, she was going to have the last.

WAIT FOR THE BEEP

"*Beep-Beep! Beep-Beep! Beep-Beep!*"

Randall's pager exploded for the tenth time in less than five minutes.

He reached down without looking and pressed a button that made the beeping stop. A young couple seated at the next table cut their eyes at him, not at all thrilled about the constant interruptions to their chicken-flavored love affair.

In fact, a number of diners at the Roscoe's Chicken 'n Waffles near the corner of Pico and LaBrea were thoroughly annoyed. Since his arrival, Randall's beeper had gone off twice during the first twenty minutes, and now it was out of control. While the customers were used to Hollywood types who came in talking on their cell phones and sporting overblown attitudes, ten beeps in only four and a half minutes was taking things a bit too far.

"Her again?" Steve asked, biting into a chicken wing. He had unbuttoned the cuffs of his white dress shirt, rolled up the sleeves, and was digging deeply into his meal.

"Who else," Randall replied. "I'm just wondering when Meredith's going to get the hint that I'm not calling back."

Randall picked at his half-eaten chicken. He was much too hyped to have an appetite, which was a surprise. After the day he'd had, he expected to be a lot hungrier than he was.

"You should have done like me and turned your pager off."

Steve reached out with greasy fingers for his glass of lemonade. "The moment I got in your car, I eighty-sixed that puppy. I'll be damned if I'm gonna let her page me to death."

"Actually, I'm kind of enjoying it, even though this crowd looks like they're about ready to lynch me."

Randall gave the couple beside him a quick glance. Thankfully, they were making eyes at each other, not him.

"What pleasure would you get out of being paged by that bitch?" Steve mumbled, crumbs dropping out of his mouth, staining his shirt with grease.

"Have some class, player." Randall smirked, watching the crumbs bounce off Steve's chest and hit the table. "Check yourself. You don't look like you're about to be one of the heads of a soon-to-be-powerful company."

Steve laughed, looking around to see who had noticed. He dabbed at his mouth with a napkin and brushed away the crumbs.

"That doesn't happen often."

"Considering how well you were brought up, it shouldn't happen at all."

"It's the company I keep," Steve replied.

Randall chuckled.

His pager went off again. The young couple flashed him a fiery look. He quickly pressed the button to silence the beeping.

"Just put it on vibrate," Steve suggested. He dug into his waffle, which was swimming in butter and syrup, and closed his eyes as he savored the bread.

Randall sighed, pulled the pager from his hip, checked the number, changed the alert to vibrate, then put the pager back in place.

"The Diabolical?" Steve asked, still smacking his lips from the syrup.

"You know it."

"Now tell me again, why is it you're enjoying getting all these beeps?"

Steve took another drink of lemonade.

"I never said," Randall replied. "Your crumbs distracted me. It's because I haven't been sweated this much since I was in college."

Steve pretended he was choking on his drink. The young couple rolled their eyes.

"*Who* sweated you in college? You were probably a nerd. You didn't get hip until you moved out here and started hanging with me."

"*Please!*" Randall laughed. "LA is *wack* and so are you! If I didn't have to live here for business, trust me, I wouldn't."

Steve snickered.

"And I was very popular in college, thank you very much," Randall continued. "All the ladies were feeling me. I had my pick."

"Yeah," Steve countered, "I figured as much, with all the women you're constantly beating off. Here comes a throng of them now."

"I guess you'd know about beating off, wouldn't you?"

"I'm choosy. I've got standards."

"Which is why you have to shave your palms so much. When was the last time you had a girlfriend?"

"Girlfriends bring drama," Steve remarked, reaching across the table for the chicken breast on Randall's plate. "You're not gonna eat this, are you?"

Randall looked down at Steve's hand as it touched the chicken.

"Nah, man . . . help yourself."

"Thanks."

Steve took the chicken and bit into it. He held up his finger for Randall to wait until he finished chewing. "Anyway," he continued, "like I was saying, I'm not trying to have any more *girl*-friends. I'm looking for someone to have a serious relationship with. I want a woman. Someone who knows what she wants, and who isn't trying to play any games."

"Lots of luck finding that in this town."

"Right. And to top it off, now that we're about to move into another tax bracket, it's going to be even harder to find someone who isn't just interested in money."

"You've always been in another tax bracket, Beverly Hills boy. What are you talking about?"

"That money belongs to my parents," Steve replied, "not me."

Two buff men in their mid-twenties walked in. Both wore muscle shirts and sweats, as if they'd just left the gym. One was reddish-yellow with freckles, all height and sinewy muscle, his hair a sandy red. The other was dark-skinned and squat, his shoulders taut and sturdy. They sat at the table across from Randall and Steve. Both men studied Steve intensely. The freckle-faced one leaned over and whispered something in a husky voice.

"What's *their* deal?" Steve muttered.

Randall glanced over at them. Both men were staring at Steve. The dark one cut his eyes at Randall, as if demanding an explanation. Randall, accustomed to the drill, shook his head and smiled.

"This is so silly. They're just posturing. It ain't nothing but bullshit."

"What are they posturing about?" Steve asked.

"Come on, man, what do you expect? You're a white boy up in Roscoe's. That fascinates everybody least once."

"Why?"

"Because, if a white person's gonna be here, he's not gonna look like you, all spiffy in your well-tailored clothing, perfectly tanned with golden hair highlighted just so. You look like someone who should be eating pâté, not sitting across from me with a ring of grease around your mouth."

Steve quickly grabbed his napkin and wiped his face.

Randall laughed.

"I was just joking. But it's good to know you follow instructions. I guess that means I get to be CEO."

"*I'm* the CEO," Steve corrected.

"You're the president," Randall protested.

"The legal documents and corporate structure have already been drafted and executed."

"Doesn't mean I can't force you to switch."

Randall's pager vibrated against his hip again. He reached down and pressed it to get it to stop, then turned his attention back to Steve.

"What difference does it make if I'm CEO? We both own equal shares."

"You just don't want a white boy having the title," Steve joked.

"And you just think all black boys want is to be *pre-so-dent.*"

The both laughed.

"Whatever," Steve said. He picked up his napkin, wiped his mouth one last time, tossed it down, and pushed away his plate. The waitress, who had been invisible, except for once, since she brought the food, returned quickly and swept everything away. She placed the bill on the table in front of Steve. He smiled and nodded knowingly at Randall.

"See. She knows who's got the paper in this place." He pulled out his wallet and threw a platinum card on the table.

Randall laughed.

"You won't get any grief from me," he said. "Actually, that's an unwritten rule with black folks. 'If you dine with someone white, they're the one who pays that night.'"

Steve's eyes widened.

"You're kidding me, right?" he asked. "That's not real, is it?"

"Do I look like I'm kidding? Besides, my card is gold, and yours is platinum. I'd say platinum wins every time."

"I wondered why I was always paying," Steve said.

"Please. Like you haven't been turning those receipts in for reimbursement."

Randall's pager vibrated again. He checked it, anxious.

"M.?"

"Yep."

"You should be hearing from dude soon, don't you think?" Steve asked, leaning back in his chair.

"I hope so. He said we should know something no later than four." He glanced at his watch. "It's a quarter till three now. I expect to hear from him anytime."

"What do you think she'll say?"

Randall leaned back.

"I hope it's a yes. This thing is win-win for her, and the contract we're offering is tight. Not many people get the kind of structure we've set up. Desi's not crazy. She knows this could work for her."

"Did you tell her agent we'll pay her a hundred just for signing?"

"Of course I did. That's how I know he'll take us seriously, and so will she. It's unheard of for a second- or third-tier actor to get that kind of money up front. We're going make this thing fly, Steve. I just know it, man. And we're going to make Desi Sheridan a big star in the process."

Steve unrolled his sleeves and buttoned the cuffs, glancing up at his good friend and partner. Randall's eyes were fiery and intense. Steve wondered if he wasn't seeing something more.

"So does she know we haven't even pitched it yet?"

"Of course not, man. That would only make her nervous, and we need her signed on, at least verbally, by the end of today. It's the twenty-fourth. Pitching season is almost halfway over. We need to be able to go into those meetings we have scheduled on Monday and throw her name around. It would have taken too long to woo and convince her if she didn't think we had a chance." Randall narrowed his eyes. "What made you ask that anyway?"

"I don't know," Steve said. "It just feels kind of funny."

"Funny how?" Randall asked, annoyed. "Getting the star to commit first can be the biggest key to getting picked up. It makes the pitch that much easier. Why am I schooling you about shit you already know? It's not like she's not getting a hundred thousand dollars, guaranteed, out of this."

"Did you lie to her and tell her we already had a network lined up?"

"No. I told her we had talked to some network execs on the quiet, and that they were highly interested."

"So you lied to her," Steve said pointedly.

"What's your deal, man? Don't you have any confidence in us as a team?" Randall huffed. "Don't you think those Emmys stand for something? A network *will* pick us up, and it *will* be the network of our choice. When I told her we had interest, it wasn't a lie. I was just speaking truth to power. Something you need to learn how to do."

Steve glanced over at the cars traveling up and down Pico.

"Tell me again why we waited so long to approach her," he said.

"I never told you to begin with."

"So tell me now."

Randall took a deep breath.

"Look, man, I like working under pressure. You know that. That's when I do some of my best work. I knew we wouldn't be able to get to her the way I wanted to by going through her agent. My homegirl Sharon Lane knew her, so that was one way I knew I could at least get her ear. Sharon was the route I expected to go, and I had planned to call her at the eleventh hour and sell her on what we were doing, knowing that she would go back and sell it to Desi on our behalf. I was going to tell her that we needed a commitment now so we could still get in for next year's season. But then this golden carrot just *drops* into my lap and made everything else fall right into place."

"What golden carrot are you talking about?"

"A golden carrot named Lansing Ward. She's a personal shopper at Neiman Marcus. She's also a friend, and someone I used to date now and then. I went by on Tuesday to pick up a new suit that had just been altered, and Lansing asked me if I knew Desi

Sheridan. Made my ears prick right up. I said no, not directly, and asked her why, thinking maybe she could get me to her. Well, she informed me that Miss Sheridan had been interviewing for a job. As a personal shopper. Lansing said her boss was going to be calling Desi late the next day to offer her the job."

"She was going to take a job at a department store?" Steve asked. "Why on earth would she do something like that?"

"Come on, man," Randall replied. "She's a black actress in Hollywood. What the hell else is she supposed to do?"

"So you got to her before the Neiman people did."

"That's right. I dialed up Sharon, gave her just enough info to make her feel comfortable enough to give me Desi's number, and then I made the call. You should have heard how Desi sounded. She had this fear in her voice when she answered the phone that was just"—he made a waving gesture in the air—"I don't know. Sad. She sounded just pitiful. So I stroked her. I said all the right things. Which was easy anyway because I'm a fan, but you know I combed the Web that night and did a little extra boning up on her body of work. When we met for lunch, I was Superfly. She was eating out my hand, and I was loving that shit!"

"You are one lying, arrogant motherfucker."

"No I'm not," Randall replied. "I'm one helluva salesman. And if you expect to have any longevity in this business, you need to drop that goody-two-shoes act of yours and learn the game, too. Look at how you handled Meredith today. Now *that* was a step in the right direction."

Steve was amazed at Randall's cool, deliberate behavior. He shook his head and gazed out at Pico.

"This *is* only about getting Desi for *Ambitions*, right?" he asked without making eye contact. "Or is there yet *another* agenda you've got going on that I don't know about?"

"I want her for the show. You and I are already on the map. Having Desi and Jet on our team will guarantee that Vast Horizons gets off to a serious start."

Steve leaned forward, rubbing his chin.

"So, um, again, you have *no* personal interest in her. None at all."

Steve's eyes were locked with his partner's.

"This is about work," Randall said in a firm tone, leaning in towards Steve's face. "This is about what you and I have been planning for months. This is about making dreams come true."

"As long as you're not talking about wet dreams, my friend."

Randall scowled. Steve threw up his hands.

"Alright, alright. I guess I'll just have to wait and see."

Randall's pager vibrated again. He glanced down and pressed the button. He squinted. He removed the pager from its sheath on his hip and brought it closer to his eyes. His tightly pursed lips softened and spread into an enormous grin.

"What?" Steve asked, piqued. "Is it Meredith again?"

"Not at all," he said, beaming.

"Then what is it?"

Randall turned the pager around and showed it to Steve. Steve read it. He snatched the pager from Randall's hand and read it again. He looked up, in a reverie.

"You Mensa-belonging, lying, scheming, *brilliant* son-of-a-bitch," he whispered.

"That's right, *potna*," Randall shouted, not giving a damn about disturbing the other patrons. "Our girl said *yes!*"

WHERE THERE'S TOKE, THERE'S IRE

"So look . . . we gon' do this or what?"

Jackson Bennett sat behind the desk in his office on Wilshire. He was leaning back in his comfortable black leather chair, a wooden chewing stick in the corner of his mouth. His hands were behind his head and his feet were propped up high in front of him, partially blocking Sharon's view of his face. He was wearing Tims. Cheese boots. A big, oversized pair.

Big enough, Sharon thought, to stuff his tiny ass all the way inside.

"The Spark," from The Roots' *Things Fall Apart* CD, was softly thumping from the speakers of the stereo system. It might as well have been thumping from Jackson's soul. The man carried East Coast flavor with him wherever he went.

Behind him she could see the brown-gray cast of smog hovering over Beverly Hills. It looked like maybe rain was threatening.

She hoped to get out of Jackson's office before the heavens opened up. She needed a break and some fresh air. He had been talking nonstop for more than two hours, and she was exhausted.

Jackson Bennett had canyon-sized lungs and a mouth to

match. When he had something to say, he didn't stop until the last gulp of air and every oxygen molecule in the room was spent.

Sharon had been interested, very interested, in what he had to offer, but she found it hard to show her enthusiasm. Her mind was scattered. She hadn't eaten that morning. Perhaps, she figured, that was why her energy level was so low.

"Count me in," she said, getting up from the draconian wooden Ethiopian chair where she had been sitting. She smoothed down the front of her white cotton blouse, then began walking around the room, her hands thrust into the pockets of her black cotton slacks.

"Where you goin'?" Jackson asked, startled by her movement.

"Nowhere. My ass is raw from those hard chairs of yours. You ever think about getting cushions?"

"No," he said proudly. "I want people to feel the same way the Ethiopians who carved them feel when they sit."

Sharon was standing at the window behind him, peering out. She glanced at the back of his head, which was sprouting twisties, his newest look. She assumed he wouldn't have the patience for the time and upkeep it took to let them grow into full-fledged locks. Another new look would probably appear inside of a few weeks.

"Do you ever have Ethiopians sitting in your office?" she asked him.

"Well . . . no."

"Then you need to get some real chairs. Shit, go to IKEA. Chairs are cheap."

"It's about style, shorty, it's all about style."

"Which is why you have on cheese boots as hot as it is outside."

"This is straight-up Brooklyn flavor. You've spent so much time out here, you're losing your New York vibe."

"I'll never lose my New York vibe, and you know it."

She stared out the window at the cars passing below. Just across the street at an angle were UPN's offices in a tannish-brown adobe-style building.

"You ever been over there?" she asked absently, her finger against the glass.

Jackson turned to see where she was pointing.

"UPN?" He laughed. "Hasn't every black person at one time or another? I heard they got a li'l Negro factory in there where they just mix us up, roll us out, bake us up like cookies, then turn us loose to be eaten by the white folks."

"Stop it." She chuckled halfheartedly, walking away from the window. "Everybody's always dissing UPN and the WB. At least they're getting black projects on the air."

"For now," he said. "Wait'll they get themselves a certified white-faced hit. Those black shows will be sent packing quicker than you can say *jigaboo*."

"You can't blame them for being all about the money," Sharon said with a listless sigh. "Who isn't? Isn't that what we've just been sitting here talking about for the past two hours? All the cheddar I'm about to make. Your thirty-million-dollar budget. Two hundred G for me, plus points. Everything is all about money and connections these days, so why shouldn't UPN and the WB be down for theirs, too?"

She was fingering the black mudcloth he had hanging against the wall. It had the stick-figure shapes of a herd of white antelope running across a beige African plain.

Jackson's heavy feet hit the floor. He leaned forward, slapping his palms against his desk, staring at her in disbelief.

"Sharon, you *must've* been smoking today, to drop some foolishness like that!"

"I'm just talking." Sharon sighed, wandering around the room again. "Don't mind me."

"Naw, naw . . . we need to talk about this," he insisted, his eyes following her. "All we need is for some white studio head to hear you poppin' that nonsense. That defies everything I stand for."

Sharon cut her eyes at him as she neared his desk.

"Jackson, you know that's something I would never say to anybody but a close, close friend, of which, I think, I only have four. Maybe five. One's in a holding pattern right now." She lethargically slapped him on the shoulder as she passed behind him again. "Come on. I'm just tired. I'm restless. I don't need no Afrocentric lectures today. I'm down for the cause, alright? Ungawa. Black power. Asalaam Alaikum, and all that shit."

Sharon stood in front of him, held up her left fist, then pounded it against her chest in a pseudo pro-black, Pan-African gesture. She contorted her face into a serious freedom-fighting scowl. Jackson laughed. She let out a deep breath and sat on the side of his massive mahogany desk, facing him.

"I don't know," Jackson said. "Sometimes I don't think you West Indians understand the plight of the African-American. Y'all don't take the struggle seriously enough."

"I dare you to go to Jamaica and say that," she replied, reaching over and picking a piece of lint from one of his twisties. She flicked it into the air. "By the time you leave, you'll have so many footprints stamped on your ass, they'll spell out Marcus Garvey."

He roared with laughter, the chewing stick dropping from his mouth onto the floor. He leaned down, picked it up, and stuck it right back in his mouth.

"Shorty, you're something else. But you know I'm right. You know I'm speaking the truth."

"Whatever," she sighed. "Like white folks know the difference anyway. We're all black, and ain't hardly none of us in this industry working."

"Bourgie island girl," he teased in a dreadful patois, "act like me nah just tell her she gwine get a check for two hundred grand in tree days."

"Keep messing me with and my people, and I'm gon' start Marcus's name off for them."

Jackson smiled.

"You know you're my girl."

"Yeah . . . well."

She toyed with a rock on his desk.

"Where'd you get this?" she asked, regretting the question almost as soon as it exited her mouth.

Jackson took a deep breath and launched into exposition.

"An aborigine gave me that. Actually, no, wait . . . I'm wrong. The aborigine gave me this didgeridoo."

He picked up a flute-looking thing and showed it to her. Sharon was mentally kicking herself.

"I got that rock from a Maori woman when I shot that Lil' Kim video in New Zealand."

Somehow Lil' Kim and New Zealand didn't seem to go together in the same sentence, and Sharon's head began to swim.

"You ever been to New Zealand?" he asked, off and running on another potentially lengthy topic. "The Maori people are amazing. Did you ever see that Maori flick where the husband was kicking the wife's ass on the regular? What was the name of it? They had a whole bunch of kids. That shit was marvelous. A Maori guy directed it. He's done some other flicks, too. What was his name? Sounds Japanese, but trust me, it's Maori. Guerrilla filmmaking, man. The real deal. Now *that's* the kind of stuff—"

"Jackson!"

"What?!" he asked with alarm, annoyed at breaking his accelerated rhythm.

"Stop. Count to ten. Take a breath. I'm not going anywhere, alright? You don't have to talk me to death all in one sitting."

Jackson pursed his thin lips together.

"You sure that Maori woman *gave* you this rock?" Sharon asked with a slight smile. "Or could it be she was *throwing* it at you? I'm inclined to believe the latter. Folks'll do anything to shut you up."

"You're lucky you know me, shorty. Anybody else would get pimp-smacked for popping some yang like that, *and* for cutting me off."

"I once saw George Will cut you off during a roundtable debate," she said, smiling.

"Yeah, and George Will almost got pimp-smacked. He saw my hand poised and itchy. That's why he didn't cut me off anymore."

Jackson had his hand pulled back, in position, demonstrating his pimp-swing.

Sharon chuckled. She needed to leave. Before the rain, and before she collapsed on the floor from sheer exhaustion right in front of Jackson's feet. Something like that would really have him running his mouth.

"Alright, shorty, what's the deal?" Jackson asked, as if reading her mind. He was leaning back in his chair again, peering at her with small black eyes. "Why are you so restless? I could tell you were kinda absent when I was telling you about the film and the budget. I expected you to be jumping off the walls. Two hundred thousand is usually enough to make me want to raise the roof."

Sharon studied the face of her longtime friend. It was a face of drama, complexity, sometimes even mischief and mayhem, but behind it was one of the most underappreciated minds she'd ever known. She considered Jackson's work genius, and his style of filmmaking awe inspiring and Oscar worthy.

If only his mouth wasn't so damn big. Maybe then some of that genius would come shining through to everyone else.

"I've got a lot on my mind, Jackson."

"You pregnant?" he flatly asked.

It was all Sharon could do to keep her eyes from stretching wide. Her heart skipped five fast beats and her pulse jumped.

"Now *why* would you say that?" she responded, feigning indifference to his pointed question.

"I'on know," Jackson said with a wave of his hand. "That's usually what's wrong with females when they got shit on their mind. It was just a wild stab."

"Don't call me a *female*, like I'm a cow or something. I hate that shit."

"Well, with you *women*, it's usually your period or the absence thereof. You know I'm right. Come on, tell me I'm wrong. That's why God made y'all the weaker sex."

Jackson was baiting her. She could tell. He wanted conversation and he would do anything to provoke a debate.

Sharon didn't respond. Instead, she picked up a framed photograph from his desk. It was a picture of Jackson and his wife, Castanza Nettles, a well-respected field correspondent for CNN. They'd met three years prior at an intimate Upper East Side cocktail party and fundraiser in support of Mumia Abu-Jamal. Sharon, in New York on other business but invited to the same gathering, had witnessed their karmic connection.

Castanza had been immediately smitten. Jackson was surprised to find her taken by his unseeming wiles. He considered himself a man who had no rap, no game. Those who really knew him knew otherwise. The five-foot-four, leanly athletic ("chickendiesel," Brooklyn heads like to call it) Jackson had spent years perfecting his game. He'd done it with his screenplays. He'd mastered it behind the lens.

His game had obviously worked on Castanza. They married within a month of meeting one another. Less than a year into their marriage, the two had a child, an overstuffed, never-sated, mealymouthed thing named Chakra whom Sharon found almost as noisy as his father. She'd asked Jackson once, during a visit to his brownstone in Brooklyn Heights, what *chakra* meant. Eager to expound on the subject of anything, he announced it meant *wheel*, then launched into a windy explanation of how it signified one of seven basic energy centers in the body. Castanza, a yoga freak, backed him up. Sharon heard them say something about "archetypes," "correlating," and "ganglia," but the rest pretty much faded to black after Jackson said "wheel." Why anybody would want to name his child Wheel was beyond her comprehension. Not even on a weed high could she conceive of such a thing.

Chakra *was* pretty round though, so she figured it made sense. There were plenty of times she'd visited with Jackson and Castanza, in both New York and LA, and found herself wanting to roll their little bad-ass two-year-old right out of the front door.

Now Castanza was pregnant again, which Jackson found appealing as hell. Those were his exact words. Her full belly was a testament to his virility. Little man or no, he wanted the world to be aware that he was of strong African stock, spitting out seed and populating the earth with a serious ferocity.

This child was a girl, the ultrasound revealed, and they would name her Kundalini.

Oh brother, Sharon had thought, when they first told her the news. It sounded a little too close to cunnilingus for her liking and she imagined that, as their daughter got older, her name would get her in a whole lot more trouble than she would probably deserve.

She never bothered to ask what *kundalini* meant. Knowing Jackson, it probably meant *kill whitey,* or something equally excessive. Maybe it really did mean cunnilingus. If she had to ask to find out, Sharon decided that she would never know.

She gently stroked the glass surface of the photograph in her hand. Jackson watched her curiously.

There was a patch of dust in the center of the picture, so faint Sharon only noticed it when the light hit the glass at an awkward angle. She ran her index finger across it, wiping it away. It seemed to mar the purity of the image beneath it.

In the picture, Jackson's right arm was around Castanza's waist. They were standing next to a baobab tree in Kenya.

(Sharon knew it was Kenya because the two had just returned from the trip in August.) Both were dressed in tribal garb. The picture was striking because Jackson was the same size as his wife, and the two looked like a perfectly matched pair. Castanza's clothing was tight across her stomach, compliments of being in the fifth month of pregnancy. Jackson's left hand was on her belly.

As Sharon traced her finger across the surface of the glass, she slowly began to smile.

Jackson's voice broke her reverie.

"We took that in Nairobi," he yammered, ruining the pristine moment. "It was our last stop after checking out Lake Victoria. Hey, did you know that Swahili is not the sole native tongue of Kenya, like most people think?"

"What?" Sharon answered, lost in the picture. His words descended upon her as if out of a mist.

"Word, it's true," he continued. "Most Kenyans have their own tribal language thing going on. For instance . . ."

He took the picture from Sharon's hand. She instinctively frowned.

". . . during this visit, we stayed with the Masai, and the language they speak is called *Maa*."

Sharon's head began to swirl again.

"Stanzi and I stayed at their *enkang* while we were there," Jackson said proudly. "I actually slept in an *I-manyat*. You know what that is?"

He knows damn well I don't, Sharon thought. *Nor do I give a damn.*

Jackson didn't bother to wait for her answer.

"It's where the warriors live. That's right, shorty, you're looking at someone who has slept amongst the warriors."

Sharon wished she'd never picked up the picture at all.

She raised up from the edge of his desk. Her head was a spinning top.

"I really do have to go, Jackson. When is our first real meeting scheduled?"

"How about the middle of next week?" he said, rising from his chair. He checked his calendar. "Let's say Wednesday the twenty-seventh. Here in my office at nine o'clock. We need to go into preproduction ASAP. And don't worry, I'll have your contract drafted up with everything just like we discussed. If I can get it for you tomorrow, do you want to sign it then?"

"Fine. Have it couriered over to Eddie's so he can look it over first and make sure it's clean."

"Why not your boy Glen?" Jackson asked. "He's pretty good, from what I understand."

"I don't mix business with pleasure."

"I hear that."

"Exactly. So, if all is cool and I sign the contract tomorrow, when can I expect my check?"

"I know you understood my Jamaican accent. I said *tree days*, not counting the weekend."

"Is that supposed to be *three* you're saying?"

"Yup."

"Jackson, nobody gets their check in three days. This is Hollywood."

"I've been waiting on this budget a long time, shorty. Now it's mine to disburse. We've got a lotta shit to do. I'm paying you first so we can get rocking on this thing."

"Bet," she said. "Is it the whole two hundred?"

Jackson nodded, gnawing on his chewing stick.

"That's perfect," Sharon said, her spirits slightly lifted. "You gonna send it over, or do I need to come and pick it up?"

"Whatever you like."

"I'll come and pick it up," she replied. "Three working days is Wednesday next week, so I can just get it when I come back for our first meeting."

She made her way to the door, feeling the energy seep from

her body with every step. Perhaps it was the weed from the night before that had drained her. She had no business smoking while she was pregnant anyway. She found herself afraid to consider what all that weed might mean for her baby.

No. Not baby. Fetus. Embryo. Zygote. Gamete.

She kept trying to reduce the thing within her to its lowest common, detached denominator, but kept coming back to the realization that it was, indeed, a baby. *Her* baby.

"What about this business with Jet?" Jackson asked. "I told him that you would call, so he's expecting to hear from you, and soon. They could use you over there, and I know he's willing to pay you well."

"I'll think about it," she said with a shrug. "And I'll definitely call him."

"Don't fuck around and let him put somebody else on, Sharon. There are plenty of people who would leap at the chance."

"I know, I know."

"Yo . . . one other question," he said.

Sharon stopped. She felt the ground sway beneath her.

"What's that?"

"Your girl, Desi. What's she got going on right now?"

"Actually, she has some irons in the fire that are looking pretty good. Why?"

" 'Cause . . . I'm really feeling her for this film. I think she could portray the hell out of Rita Marley. I'd prefer not to even have to go through the process of auditioning other actresses, that's how strongly I'm feeling her for the role. I know her steelo, so ain't no worries there. Put a bug in her ear for me that if she wants the part, it's hers. She'd be one of the lead characters."

"Alright, I'll tell her," Sharon replied, "but don't even front and try to offer her scale."

"Come on, Sharon. Who am I?"

"I'm just saying. If she does take it, you need to come correct with her pay."

"No doubt, no doubt. But, yo, answer me this," he said, chawing on his stick, "does Desi blame me for how the public treated *Flatbush Flava?* 'Cause I know she had to realize that was just some straight-up playa-hatin' the media did on me and the film. I've offered her parts since then, but she hasn't bitten."

"They've been small parts, Jackson," Sharon said, desperate to leave. "She's got a name. People know her face. She'd rather pass on a bit part than go back to square one."

"Then why'd she do that burger commercial?"

Sharon waved her hand in the air and made for the door.

"I'm out. I'll be sure to tell her what you said."

She took three steps, then swooned a little. She stopped and leaned against one of the Ethiopian chairs.

"Shorty," Jackson asked, getting up, "are you sure you're alright?"

"Yeah, yeah," Sharon said, the room spinning around. She held on tightly to the hard wooden chair. "Just let me rest here for a minute. I should have eaten something this morning. I think my sugar is low."

"You hypoglycemic?"

"I don't know. I suppose I could be."

Jackson walked around the desk to Sharon, then led her over to his cushiony leather chair. He gently pushed her into it. He knelt in front of her.

"Hypoglycemic people know they're hypoglycemic. You want me to order in some food?"

"No, no," she protested, raising her palm. "Really, I'm okay. I had a rough sleep last night, and I think all I need is a quick energy boost. Maybe I'm just carb-depleted."

She opened his desk drawer, rooting around through the paper clips, pens, chewing sticks, and assorted invitations to movie premieres.

"Don't you keep any candy in here? All I need is something to munch on."

"That's it. I'm ordering you some food." He pressed the intercom button on his phone. "*Khalilah!* Bring those menus in here!"

Sharon mustered enough strength to push herself up from the chair. She stepped around him.

"I'm out, Jackson. I'm supposed to be meeting somebody in"—she glanced at her watch—"thirty minutes anyhow. If I rush, I can make it."

"With the way you look now, you don't need to be rushing anywhere. You want me to call you a car?"

"It's not that hectic, Jackson. I gotta go."

She gave him a quick, sincere hug, and cautiously made for the door. Khalilah came in with the menus.

"Never mind about those," Jackson told her.

Khalilah, used to his antics, spun around on her axis and disappeared as quickly as she had arrived.

"Thanks for looking out for a girl," Sharon said as she stopped at the door.

"Always," Jackson replied. "We go too far back. You're cool peoples, shorty."

"Ditto."

Just as she was about to leave, she remembered something.

"Oh yeah. The name of the movie you were talking about with the Maori people is *Once Were Warriors*. The director's name is Lee Tamahori."

Jackson smacked himself against the forehead, opening his mouth to speak.

Before he could utter a sound, Sharon was gone.

She could barely keep her eyes open as she turned from La Cienega onto Centinela, then into Ladera Plaza. Sharon pulled into a parking space in front of the Fatburger that was next to Starbucks, shut the car off, and rested her head against the steering wheel of her bronze Lexus GS400.

She had been driving in silence ever since she left Jackson's office, forgoing the usual comforting sounds of soft reggae or churning hip-hop filling the car. Music would have been too much of a distraction. She needed all her concentration just to make the drive. Her lids were so heavy, it took everything she could manage to keep them open. She had dozed off during a red light at the intersection of Wilshire and Doheny. The cars behind her blared their horns in unison like a cry from hell. The noise terrified her. Sharon's eyes popped open and she floored it, her tires squealing in surprise as they spun hotly against the baking asphalt.

That was enough to scare her awake. She had cranked her air conditioner up high, directing the vents towards her face in a full-freeze blast, in the hopes that it would keep her conscious. The drive seemed to take forever, giving her time to ponder her situation. Her thoughts were thick and murky, filled with dread and expectation. Instead of dwelling on the good news she'd just received from Jackson, all she could picture was the face of Glen.

It was a dour face. The one he would have *after* he learned that she was pregnant.

She kept hearkening back to the photo of Jackson and Castanza in Kenya. They appeared to be so happy and Jackson's expression was teeming with pride. Sharon ached for the feeling that seemed to rise from their images. It spoke of love and unity, something she wanted so badly and almost seemed close to getting, until this.

Glen always treated her lovingly, but she had witnessed behavior from him with others that indicated he could be cold and aloof. If he knew she was pregnant, would he be as proud as Jackson was in the photo? Or would he respond with that steel voice she'd heard him use on the phone once with his younger sister, Kell.

She doubted Glen would be happy and proud. He had too much going on to want a baby right now.

If Glen knew she was pregnant, she wondered, would he even

stick around? That's when things always got shady. Other than great sex, a mutual appreciation for premier wines, Glen's weakness for her island-style cooking, occasional sleepovers that sometimes lapsed into days, and the foot thing, they had no real foundation or ties. Not any that bound them together in a serious way.

Sure, she made him happy. So he said. But he had never used the L word. She hadn't used it either, not with him, but she was in it—deep—without a doubt.

She added their age difference to the whole mix. A baby would be the real litmus test, she knew, because it would mean that he would have to decide if he really wanted to be with an older woman. He was always saying that her age didn't matter, but it was easy to talk about what mattered and what didn't when the situation was cool.

The situation was definitely *not* cool anymore.

She would be his baby's mama. And, more than likely, that was *all* she would ever be. She couldn't remember how many times Glen had jokingly, and seriously, talked about how he loathed the phrase *my baby's mama,* and discussed with disdain the state of a society that allowed so many baby's mamas to flourish. Whenever he saw a young single mother with a string of kids in tow, he immediately had something flip to say about it.

Sharon vividly recalled his comments one particular afternoon, just a couple of months before. She and Glen had just left a barbecue at a mutual friend's home in Carlton Square. They were sitting at a red light, in Glen's brand-new silver Jaguar S-Type sedan, at the intersection of Manchester and La Brea. A young black girl—she couldn't have been more than fifteen—was standing at the corner, waiting for the light to change.

Her small hands tightly gripped the handle of a stroller, and her belly was round and ripe. The child in the stroller seemed barely a year old.

"You see that?" Glen had commented with disgust. "Now

that's just straight foolishness. What kind of life does a person like that have?"

It was then that Sharon realized just how out of touch her well-bred boyfriend was.

"My parents didn't raise us like that," he said. "We knew better than to be messing around with hoodrats who spread their legs for any- and everybody. Girls like that have three and four kids, all with different daddies. Their life is nothing but a series of paternity tests, child support—which they probably don't ever collect—Pampers, and Jerry Springer. What kind of dismal way is that to live? Most of these girls don't even know there's a whole, big, baby-free world going on around them."

Sharon had remained quiet as he spoke, studying the girl, wondering what her life *was* like, and what she would ultimately become.

"When I was in high school," Glen had ranted, "I wasn't even *trying* to get caught up in that mess. There's just too many things I want to do with my life."

The light changed, and Glen sped off. Sharon glanced back to see if the girl had been able to safely cross the street. She saw her pushing the stroller towards the opposite corner.

Who was he to call her a hoodrat? That young girl could have been anybody, she imagined, with circumstances that had just ballooned out of her control.

"It's really not nice to judge situations you don't understand," she had said to Glen. "That business about walking a mile in a man's shoes is true. That girl could be a gifted artist. You're coming to a conclusion about her based solely on what you think you see."

"Yeah . . . ," he exclaimed, "I think I see a hoodrat! I'm trying to tell you, Sharon, the ghetto is taking over everything. You'd better listen. You've got to protect your neck. There's a certain standard of living that I refuse to step down from. I'm not trying to have the hood encroaching on my backyard, baby's mamas hanging all off my fence and dirty-diapered crumbsnatchers dangling from my satellite dish. Baby's mamas need to stay in the ghetto with their baby's daddies, where they belong."

Welcome to the real world, Glen, she mused now, bitterly. *Where baby's mamas aren't just in the ghetto anymore.*

Sharon gently butted her head against the steering wheel in an attempt to scramble her thoughts.

She was startled by a rap at her window. She struggled to raise her head. It seemed to weigh a thousand pounds.

Desi was standing there in a pair of khaki cargo shorts and a white T-shirt, a look of concern on her face. She gestured for Sharon to let down the window.

Sharon opened the door and got out instead.

"Are you okay?" Desi asked, searching her face. "Why were you just sitting there like that, banging your head against the steering wheel?"

"I'm fine, Dez," Sharon said in a dragged-out voice. "I'm real tired and hungry, though. I'm gonna get something from Fatburger. Maybe some fries or something, and take it with me into Starbucks."

Desi grabbed her by the arm.

"You look terrible!"

Sharon smiled weakly.

"Thanks. That's exactly what I needed to hear."

"I don't mean it that way," Desi said. "I mean you almost look as though you're ill."

Sharon triggered the remote for the Lexus's door locks and security system. She stepped up on the curb and stumbled into Fatburger, Desi close on her heels. Once she got inside, she sat down at the first table she reached.

"Could you do me a favor and order me a large fry and a burger?" she asked weakly.

Sharon zipped open her purse to retrieve the money, but Desi, now genuinely worried, had already gone to the counter and was placing the order. She returned with the food and set it in front of Sharon.

Desi watched in amazement as Sharon's lassitude was replaced by ravenous hunger. She stuffed fries into her mouth five and six at a time, barely catching her breath. She packed the chewed potatoes in a ball in her jaw, savoring the sensation of munching as many as she possibly could before allowing herself to swallow.

Desi pushed a large cup of Coke in front of her, hoping she would wash the food down. Sharon kept stuffing fries into her mouth until her cheeks were puffed circles and there were no more fries to be had.

She reached for the Coke and sucked desperately on the straw. She gulped, drank, gulped, drank, and gulped again until her mouth was empty. Sharon was panting, a dazed look on her face.

Desi remained silent, watching her friend decimate the meal.

Sharon snatched up the burger and went to work. She took enormous bites, but still didn't swallow, chomping and chomping until the burger was half gone. After a few more sips of Coke, and a couple of quick gulps, she began again.

A young man in running pants passed by them, cutting his eyes at Sharon as she ripped into the food.

When she finished, there was only paper, a few crumbs, a splatter of ketchup, and a half-finished soda. Sharon was still panting. She drank more of the Coke, pacing herself, and, gradually, her heightened breathing began to calm.

"Man!" she said. "I was *sooo* hungry! I don't think I've *ever* been that hungry in my life!"

Desi's lips were pursed and her brows were knitted.

"Why are you looking at me like that?" Sharon asked.

Desi was still frowning.

"It's no big deal, Dez. I just needed to eat something."

"You need to take better care of yourself." She leaned in closer to Sharon, lowering her voice to a whisper. "I swear, I just don't get it. It's like you're walking around in a daze. What are you doing, starving yourself? Is that how you plan on dealing with the baby?"

"Nooo . . . ," Sharon replied, wondering how Desi's mind worked. "It's really not that hectic. The day just got away from me. I've been caught up with Jackson since noon."

"Was he too cheap to take you to lunch?"

"I didn't expect to be there that long."

Sharon took another sip of Coke, not at all pleased with the way Desi was grilling her.

"You should see yourself," Desi reprimanded.

She reached into her purse and pulled out a palm-sized mirror, then aimed it in Sharon's direction. A large mustard stain had tap-danced down the front of Sharon's white blouse. There was ketchup on her left cuff. Desi raised the mirror a little higher so that Sharon could see her face.

Her eyes seemed lifeless, and there were dark sunken hollows beneath them. A few errant crumbs had gathered around the edges of her mouth. Sharon had to admit, if only to herself, that she looked rather ill. But that was *her* issue, not anyone else's.

She wiped her mouth with a napkin.

Desi put the mirror away.

"If you're not going to take care of yourself," she scolded, her voice once again low, "you should at least acknowledge the baby. It deserves better than this."

Desi had already decided that Sharon was having this baby. In her mind, there was no other option or discussion necessary.

"Do me a favor, Dez. Stop with all this 'the baby' shit, alright? You're speaking in hushed tones like I'm a leper or something. I'm not even sure I'm pregnant. I haven't taken a test yet or anything."

"You know you're pregnant."

"What*ever*," Sharon replied, annoyed. Now that she had eaten, she was beginning to feel much better, but Desi's pointed attacks threatened to bring her down. She was determined to reroute the conversation. "Did you hear back from Randall and his partner?"

Desi knew why Sharon was changing the subject. She didn't want to take the conversation any further than it had already gone. Desi went along with it, thinking her good news might help the vigor return to her friend's face.

"I'm going to do the show," she announced, sitting back. "I like the terms they presented, and they're giving me a nice amount of money up front as a signing fee."

"Now, see," Sharon exclaimed, "that's really good news! So there's no reason for you to be sitting across from me with your face twisted, all up in *my* business, when you should be running up La Cienega right now, doing the Humpty-Hump."

Desi grinned, relaxing a little.

"The Humpty-Hump is so played out."

"Well, if I was you, I'd be running up the street doing *something*. The Freak, the Spank. Ooh, I know! You could just break out and do the Running Man. People would think you're jogging."

"Or having an epileptic fit," Desi said, giggling at Sharon's unexpected silliness.

"Go 'head, girl," Sharon insisted, her energy level rapidly rising. "Get out there on that street and do something. Bust one good split. Show the Lord you appreciate all the hard work He's done for you." She reached across the table, semiseriously nudging Desi to get up. "Go on. I'll get everybody to watch. La Cienega awaits. Go bust a move for the people!"

"Stop it!" Desi squealed. "Have you lost your mind?!"

"*Shiiiiit,*" Sharon droned, sounding completely like her old perky self again. "If I wasn't so drained, I'd be out there doing splits right behind you."

She burst into song.

"*Well, we're movin' on up!*"

A couple of heads turned their way. Desi smacked Sharon gently on the hand.

"Stop it, I said," she said with a laugh. "You act like you're on Prozac!"

Sharon might as well have been. Her attitude had done a complete one-eighty. Her eyes were no longer wan and lifeless. Now they crackled and popped with a girlish playfulness. All she'd really needed was a bite to eat, she realized, and everything was alright again. Even her gloominess and the dark brooding about Glen seemed to have faded.

She was also genuinely happy for Desi. She'd watched her struggling for breaks for a long time.

Being happy for Desi made Sharon give herself permission to celebrate her own good fortune.

"Jackson just got a green light for a film based on the life of Bob Marley," she blurted.

"Oh, really?"

"Yep. It's got a thirty-million-dollar budget. This is going to be the one that does it for him, I just know it. He's been talking about it for years. Anyway, he wants me on the project."

"Oh, Sharon!" Desi squealed, reaching across the table and grabbing her friend's hands. "That is *so* awesome!"

Sharon realized that, indeed, it was.

"I'm pretty pleased about it," she said. "Funny, when I was in his office, I couldn't muster up the energy to get that excited, but you know what?"

"What?"

"Being around you is actually making me get a little bit hyped."

"Good!" Desi replied. "You ready to go bust those La Cienega splits?"

"Hold on . . . I'm not finished," Sharon said in a conspiratorial voice as she leaned in towards Desi. Their hands were still together. "After I tell you this, though, you might want to bypass La Cienega altogether and go bust a string of splits on the 405."

Desi leaned closer, her eyes bright with excitement.

"What? You and Glen are getting married?"

Sharon froze.

"Now where did *that* come from?"

"I don't know," Desi replied, shrugging her shoulders. "I'm a hopeless romantic. Forget I said it."

"I already have. Anyway, get this: Jackson wants you to play Rita Marley. It's one of the leads. He said the role is yours if you want it. No audition necessary."

Desi's eyes were locked with Sharon's, but she gave no response.

"Did you hear what I just said?" Sharon asked.

Desi nodded, unable to produce even the tiniest sound. She opened her mouth to speak, but nothing would come out.

"Does the fact that you seem catatonic mean that you're happy, or that you just don't give a fuck?"

Sharon saw the glimmer in Desi's eyes at the same time she noticed that her hands were trembling.

"Oh, no . . . wait. You're not *crying*, are you?"

Two ripe teardrops fell onto the table. By the time they landed, Desi burst into full-scale tears, completely confusing Sharon. She covered her face with her hands. Fatburger patrons began to take notice.

"Dez, what's up?" she implored. "I thought I was giving you good news."

"You did," Desi said, grinning broadly through her tears. "I just can't believe this is happening." She picked up a napkin and wiped at her nose. "I never talked to you about this, but, Sharon, girl, I was just about to go broke."

"Oh my goodness, Desi, are you serious?"

Desi nodded.

"About as serious as you can get. Just a couple of days ago, I was seriously thinking about taking a job at a department store, or going back home to Jensen. Then this show *Ambitions* comes up, and now there's Jackson's movie."

Sharon didn't know whether to be sad at not knowing what had been going on with her friend, or happy at the positive turn of events.

Tears were still falling from Desi's eyes.

"It's okay now, Dez," Sharon said softly, her voice reassuring. "Things are starting to look up for both of us."

"I know," Desi replied. "This is just such a blessing. Girl, I had been praying like a fiend, asking God not to send me back home. I feel like, after all this, I'll never doubt Him or lose faith again."

Sharon smiled, wishing her shaky faith was as strong.

"Jackson was afraid you were going to turn down the part."

"Why would he think that?"

"He wasn't sure if you were mad at him about what happened with *Flatbush Flava*."

"That's ridiculous," Desi said, waving her hand. "What happened happened. If anything, I was angry at him for offering me all those bit parts. I don't think he ever considered how insulted I felt."

"I don't think he meant any harm," Sharon said. "It's so hard for black actors to get work, and Jackson is so hell-bent on changing all that. He probably thought he was doing something nice by offering you those roles."

"I figured as much. I assumed his heart was in the right place."

The Fatburger, empty when they first arrived, had now become noisy and crowded. A group of five teenage Mexican boys was sitting at the table behind Desi and Sharon, laughing loudly and flirting with three teenage girls waiting for their order. A young black woman walked in, followed by her four boisterous children.

A baby's mama. Sharon felt a sudden chill pass through her body. Desi noticed it.

"Let's go next door and get some chai tea," she suggested.

"Great," Sharon said, "but I can't stay long. I have something really important I need to take care of."

Magic Johnson's Starbucks was a popular watering hole within the African-American community. It was a warm, inviting place filled with positive vibes and interesting people, a number of whom were regulars.

Popular authors often parked at tables for hours with their laptops. Celebrated litigators, agents, and producers power-sipped double lattes and brokered deals. Hip-hop heads munched on chocolate hazelnut biscotti and talked shit over a game of chess. Desi and Sharon loved meeting there because they could sit back in the comfortable chairs, enjoy the pleasing atmosphere, and just linger, talking about nothing and everything. There was never any rush once you passed through the doors. Something about the place made people want to slow down and relax.

Sharon was at the counter, checking out the desserts.

"What's that?" she asked the young girl behind the register.

"Lemon pound cake."

"Is it good?"

The girl gave a furtive glance to her left, then wrinkled her nose.

"It's alright," she whispered. "I don't really like it that much."

"Then it's *not* alright," Sharon said in a sarcastic tone.

"No, I guess it's not," the girl replied, somewhat offended.

Sharon snickered, shaking her head.

Why is it so hard for people to say what they really mean?

"Alright," she said, "let me get one venti chai tea with vanilla, two vanilla almond biscotti, and one chai iced tea with double vanilla."

"Venti?"

"Yeah. I just said that."

"For one of them. You didn't say what size for the other."

"Oh. Well, I thought I did."

"But you didn't," the girl mumbled under her breath as she walked away from the register to get the biscotti.

I know she's not giving me attitude, Sharon thought.

The girl returned, flashed a pleasant smile, took the twenty Sharon offered, and gave her the change and the biscotti.

The moment Sharon stepped aside to wait for the rest of the order, the girl rolled her eyes.

"You must have really rubbed her the wrong way," a voice whispered over Sharon's shoulder.

She turned around. It was her friend Shaun Robinson, one of the hosts of *Access Hollywood.*

"Hey, you!" Sharon exclaimed, giving Shaun a big hug. "It's been a minute since I've seen you last. What's been going on?"

"*Girl . . . ,*" Shaun began, breaking into that voice that immediately put those who heard it at ease, "I've been flying around so much, I'm about to sprout wings! I did the MTV Video Music Awards, the Emmys. I *just* got back from a spa vacation in Palm Springs."

Shaun was a sophisticated beauty who was slender, fit, and full of vivacity. Café au lait with dark shoulder-length hair with burnished highlights, she had a warm and winning personality that made it easy for celebrities to relax around her, both on and off the camera.

Sharon enjoyed hanging out with her. Shaun was quite witty, with a knack for good conversation. They used to do lunch or dinner at least once a month, but that dwindled after Sharon began dating Glen. She had seen very little of Shaun of late, other than on TV, although they still talked on the phone every few weeks.

"You look great," Sharon said, reaching for the two orders of tea.

"Girl, I *feel* great. There's nothing like being pampered for days on end to rejuvenate your perspective."

"Maybe that's what I need," Sharon replied. "I've been feeling pretty whooped lately."

"Do it!" Shaun said. "In fact, I'm going again next month. If you want, we can make it one of those girlfriend trips and play catch-up with what's been going on."

"That sounds cool. Make sure you call me and remind me."

"I will. How's work?" Shaun asked.

"Looking pretty good," Sharon said. She suddenly realized an opportunity. "Actually, if you call me at home in about an hour and a half, I can give you a heads-up on some skinny that should be kicking around town soon, if not already."

Shaun beamed, excited.

"Is it juicy stuff?" she asked.

"Well, it's not Brad Pitt or Denzel, but it's definitely something important enough for you to use on the show. You can probably break it before the folks at *Entertainment Tonight* get wind. After you guys, it'll mostly show up in the industry mags."

"Wonderful! I'm definitely going to call you." Shaun checked her watch. "Is five o'clock okay?"

"Yeah, that gives me plenty of time to finish up here, run an errand, and get home."

"Alright, girl. I was over in the corner and saw you standing here, and thought I'd come up and surprise you real quick. But now I gotta run! Gimme some love!"

Shaun gave Sharon, who was awkwardly holding the teas and biscotti, a quick embrace.

"Alright! I'll talk to you at five o'clock."

Shaun waved goodbye, and dashed off.

Sharon carried the chai teas and biscotti to the lounging area. Desi had already staked out a table with two chairs. Sharon handed her the iced tea, then sat down in front of her own steaming cup. She placed the two biscotti on a napkin in the middle of the table.

"I just ran into Shaun Robinson."

"Really? How is she?"

"Dez, she looks fantastic," Sharon said with a hint of envy. "She was this firecracker, bursting with energy. She just came back from a spa treatment and everything about her was glowing. I think maybe that's what I need to get me going again."

Desi nodded, drinking her tea.

"Just knowing that I'm going to be able to sink my teeth into some quality acting again is good enough for me," she said. "Sharon, my mind feels so much lighter. All I've been doing is stressing money. I couldn't even focus on the craft anymore to attract the right role. I was in too much of a panic, I think."

Sharon bit into one of the biscotti, agreeing with her.

"I definitely believe the way you feel inside can affect what comes to you."

"Exactly," Desi said. "I was probably blocking my own blessings by carrying around all that panic and fear. Not that I'm saying I'm healed and holy-rolling and won't ever be fearful again. I know that's not the case. But at least I see a direct correlation between my actions and how the resolution came about. Now that I'm going to be able to handle the financial situation, I'll be free to get back to who I am and what I've been out here trying to do in the first place."

She picked up the remaining biscotti and took a small bite.

"*Mmmm.* These are so good."

She drank some of her iced chai tea. Sharon observed how free Desi seemed. She had a glow, too. Even the way her hair looked was different, not the way she was used to seeing it styled.

"I like your hair like that."

"You're just noticing my hair?" Desi asked, fingering her curls. "I haven't been blow-drying it like I usually do. I just rub it with a towel after I get out of the shower. I've been wearing it like this for a couple of days now."

"It works for you."

"Thanks. Randall said the same thing."

Sharon sipped her tea, noting how familiar Desi sounded as she spoke Randall's name.

"Sharon, aren't you excited?!" Desi squealed. "I'm so freaking hyped! I mean, imagine . . . people are going to be seeing me on TV every week!"

"So they've already pitched the show and been picked up by a network?"

"Randall said it was practically a done deal."

Sharon knew Hollywood well enough to know nothing was done until it was done. Anything could happen. All kinds of pitches were being made this time of the year.

"You said they're paying you just for signing, right?"

"Yep. A nice chunk of money. Enough to keep me covered for a while."

Desi's face was beaming. It was infectious. Sharon began beaming, too. She decided not to say anything about the network situation. If Vast Horizons felt confident enough to pay Desi big money up front, they might have already inked their network deal. She kept her dark thoughts to herself.

"That's great, Dez, it really is," Sharon said. "And don't forget about the movie. That should be serious exposure for you."

"Oh, I'm not forgetting it for one moment," Desi said, smiling.

"Make sure you call Jackson and talk to him. Just to let him know that everything is really cool between you two. And I already told him he's gotta pay you well for this, so if he pops any noise, you just route him back to me."

"Thanks, Sharon. You've done so much for me already."

"You just make sure you rock this role when it's time for us to shoot."

"Oh, most definitely. I'm giving it everything I got."

Sharon dipped her biscotti in her tea, then bit it.

"So are Randall and Steve going to be writing for the show full-time?" she asked, her mouth full of cookie.

"At least the first year," Desi said, "and that's all I have to commit to for now. It's really a good contract. A great contract, actually."

"You know, at some point, you should consider getting a producer's credit worked in."

"But I don't want to produce," Desi replied.

"How do you know?" Sharon answered. "You might enjoy the role so much, and be such a big draw, that you want to take a more active role in what's happening with the show. It's too early for that now, but keep it in mind as things progress down the road. Not only do you have more overall involvement, it's also a whole 'nother check you'd be receiving. If a show like that lasts long enough to go into syndication, you could potentially hit the jackpot. The more titles and involvement you have, the bigger your share of the booty."

"Wow," Desi said. "It's amazing how much I don't know. Randall schooled me on the business all through dinner last night."

"Just be sure he's schooling you right," Sharon said. "Remember, he's got a potential vested interest in you, so he's not going to tell you everything you need to know."

Desi hesitated.

"But I thought you said he was cool."

"He is, but business is business."

Sharon felt her dark side squirming its way out. Desi sat across from her now, no longer drinking her tea or eating the biscotti, looking as if she didn't know who to trust or what to believe.

"Are they putting in writing everything Randall mentioned at your dinner meeting?"

"Yeah," Desi said. "Hey, do you still think that Glen could maybe look over the contract for me before I sign it? You've got me extra nervous."

The mention of Glen cast a shadow over Sharon's face.

"Yeah, I can ask him. I'm sure he won't mind."

Her tone was flat. There was no enthusiasm at all.

Desi saw the shadow.

"It's no big deal if you can't get him to do it," she said. "Maybe I can get someone else to look at it. What about your friend Eddie?"

"Eddie will charge you," Sharon replied. "He charges me."

"Really?"

"Really. He's good, but he's high. Save your money. I'll ask Glen to look over it for you."

Sharon's expression was as if she'd just been drafted for war. She took another sip of tea.

"Just the thought of talking to Glen seems to make you uneasy," Desi observed.

"Am I that transparent?" Sharon asked.

"Yes, and it's coming out in other ways. Like making me worried about this television deal."

Sharon sighed.

"Sad, but true. I'm sorry about that. I'm sure Randall and his people are on the up-and-up." She put her hands in her hair, pulling her locks back into a ponytail. "It's just that you're so upbeat, and Shaun just bounced out of here slaphappy as hell. All of us have positive things going on, but, try as I might, I just can't keep my spirits up. Why can't I let my soul glow, too?"

"Just a few moments ago, you said you believed that how you feel inside can affect what comes to you. Change how you feel inside."

Sharon let her locks fall free.

"Dez, baby, it ain't that easy. This Glen thing is dominating everything I do."

"He's just a man, Sharon. Why are you making this seem like the end of the world? Unexpected pregnancies happen all the time. You cope with it. You're a grown woman, you should know that by now."

"Look, Dez, just because you found Jesus, don't make it seem like everybody else around you should be seeing visions, too. The answers don't come that easy for me."

"I didn't just find Jesus. All I'm saying is have a little more faith."

"Can I get some on loan?" Sharon chuckled. "My stash seems to have run a little dry."

Desi had her lips pressed together as she stared at the table. "I guess I'm still kind of confused," she began. "You said your period is three weeks late, right?"

"Yep."

"Yet you've been seeing Glen that whole time, laughing and having fun and sexing him and everything else. Last night, you could barely talk to me on the phone for him pawing at you. I don't get it. You were obviously suspecting that you were pregnant during all of that time, right?"

"Yeah," Sharon replied, "I suspected it. But I refused to let myself think about it. I kept pushing it out of my mind, and proceeding like it was business as usual." She toyed with one of her locks. "It was almost like I tricked myself into believing that if I didn't think about it, it would just go away."

"What made you suddenly want to acknowledge it today?"

"That stupid dream last night with the fish sandwich and the red Expedition. My conversation with you this morning and the reality check you slapped me with."

Desi smiled, pleased to know her words had not been in vain.

"There was a picture I saw in Jackson's office," Sharon continued. "Then there was that chick in Fatburger who came in with four kids. All kinds of crazy shit lined up today. It's getting too heavy for me to keep on my mind. It's time that I acknowledge this situation to myself, and to him."

"That scares you, doesn't it?" Desi asked.

"Yeah. It scares me to death. I have this feeling that, once I tell him, everything will change. My relationship with Glen will never be the same."

Sharon's face was riddled with pain.

"So you really do love him."

"Apparently so. And I know he doesn't want kids, so things

will have to change between us, one way or another. If he tells me to get an abortion, I'll resent him for being so insensitive. If he blames me for getting pregnant in the first place, it won't be long before he's gone."

"Sharon, you didn't get pregnant by yourself."

"Yeah, but I'm older than he is. Like you said this morning, I should have been more responsible."

"I said both of you should have been."

"Yeah . . . well."

The Starbucks was bustling with people. Sharon checked her watch.

"So the chances of him being happy about the baby and wanting to settle down with you are that remote?" Desi asked.

Sharon snickered.

"I can't see it," she said. "He's never even told me he loves me."

"Wow."

"Yeah. Wow is right." Sharon finished off the last of the biscotti. "I've gotta get going. I want to get home early enough to relax my mind and prepare myself."

"He's coming over tonight?"

"He comes over almost every night. But I'm going to tell him. It's been messing with me all day. I feel like I'm on death row. I just want to get it over with, deal with the situation, and move on."

"Keep in mind," Desi said, "there's always a chance things just might work out for you guys. Look at how things worked themselves out for me."

"Again, Dez, if you've got some spare faith lying around, please send it my way." Sharon brushed a lock from her face. "I'm ashamed to admit that I'm not as strong about this as I wish I was. Let me tell you, there's nothing worse than being afraid all the time, dreading what may or may not happen."

Desi was surprised. For as long as she had known Sharon, *fearful* was not one of the words she'd choose to describe her.

"It's going to work out, Sharon," Desi said with conviction. "I know it. You just have to believe it, too."

"Well, say one of those prayers of yours for me. Pray for me to strengthen my faith. That way I won't care what happens if Glen, or any other man, ever walks away from me."

"You'll still care," Desi said, "but you'll know that you'll be alright, no matter what."

"Yeah . . . well." Sharon got up. "I'm out. You heading home soon?"

"Actually, no. I'm going to meet Randall over at the Martini Bar."

"The Martini Bar?" Sharon's head reared back. "Is this business or pleasure?"

Desi pursed her lips and sighed.

"He wants me to meet his partner, Steve Karst. Now that it's almost official, Randall suggested we get together so we can at least become comfortable with one another."

"Alright, now," Sharon teased. "You better watch that Randall. That's the Bronx in the house. You know how we do it."

She walked away, her palms facing up, pushing the air.

Desi smiled, shaking her head.

"It's just business!" she called out.

Sharon ignored her, singing as she opened the door.

"*Uptown, baby, we gets down, baby . . .*"

Desi was pleased that Sharon was leaving on a positive, if artificial, note.

She silently said a prayer, for Sharon's sake, that things would be alright.

Sharon was in Sav-on, trying to find the aisle where they kept all the feminine stuff, talking on her cell phone.

"Jet Jonas, please."

"May I ask who's calling?" a woman's deep voice asked.

"Sharon Lane. He's expecting my call."

She grabbed some deodorant, remembering that she was running low. Realizing she might need a handbasket, she turned and headed back towards the front of the store.

"*Sharon Lane!*" bellowed the voice on the phone. "Well, well now! That means I can finally believe Jackson Bennett's not as full of shit as everybody says he is!"

"Jackson's a good guy," Sharon said, chuckling. "And, every now and then, his mouth and his mind do manage to meet up."

"*Heyyyy,* I like that! Don't be mad if you hear me use it!"

"Have at it."

She grabbed a blue handbasket and headed towards the pharmacy section of the drugstore.

"So, Miss Lane, sounds like you and I need to talk dollars and cents."

Sharon had almost forgotten how bombastic Jet Jonas was. He was about six feet two inches, one hundred and eighty-five pounds of pure sinewy pecan-tan muscle. He had a mind that was quick with numbers and fierce with contracts, and fleet feet that had made him the leading rusher in NFL history.

His voice was larger-than-life. It seemed much too big to come out of his body.

During his time with the Los Angeles Lords, Jet had played it smart, not relying solely on his body for his success. His empire was formidable then. Now, three years into his retirement, it was even stronger. He was a well-respected, business-savvy, multi-multi-multi-multimillionaire. He was thirty-nine, just one year older than Sharon.

What a difference a year makes, she thought.

"Shouldn't we talk business first before anything else?"

She grabbed a Reese's peanut butter cup as she passed through the candy aisle.

"Oh, I already know we're gonna bring you on board here," he said. "I've gotten it from good authority, and I don't mean just Randall James and Jackson, that you're the one we need over here at our helm."

"Oh, really?" she replied. "And just who would these good authorities be?"

Jet laughed. "You're testing me, right? Well, let me tell you something, Sharon Lane. I didn't get where I am today by not doing my homework. I'm big on it. It always gives me that extra edge. And what I learned most when I was doing my research on you is that a lot of people have some really good things to say about you."

Sharon was tearing into the candy. Her mouth was full when she spoke.

"Oh yeah? Like what? I could use a little ego stroking right about now."

Jet paused.

"Well, for one," he said, "I can see you're just like folks say you are. Straight and to the point. That's how I work, and I like surrounding myself with people who operate the same way."

"It's the only way to be. Now how about that ego stroke?"

She grabbed a bag of cotton balls and tossed them into the basket.

Jet made a gurgling sound that Sharon realized was laughter.

"I think the best one went something like, 'She's the shit.'"

"Hmmm. Alright. I can deal with that."

Sharon found herself in front of what she came into the store for: home pregnancy tests. She picked out two, First Response and E.P.T., and dropped them into her basket. She wanted to be extra sure.

"So, armed with all that information, I know we can't go wrong having you here. Therefore, the next step is determining what it's going to cost us to do it."

Sharon stood in line for the register.

"First of all," she said, "I don't even know what the position is you're hiring for. And secondly, I just starting another project, Jackson's film, and that's going to take up a lot of my time until it's finished."

"I see. I thought Jackson had briefed you on everything he and I talked about."

"He didn't. He just told me to give you a call."

"Well, the position is vice president of Entertainment. You'd be the number-four person in command over here, behind me and my two partners."

Sharon advanced in the line.

"And I already know about you working on the film. We're willing to be flexible with you, as long as we know you're ours once the project is done."

"Well . . ." was all she could say.

"Is that well good, or well bad?"

"Look, Jet, I don't like to discuss business on a cell phone," she said, placing her items on the conveyor belt. "Give me an idea of what the general starting range is you're looking at, and from there I think we can determine if we should even meet at all."

"How about two-fifty a year, plus full benefits, perks, and an attractive bonus package," he immediately responded.

Sharon held her tongue.

"Now that's just a floor," he added. "We can talk about things further and see how we can meet at a common ground."

Sharon smiled as she fished in her purse for money.

"Are you free on Monday?" she asked.

She heard him flipping pages.

"Actually, I'm going to be in pitch meetings with my partners for most of the morning and afternoon. I sure wish you were on board with us now. We could probably do with some of your expertise that day. We've got a meeting with NBC at nine, Fox at eleven-thirty, ABC at one-forty-five, and CBS is at four."

"What kind of projects are you pitching?" she asked.

"Just one, for starters. It's a drama called *Ambitions*. There's nothing out there like it on television, Sharon. I expect it's going to be snapped up right away."

"I see," she replied. "Is there any advance interest? Any buzz?"

"Oh no," he bellowed. "We're going in there cold. This will be their first chance to check it out. I'm sure there'll be a big buzz about it after today."

"I understand."

She handed the cashier two twenty-dollar bills and her Lucky/Sav-on Rewards card. The cashier handed her the change and the card. Sharon gathered up her bags and headed for the exit. She suddenly realized that she hadn't paid for the Reese's peanut butter cup.

Oh well, she thought.

"How do you feel about us meeting tomorrow?" Jet asked. "I'll be on the golf course at eight o'clock. It's cool if you play. If you don't, we can just talk while you watch me do it. I really want to see you as a part of Vast Horizons, Sharon. I'm going to do everything I can to persuade you to join us."

"Specifically so I can be on board by Monday, right?"

"That's what I like about you, Sharon Lane," he said with a chuckle. "You don't cut any corners. You get right to the point."

Sharon was sitting on the toilet, peeing on the second pregnancy strip, when the doorbell rang.

The first one was positive. This one was rapidly reaching the same conclusion as she flushed the toilet and fixed her clothes. She washed her hands and dried them.

She had no idea who could be ringing her bell. It wasn't even six P.M. And it was Friday. Most people were stuck in traffic, just trying to make it home.

Shaun had called at exactly five, and Sharon had already given her the scoop on all the things that were going on, from the situation at Massey-Weldon to Jackson's new film.

Other than her conversation with Shaun, everything had been peace. (Except for a hangup call when she first walked in, but that didn't count.)

The house smelled like weed. Despite her better thinking, she had taken a toke to prepare for the results of the pregnancy tests.

She couldn't let anyone in with her house smelling the way it did.

She checked the peephole. It was Glen.

Sharon opened the door.

"Hey. What are you doing here so early?"

Glen bent down and kissed her.

"It's good to see you, too," he said.

He handed her a large bouquet of delicate pink roses.

"What's this for?" she asked, still standing in the doorway.

"They were so soft and pretty when I saw them, they immediately reminded me of you. I had no choice in the matter. They were calling out your name."

Sharon looked into his eyes. They were bold and sincere.

"Can I come in?" he asked.

"Yeah, sure," she said, stepping aside.

She closed the door. When she turned around, he pulled her into his arms.

"God, baby," he moaned, "I thought about you all day at work. I mean all day. I didn't get a damn thing done."

Sharon was trembling from her crown to her feet.

"What's the matter?" he asked, pulling her tighter, trying to still her body. "Why are you shaking like that? Is something wrong? Did something happen to you today?"

He squeezed her closer.

"Could it be that you were missing me?" he asked in a playful voice.

Sharon freed herself from his grip and took him by the hand. He willingly followed. She led him to the couch and pushed him down onto it.

"What's up?" he asked.

"Stay right there," she commanded, flinging the roses onto the coffee table.

She walked across the living room, through the short hall, into the downstairs bathroom. She came out with both pregnancy tests.

Her eyes wet, she marched over to Glen and thrust them at him. At first, he was unsure of what she was holding in her outstretched hands. His eyes focused. Within seconds, he knew.

"Now get out," she said.

"What?"

"I said *get out!*" She flung the pregnancy tests at him.

"Sharon, what's the matter with you? How are you going to shove these things at me, and then just throw me out of your house? What kind of ghetto shit is that?!"

"Get out of my home, Glen."

"*Fine!*" he shouted, standing up from the couch. "Let me get the fuck out!"

Furious, he made for the front door. Sharon ran up behind him and shoved him, face forward, into it.

"*Get out of my house!*" she screamed. "I fucking *hate* you!"

Glen looked back at her, his eyes smoldering.

"*Get out!*" she cried, pounding his back with her fists. "*Get out, get out, get out!*"

"Step away from me, Sharon, and let me open the door." Glen's voice was icy steel, just like she'd heard him speak to his sister. "I will gladly leave you and your home, if you'll just give me a chance."

She raced into the living room and grabbed the flowers from the coffee table. Glen was just opening the door. He looked back when he heard her approach, expecting the return of her fists. She smacked him hard across the face with the flowers, the beautiful petals stinging his skin as they scattered around and across his head. A welt rose up on his left cheek where one of the rose stems had landed. Sharon watched it take shape and stretch diagonally all the way across his face.

Glen stood before her, his fists clenching and unclenching. His top lip quivered in an attempt to contain his mounting rage.

"Now *get* out," Sharon snarled, and pushed him through the door.

She slammed it closed behind him.

She stood with her back against it, feeling something violently lurch its way up her insides. The lurching continued until it reached her mouth and forced it open. First a gasp escaped, then the contents of her belly, followed next by an anguished howl.

Sharon slid to the floor, hysterical. She collapsed in a crying heap amidst a grotesque blend of her own vomit and the tattered pink petals and broken stems of Glen's roses.

WADE IN DEEP WATER

You still haven't explained to me how this happened."

Wade was pacing around his penthouse office in a pair of off-white boxer shorts. His clothes were mingled with Meredith's in assorted heaps around the room.

It was nine P.M., the lights in his office had been dimmed, and his wife, Anna, had left that morning on a flight to London for a weekend visit with some friends.

He thanked God for that. He needed some time to form an action plan. He had to find a way for Massey-Weldon to save face.

Under Meredith's care, the company was now suffering a serious professional flesh wound. Massey-Weldon had experienced them before—accusations of racism, bogus charges of sexual harassment—but they always healed. This wound was ugly. It threatened to gape open and bleed for everyone to see.

Wade realized, too late, that he'd been too hands-off. He didn't know the true state of affairs of his own company. His wife didn't either. She had been spending far too much time coddling and placating the stars of their most popular shows.

That left only Meredith to deliver any real answers. She had been with him, in his office, for the past six hours. Wade found himself no closer to the truth than if he'd asked a stranger in the hall.

During those six hours, Meredith had supplicated herself to him, first with defensive statements, then hysterical cries. When those tactics didn't work, she disrobed completely and dropped to her knees.

Wade, physiologically unable to prioritize passion and profession, went for the first and released his anger inside her mouth.

Between the hours of three and six, he'd been called by *TV Guide*, *Variety*, *The Hollywood Reporter*, and *Access Hollywood*. After someone called from E! Entertainment's *Gossip Show*, he had his assistant JeJeune turn the phone calls away.

When he first summoned Meredith to his office, she served him up a plate of red herrings that led nowhere. All he knew was that he kept winding up in her and on her in an assortment of sexual postures. Each time they finished, nothing was resolved and no explanations prevailed.

The day had turned into night, and more critical changes had already taken place.

Bettina, a receptionist he had been most fond of, had been fired. He had been biding his time when it came to her, planning to approach her soon for an old-times'-sake rendezvous. Now she was gone. He regretted never getting the chance to savor her black nectar again.

He had fired her on Meredith's word, after the fellatio, but before the first episode of sex. Meredith had proof, she claimed, that Bettina was a part of the whole Randall and Steve breach conspiracy.

Bettina was remanded to his office. Visibly shaken at being summoned, she listened as Meredith rained a litany of charges upon her. Some were real, some were suspected, most were fabricated. Bettina did not deny any of it. She realized that she was in way over her head. She surrendered her access card and other company-owned items and was sent packing without a penny of severance.

Executives from both ABC and NBC, wanting to know about

the future of *Stickies* and *Westwood*, had tried, to no avail, to reach Wade before the day's end. He hadn't taken their calls, either. He needed the weekend to organize and assess.

"Meredith, why didn't you come to me sooner and let me know that Steve and Randall were getting restless?"

She was stretched out on his black leather sofa, wearing only a pair of leopard-print Victoria's Secret panties.

"Wade, I never knew a thing," she lied. "They never said a thing to me about being unhappy."

She was no longer as pressed and fearful as she had been when he first demanded she come to his office. Once she realized that she could find a way to maneuver him between her legs, the day's fiasco could be saved. A seed of an idea had planted itself in her brain. It was doable, she just didn't know to introduce it.

As long as Wade was willing to fuck, Meredith knew she could work the situation to her favor, and her opening would come.

"Why didn't anybody catch the lapse of the time frame in their contracts?"

"Wade, honey, I'm telling you . . . I don't know. I'm beginning to believe that perhaps they tampered with files. Legal has an excellent automated tickler system. There's no way something like that could slip through their cracks."

Meredith also had no fear of legal repercussions, not from Randall and Steve. Now that she knew they had no intention of suing the company, that they merely wanted to exit to form their own, she was free to fictionalize their situation as creatively as she was able to conceive it.

Wade continued to pace nervously in front of the window, his taut, tanned, athletic body a silhouette against the evening sky.

"There's no way they're taking Carlos with them," he said. "Anna won't let that happen. He's been with us from the very beginning."

Meredith watched him build himself into a tizzy.

"How quickly do you think we can assemble writing teams for these shows?" he asked.

"A couple of days. Five at the most."

"That long?"

"That's not a long time," she said reassuringly. "We are going to have to get the best, though, since it's such short notice."

"If we have to do it, we just have to do it," he declared.

He turned towards her.

"There's no way we can put together new writing teams before Monday, is there, before the networks start to call again?"

"Wade, darling," she cooed, "honey, you're not thinking. That's just not possible. People are gone for the weekend. The networks are just going to have to wait."

"Yes, Meredith," he replied curtly, his voice aquiver. "Make the networks wait. Be sure to tell that to the judges when they drag us to court."

"Nobody's going to court," she said. "The networks are not going to let this thing spin out of control. Neither are we."

Wade kept moving around nervously, staring at the floor as he paced. He didn't know what to do. This type of predicament was best handled by Anna, but she was away. Without her as his touchstone, he was at a loss for direction.

Meredith saw her opening, the one she had been waiting for, yawning its opportunity before her.

"I might even have something that will placate the networks in the face of all this."

He looked up, frowning.

"Placate them how? They don't want to be placated. They want fucking solutions!"

She sat upright on the leather couch, her breasts pointing towards him like two cannons about to fire.

"Remember when you told me once that if I brought you a show, a really *good* show, you would let me have a creator's credit and get my chance at building my own little kingdom?"

He frowned deeper.

"Yes, yes," he replied with irritation, "but what does that have to do with what we're talking about now?"

"Well . . . I have said show. Something that will make the networks' mouths water. It's diverse, and you know how uptight everyone is with all the issues about diversity in Hollywood right now. The networks are under pressure to provide more representation."

Wade's face was a scowling outline in the dim shadows where he was standing.

"Go on," he grunted.

"It's a dramatic series, based in Los Angeles, revolving around five characters in a restaurant setting. They're rich, they're middle class, they're black, white, and everything in between. Each of them has a struggle of the mind and heart. I've got it all laid out, and, Wade, the demographics it will reach—you can't even imagine!"

Wade listened, desperate for a solution.

"How come you never told me about it before?" he grumbled.

"Timing, honey. Timing is everything. I just worked out the full proposal a few days ago. How ironic it is that we may get to use it now."

Meredith was up, sauntering across the room to him. She slid her arms around his shoulders, pressing her full breasts against his back. The two were dim silhouettes against the flickering lights of the houses in the hills behind them.

"I don't know, Meredith," he said with a heavy sigh. "This situation has to be resolved, and I'm not so sure that this is the way to do it."

"Wade, calm down," she whispered. "This situation can and will be handled, and this is *exactly* the way to do it." She slid her hands down to his chest, gently tweaking his nipples.

"First thing Monday morning," she said, "we call up the networks. We won't wait for them to call us. We tell them we're already culling new writers for *Stickies* and *Westwood*, only the best the WGA has to offer. We give them an action plan for both shows."

"Are you going to come up with the action plan?"

"I already have it under control."

She slid her hands downward, running her fingers across the ridges of his tight abdominal muscles.

"We let them know this was an internal fracture that may have temporarily impacted the company, but that the company had nothing to do with it and we can immediately recover."

Her wandering hands were now down around his boxers.

"Then we show them the proposal. We tell them it's what we believe will be our next big hit, something we had been keeping under wraps, but now we want to offer it as a good-faith gesture of our commitment to excellence in television programming. Then we see if we can pitch it to them and get things rolling."

Her fingers were rolling across the vent in his shorts. She pressed down firmly, feeling his hardness spring forth.

"And you have the proposal ready?" he groaned.

"I do. It's on my computer at home. All I have to do is print it out and package it as a company presentation."

Wade, unable to resist his body's call, closed his eyes and leaned his head back against her. He reached back, draping his arms around her, resting his hands in the small of her back. He ran his finger across the tiny, delicate, fleshy ridge, her spot, and she moaned with pleasure. His hardness caused his shorts to tent, creating an interesting reconfiguration of their silhouettes against the sky.

"What's the name of this show?" he asked.

"*Native Suns,*" Meredith replied, triumphant. She was impressed at her ability to come up with a name so quickly. She cupped him in her hands, massaging him with her fingers and her words.

"We can do this, Wade. You and I, together. We'll restore Massey-Weldon's good name. And everything will be just fine. Even better."

Wade was weak, almost faint, as he surrendered to her hypnotic touch. It all made sense. Everything she was saying had an absolute order.

As the hormones rushed from his pituitary to his privates, he began to envision Meredith as the company savior, an ideal he reserved exclusively for his wife.

If Meredith had suggested at that moment that they leap, hand in hand, from the office window because they could fly, Wade would have happily submitted, so strongly did he believe her words.

"We'll pitch it on Monday," she whispered, gently kneading his groin. "Together. You and I."

"Yes, yes," he moaned in submission. "You and I will pitch it."

"The hell you will!" Anna Weldon proclaimed.

Meredith backed away from Wade, jettisoning him without a second thought. Her hands were covering her breasts. Wade remained frozen, the tent in his pants still prominent.

Before he could even respond, Anna, a petite woman, was using her dainty hands and feet to restore order back to the company she co-owned. She ran her fingers through her bobbed thick black hair and assessed the chaos of the room. A woman of refined confidence and pragmatic spirit, she began switching on lights as she walked about the office, announcing to them what would be done.

"If anybody's going to present this *Native Suns* deal, it will be me and my husband," she said.

Anna had obviously been in the room for a while to know the title of the project.

"You have the proposal at your house?" she asked Meredith.

Meredith nodded.

"Put it together and have it couriered here to the front desk by Sunday morning. Send the action plan you talked about as well."

Meredith nodded.

Anna turned to Wade.

"I've already requested a meeting with our people at NBC. The president will also be there. We're scheduled for two o'clock. We'll pitch it to them then, and get the rest of this debacle cleared up. We'll talk to ABC next."

She turned back to Meredith.

"Please gather up your clothes and leave my husband's office. I'll contend with you on Tuesday. Don't come back until then."

Meredith, burning with humiliation and outrage, picked about the room like a hen, searching for errant articles of lingerie, her skirt, blouse, jacket, and black block heels.

Anna stood sentinel, waiting until she had collected everything. Her eyes met Meredith's. Meredith slunk from the room.

She disappeared into the hallway, hovering in the shadows just outside Wade's office. She watched as Anna approached him, stopping just a few feet away.

Wade's head hung to his chest like a forlorn child. After a few chill moments, Anna opened her arms. Wade rushed into them and began to cry. Anna's arms closed around him, wrapping him up within her bosom as if she were a guardian angel.

Anna glanced up, out into the hallway. She saw Meredith in the shadows, watching. For a moment, their eyes met.

Meredith turned away, still naked except for her panties and the bundle of clothes she held close to her body. She made her way down the hall, then stopped to slip back into her clothes and shoes.

Anna wouldn't get away with this.

Meredith realized that she had lost the fight for Wade. She saw now that she had never stood a chance to begin with.

Anna was a different story.

And when it came to her, Meredith noted, Anna obviously didn't know exactly who it was she was dealing with.

MIDLOGUE #2

"You can't stay here. I can't handle this anymore. I'm tired of all the boys and the drugs. And turn that TV off!"

Fine, *Alicia thought as she kept flipping through channels.* The boys and the drugs are tired of your ass, too.

It was time she cleared out of this shitty old space.

"I don't have to stay here," she yelled in the direction of the bedroom. "I'm grown, whether you choose to believe it or not. I'm about to break out and go to California!"

"California? For what? What's in California for you but more trouble?"

"I guess trouble follows me everywhere I go," Alicia sang under her breath.

She flipped through more channels, stopping on Ricki Lake *to check out a sexy guy sitting onstage between two feuding women.*

"Ooh, he is too fine," she said to the television as she licked her lips.

"Haven't you had enough trouble in your life as it is?"

Alicia rolled her eyes.

"What you got, a seven-second delay or something? Ain't nobody even talkin' 'bout that shit anymore."

"Stop cussin' in my house."

"Stop giving me reasons to cuss."

A wailing sound came from the back of the room. Alicia shook her head, clicked off the television, and got up from the recliner.

"I'm outta here," she yelled. "Thanks for raising me by your damn self after Gramps died. California here I come!"

"Where will you get the money?"

"Don't worry about that, I already got loot."

The wailing wafted down the hall and filled up the living room.

"I will not miss this shit," Alicia mumbled.

She walked to the closet and grabbed her FUBU jacket. It matched the FUBU overalls she wore.

She pulled a skullie over her starter locks. Some of them were unraveling because her hair was too fine and too curly. It was chilly outside, and it was a far walk to the station. She pulled the skullie all the way down over her ears.

She felt her left pocket. Inside was twenty-five hundred dollars, compliments of her current boo.

Alicia was gonna miss him, he could pack a mean blunt. But a rolling stone like her had to keep moving before she gathered too much moss.

She wasn't taking anything but what was on her body and in it. She was making a fresh start, in a fresh place, with fresh cash.

She reached into her right pocket. There was a slip of paper with a phone number scratched on it. Alicia had gotten it from the Internet. She was a whiz on the Net. She'd found the phone number when she found out all that other business, the time she was online looking into her birth records. The discovery shocked her, but filled her with interest and intrigue. Many searches and discoveries later, she was seriously piqued. Enough to make her want to take the show on the road, all the way to California.

Every now and then, she dialed the phone number and hung up.

Once she got to Cali, she would use it for real.

I'm feeling a little hellafied, *she thought as she left the house and headed down the street.* I think it's time I give my dear sweet mama a good old-fashioned wake-up call.

Part Three

Change

PERSON TO PERSON

"Are you alright?"

Bettina was in bed, on the phone. It was the same tainted bed she had vowed, just yesterday morning, to replace. Now she couldn't afford to do it. She was out of a job and needed to hold on to as much of her money as she possibly could.

She still hadn't replaced all the underwear she'd thrown away. It had been her plan to go shopping for new items after work yesterday, but that never came to fruition, either.

After she'd been summoned to Wade's office, then accused by Meredith, everything else had gone downhill.

She was escorted from the Massey-Weldon building like a common thief, in front of everyone. Humiliated, she jumped into the Viper, closed out the world, and got from Century City to Santa Monica in record time, in spite of the Friday traffic. Once she entered her condo, she stayed there. She had been in bed sulking ever since.

Bettina would still have to buy underwear. There was no getting around it. She would just have to use her credit cards.

The beginning of a new month was also coming around in a few days, and with it came a new cycle of bills. She was going to have to use her credit cards to pay for most of those. She didn't have any backup options, especially since she had kicked all her well-heeled lovers to the curb.

She was in a big blue Spelman T-shirt and had on a pair of white footies. She didn't have on anything underneath the T-shirt.

She had the remote in her hand, flipping channels. When the phone first rang, it startled her. Once she realized it was Steve, that surprised her even more.

"How did you find out what happened?" she asked.

"I got a call from Nina Swanson," Steve said.

"Today?"

"Yeah, actually, this morning around nine, before I went to the gym."

It was now one o'clock in the afternoon.

"Why would Nina call you on a Saturday and tell you I got fired? Are people that starved for gossip that they're willing to give up their weekends for it?"

"No, Bettina. It wasn't anything like that."

She flipped the TV from channel to channel, not even registering the images as they passed across the screen.

"How was it, then?" she asked. "Explain it to me."

Steve cleared his throat.

"I was thinking about you a little yesterday after we left. So I called Nina and left her a voice message telling her to have you call me. I didn't want to bother you while you were working the phones."

"Didn't you have to talk to me when you called there for her?"

"No. I dialed her direct extension."

Bettina sighed listlessly.

"What's wrong?" Steve asked. "Am I keeping you from something?"

She flung the remote on the bed.

"No, Steve, you're not keeping me. I'm just worried, and a little stir-crazy, and a whole lot of other things. I don't know what to do, now that I don't have a job. I've never been fired before, do you know that?"

"But you were leaving anyway."

"Yeah, but on my own terms. I wasn't expecting them to fire *me!*"

Out of nowhere, she burst into tears.

Steve was on the balcony of his apartment in Beverly Hills. He had debated and debated with himself before he mustered the nerve to dial her number. Once they started talking, he began to relax. He was wearing a blue windsuit and Nikes, and was leaning back in a canvas director's chair with his legs stretched out in front of him. When he heard her cry, he sat up in a panic.

"Bettina! Bettina!"

"What?" she wailed pitifully. "Stop screaming my name like that. I'm alright . . . it's just tears. Haven't you ever heard a woman cry before?"

"I don't deal with tears very well," he admitted.

"Well, then, maybe you ought to hang up." She sniffled, dabbing at her eyes with her comforter. "What did you call me for, anyway? Why all the sudden interest in me?"

"I was worried about you," he said.

"Oh. Thanks. I appreciate it."

Steve hesitated.

"I was also thinking that, maybe . . ." His words trailed off.

"Maybe what?" she asked, reaching for the remote again. She needed something in her hands to make her feel busy. Somewhere to send all that extra nervous energy.

"You know, I was wondering if, perhaps, you'd be interested in . . ."

"Hold on a sec, my phone just beeped."

Steve was staring down from the balcony at the cars passing below on Wilshire Boulevard.

"I'm so tired of whoever it is that's doing that," Bettina announced, clicking back over. "If you're gonna call my house, dammit, speak. I got five years' worth of hangup calls working at that front desk."

"See," Steve said. "A few minutes ago you were crying because you were fired. Now here it is, you're complaining about the job."

Bettina smiled a little.

"Yeah, I guess you're right. It's more my ego than anything. I take pride in my work, even if it is just answering phones. Actually, that sounds even worse. All I did was answer phones, and I got fired from that."

"Stop reaching. You were moving on anyway. Think about the fact that you'd been there for five years and never got promoted."

Bettina thought about it.

"True. But that's all the more reason why *I* should have walked out on *them*, and not let them send *me* packing. Do you know that I was just about to—"

"Would you mind having lunch with me?" he blurted.

He gripped the edge of the balcony, closed his eyes, and waited for the blow.

"What did you just ask me?" Bettina whispered.

Steve sighed, not wanting to have to say it again.

"I wondered if you'd be interested in having lunch."

"But it's already after one o'clock."

"I eat late on the weekends. And I thought it would be good for you to maybe get out into some of this beautiful LA smog."

Bettina leaned back against her pillows, smiling.

"Is this a boss asking a new employee out to a business lunch?" she asked.

"Uh-uh," he said.

"Is this a man asking a woman out on a date?"

He breathed heavily, the top of his lip breaking out in a sweat.

"I suppose it is."

Bettina was quiet.

"I know it probably seems awkward," Steve said. "You're black, I'm not."

"Actually, Steve, that doesn't bother me," she replied. "I think you're a handsome man. Color can't take away from simple fact."

Steve leaned against the balcony, his eyes still closed. He couldn't tell where she was going with her comments. Was she about to say yes?

"Thank you, Bettina. That does wonders for my ego."

"I'm sure your ego gets along just fine."

Bettina took in then released a deep breath.

"What's wrong?" he said.

"Steve, this is so fucked up. It really is. I was just beginning to get my life together. I was making all these positive changes. I don't know how much you think you know about me, but I've lived a little. A lot. Yesterday, before I got fired, was a big deal for me. I declared myself celibate yesterday morning. I've made too many mistakes with men. I decided that I'm not going to get involved in any more crazy scenes with men who only want to know me for one reason."

"Bettina."

"Yes."

"I want to take you to lunch, not the Holiday Inn."

Bettina chuckled.

"You're getting kinda serious on me," he said. "I don't move that fast. Just because I'm blond, that doesn't mean I'm easy."

She laughed out loud.

"Wait a second . . . you're not taking me to Roscoe's for fried chicken, are you?" she asked. "Are you asking me to lunch because you need me as a passport into a black restaurant?"

"No," he protested. "I would never do that. Besides, on the seventh day, I give the bird rest."

"Well, I'm sure chickens worldwide heave a sigh of relief over that."

They both laughed together.

"Do you like fresh seafood?" he asked.

"That's the only way to eat it."

"Alright. How about I pick you up in an hour and we go someplace casual?"

"Well . . ." She was unsure if she wanted him to come to her home.

"I'm telling you again though, Bettina: This is strictly on the level. I don't want any of your fast moves. I like to take it slow. I've been hurt a lot in my life, and I'm not having it anymore."

She grinned.

"Do you have a problem with that?" Steve asked. "Because if you do, you need to let me know right now, and we can put an end to this before your shenanigans even start."

Bettina was still laughing.

"No, Steve. I don't have a problem with that at all."

By three-thirty, Bettina and Steve were strolling around inside the shops at the Redondo Beach Pier. They had already eaten two big plates of Dungeness crab, and washed it all down with beer and laughter.

Their conversation was carefree and easy, almost as easy as it was for Steve to reach for Bettina's hand. As easy as it was for her to allow him to hold it.

She pulled him into novelty shops and stuck too-large sunglasses onto his face. He bought churros, one for her and one for him, and they quickly bit into the warm sugary breadsticks in a race to see who could finish eating first.

Steve had been nervous when he first picked her up at her place in Santa Monica. He knew exactly where she lived when she gave him the address. His family, real-estate titans with more than five billion dollars in property worldwide, owned an office building just two blocks away from Bettina's condo.

She had asked him to not come up, but to call from his car when he arrived. He did, waiting for more than ten minutes, filled with panic at the thought that maybe she had changed her mind. The feeling of panic surprised him, as he realized how much weight he had placed on her saying yes.

His interest in Bettina had not been sudden. It had been lurking for years, a feeling that hovered in the background of his conscious and subconscious mind from the moment she first arrived at Massey-Weldon. She came to the company three months after he was hired, her natural, radiant beauty capturing his attention the moment he first walked into the building and saw her behind the reception desk.

Steve was in a relationship then, one that was taking far more from him than it would ever hope to give. Bettina's winsome face first thing in the morning got him through and out of that relationship, and others that followed, without him even being aware of it. He only knew that, with something as bright and beautiful in the world as her face, there was no reason to aspire for anything less.

Bettina had never done anything to make Steve believe the regard went both ways. She knew him well enough to have brief conversations that lasted until someone else came up to chat with her. Those brief conversations, he knew, were merely the result of the familiarity of her seeing him at work every day for five years. She was naturally gregarious. Almost everyone seemed fond of her and drawn to her presence. Because of that, he couldn't interpret her behavior towards him as anything more than professional friendliness.

It didn't happen often, but every now and then, as she was on a call and he was just walking into the building, her eyes would land specifically upon him and her face would suddenly light up. Whenever it occurred, it was a brilliant, unexpected, almost shocking thing that made his heart, and feet, race, as he hurried to the elevator, away from its near-nuclear glow.

The feeling always left him warm and happy inside, making him wonder if he was truly capable of being the inspiration of something so lovely. He liked that feeling. It was what he hoped for with each new woman he met. It was something they could never quite match. By presence alone, again without him realizing it, Bettina slowly raised the bar on Steve's ideal.

It had been two years since he had dated. His tolerance for empty conversations and shallow women was gone. He immersed himself in two things that were most constant, his career and his health, and there he found satisfaction. He went to the gym five times a week. That way, he could eat what he wanted and still remain fit. His career was flourishing, and, with the new venture of Vast Horizons, he was ready to take it to the next level.

When Randall, who was actually friends with Bettina, asked him what he thought about her coming over to work for them, Steve was delighted. It pleased him to know that she would be there, providing for him a sense of familiar anchoring.

It was only after he and Randall quit the day before, as they lingered at the reception desk sharing a laugh with her, did he admit to himself that he wanted to actively pursue something more. He didn't know if it was wise, especially since Bettina would soon be his employee. But he really didn't care about that. Not enough. What he did care about was how good he felt when he was in her presence. And that alone was enough to make him decide to take the risk.

When Bettina finally came down and got in the car, he knew he had made the right decision. She was wearing an airy sundress, beige with soft pink and green flowers, and had a beige sweater tied around her waist.

She smiled apologetically, and his heart began to soar.

Their conversation was light, almost halting at first, then began to flow as Steve maneuvered his gray Mercedes sports coupe through the streets and onto the freeway.

"Where are we going?" she asked.

"It's a surprise."

On the way to the surprise, Bettina had him stop at a Target on Sepulveda in Manhattan Beach. She ran inside, bought a pair of panties, and put them on in the restroom. When she returned to the car, she was carrying her beige sweater. After that, she became even more at ease.

Bettina's hand was still nestled in his as they walked out to the edge of the pier and leaned against the railing. The cool ocean air washed over their faces, invigorating their lungs and spirits with its salty scent.

"This is nice, isn't it?" Steve asked. "There's something so restorative about the smell of the sea. Nothing can compare to it."

Bettina breathed in deeply and exhaled.

"I love it here," she said. "Thank you for bringing me. This place is beautiful."

Steve looked at her, his hair whipping across his forehead.

"You've never been here before?" he asked, surprised.

"Never," she answered. "I didn't even know it existed. My dates never really took me out, as much as they kept me in."

Steve casually slipped his arm around her waist.

"I have to bring you here when the gray whales run."

"Whales come here?" Bettina asked with fascination.

The wind rippled the surface of her hair. Steve studied the way it moved in waves across her head.

"Yes, and, like you, it's stunning to watch."

She blushed, gently bumping him with her hip.

"Stop it," she said with a coy smile. "Tell me about the whales."

"Alright," he said. "Well, every year Pacific gray whales do this ten-thousand-mile migration."

"Ten thousand miles!" she exclaimed. "Are you serious?"

"Oh, I am most serious. That's how far they travel, round-trip. Can you imagine swimming that long and that far?"

They gazed out at the waves breaking on the ocean surface.

"I can't even imagine doing a mile," Bettina said with a chuckle.

"Well, every winter, these whales go from the freezing Arctic waters of the Bering Sea down to the warm lagoons of Baja to have their babies. Then they head back up to the Arctic." Steve stared out at the ocean as if he could see the whales going by. "It's the most breathtaking thing you ever want to witness. When you see them on their way back, the newborns are swimming alongside them."

"And you can see them here?" she asked.

"Right here," Steve said. "They pass real close to the Redondo Beach shoreline. I've been coming here to see them since I was a kid."

Bettina looked up at Steve, who was blissfully watching the sea. She leaned against him, feeling, in that moment and in that space, safe and free.

Steve gazed down at her and smiled.

"Don't you get fresh with me," he warned. "I told you before, I'm not that kind of guy."

Devin could see Bettina from where he stood on the street overlooking the pier. He noticed the way she was leaning into the white guy.

So that was the reason, he thought.

It wasn't about him being married. Bettina had apparently jumped ship for another reason. Now she wanted someone white.

Devin gave a bitter laugh, watching her bump playfully against the man.

He had already succeeded in getting her fired. He wasn't going to stop until every ounce of her dignity was gone.

Then she would know how he felt when she turned him away.

All Devin had to do was get to the guy. From there, everything else would be easy.

Then Bettina would come crawling.

He smiled, imagining that moment.

If she begged hard enough, he just might take her back. But only if she begged.

And did that thing with her nails that he loved so much.

Steve and Bettina were sitting in his car in front of her building. The engine was off. They had been there for more than an hour, and the night air had taken on a deep chill.

Bettina draped her sweater around her shoulders.

"Are you alright?" Steve asked. "Are you comfortable? Do you want me to turn on the heat?"

"I'm fine," she said softly. "I have to head up in a minute."

Steve nodded.

"Thank you for getting me out of the house. I would have gone crazy if I stayed in bed all day. I was beginning to panic about stupid things, things I already had a solution for."

"I don't know why you were sulking. It's not like you don't have another job to go to. You can start work with us on Monday. Jet already has the new offices set up."

"I know. I think I just felt like sulking."

"Sulking's no fun."

"No." She smiled. "It isn't."

"Then don't do it anymore. You're much too pretty for that."

Bettina blushed, then began toying with the sleeves of her sweater.

"Steve, I know you guys hadn't expected to take me on this early. Randall told me that Carlos was coming on board first."

He shook his head.

"Not anymore. Anna Weldon got to Carlos and convinced him to stay. I don't even know how she knew he was leaving."

"Are you serious?"

"Yes. He's got a new baby on the way. He's been with the company a long time and Anna considers him the best in-house attorney they have. She offered him fifteen percent more than what we were going to be paying him at Vast Horizons."

"How did you find that out?" Bettina asked.

"He called me at home this morning and told me."

Bettina laughed.

"Damn, Steve. You may as well be running Massey-Weldon's switchboard. Everybody from there seems to be calling you up."

"It sure looks that way," he said.

Bettina repositioned herself on the seat so that she was facing him.

"I wonder who told her," she said. "Other than me, you, and Randall, who knew that Carlos was leaving?"

"No one, other than Jet. None of us told anyone about it. Besides, who, outside of our circle, would care?"

"I certainly didn't tell anybody," she said. "Oh, shit . . . wait a minute."

"What?"

"No. He wouldn't do something as stupid as that."

"Who are you talking about?"

Bettina sighed. "Damn! I didn't even make the connection, but now it all makes sense."

"What, Bettina?" Steve asked in frustration. "Was it someone in the building?"

Bettina reached for his hand.

"Steve, I am so sorry. This is probably all my fault. There was this guy I was messing around with. Someone I had no business dating in the first place. It was just pillow talk. He told me what was going on with his career. I talked about what was going on with mine."

"I see," Steve said, casually moving his hand away. "Are you still seeing this guy?"

"No. That's the problem. I broke things off with him yesterday morning. I'll bet he's the reason Meredith found out about my leaving to go to work for you."

"How would he know to call the Diabolical Miss M.?" Steve asked.

"That's what you call her?"

He chuckled.

"Yeah. That's kind of an inside joke between me and Randall."

"Oh . . . well, it's very appropriate," Bettina said. "Anyway, Devin knew who she was because I told him. I don't have a lot of friends. Actually, none. So I used to talk to him about everything, including the people at work. He knew I hated Meredith. She was the perfect person for him to call so he could get back at me."

Steve fidgeted with the steering wheel.

"Devin, huh?"

"Yeah, Devin. I guess he took things harder than I expected him to."

"You ever say anything to this Devin character about me?" he asked, twisting the steering wheel.

Bettina watched him.

"Yeah. I told him you were one of the guys I was going to work for."

"How'd you describe me?" he asked.

"I didn't," she answered honestly. "Not physically. I told him how you and Randall have won Emmys, and that you guys are really good writers. Other than that, that's all he knows."

Steve nodded.

Silence hung between them.

"I'm sorry I messed up things with Carlos," she said, breaking the silence. "I guess this is just another reminder about the company I keep."

"We all make mistakes."

She snickered.

"Steve, I think I got the mistake thing down pat."

She shivered, pulling her sweater around her tighter.

"Don't worry about Carlos," he said. "We can get another attorney. This town is full of them. Jet might even know someone that he wants to bring on."

"I'm still sorry," she whispered. "I feel like this is all my fault."

"It's not. You don't know for sure if this Devin guy is the reason you got fired and Anna found out about Carlos."

"I'm willing to bet on it, that's for damn sure."

Bettina rubbed her eyes. It had been a long day, packed with far more than she had expected.

"I've got to go," she said, placing her hand on the door handle. "I really do appreciate you getting me out of the house, Steve. My whole attitude has turned around, thanks to you."

He nodded, a strained smile on his face. She opened the door.

"Do you still love this guy?" he couldn't help asking.

"Who?" she questioned, looking back at him.

"This Devin character."

That killed it for Bettina. She sighed, shaking her head.

Why were men always so quick to want to lay claim, she wondered. She had just spent a wonderful day with Steve, and already he was acting possessive. She understood now, more than ever, why it was important for her to reclaim herself through her celibacy.

"I never loved him to begin with," she remarked in a flat tone. "Goodnight, Steve."

Bettina got out of the car and closed the door. She didn't even look back as she went up the walkway, pressed the code, and entered her building.

Steve started the engine, revved it a few times, and pulled off.

As he drove away and she rode up the elevator, neither one of them could figure out how such a beautiful day had gone suddenly wrong.

PANTS ON FIRE

Hello?"

Desi's voice was thick when she answered the phone.

"Oh, God . . . I woke you. I'm so sorry."

She was surprised and pleased.

"No you didn't. I should have been up anyway."

"I figured since it was Sunday, you'd be getting ready for church," Randall said.

"What makes you think I'm the churchgoing type?"

"You're from the South. And you seem to have a strong moral center. It just makes sense that you'd be a churchy kind of girl."

"Churchy, huh?" She chuckled.

"Yeah. That is a word, isn't it?"

"Not any that I've heard."

She sat up in the bed and glanced over at the clock. It was eight-thirty.

"Why are *you* up so early?" she asked. "Are you a churchy kind of guy?"

"No," he said, laughing. "I get some of my best writing done in the morning."

"I see. Are you working on something for *Ambitions?*"

"Yeah. I'm going to e-mail it over to Steve in a minute so he can put in his two cents."

"And you called me because . . . ?"

She waited for an answer.

"I wanted to see if you got home okay."

"From when? Friday night after the Martini Bar? That was two nights ago. I sure would hate to have to depend on you to be worried about me!"

"Alright, alright, I just wanted an excuse to call. I really just wanted to tell you again how excited I am that we're going to get to do this project together."

She smiled.

"Thank you. I'm excited, too. I'm anxious to get back into a really good role."

"Great!" he replied.

She waited to see if he had anything else to say. There was a moment of silence as they lingered on the phone.

"Well," he finally said.

"Well," she said in return.

Desi rubbed her eyes and yawned.

"Oh," Randall exclaimed, "I knew there was something else I wanted to talk to you about!"

"I would hope so. The thought that you'd call me up first thing in the morning and have nothing to say is kind of disturbing."

"I was feeling a little awkward just now," he said in defense. "Sorry about the dead air. I'm still trying to become familiar with being in your presence."

"Spare me the grandiose treatment, Randall. I thought you considered me down-to-earth."

"I do, but you are still Desi Sheridan."

"What was the other thing?" she asked.

"You must be pretty happy about the big news."

"And what big news is that?"

Randall was sitting in front of his PowerMac in his office at home. He was leaning back in his chair with his feet propped up on his glass-and-aluminum work desk.

"Desi, come on . . . I know you guys talk. I figure you were probably the first person she called."

"Who?"

He realized that she didn't know.

"Sharon didn't call you?" Randall asked.

Desi reached for the remote beside the bed and clicked on the TV.

"Exactly what would she be calling to tell me?"

"She's going to be working with us. She and Jet had a meeting yesterday and made it official."

"She's *what?!*"

"Yep," he replied proudly. "Sharon Lane is the new vice president of Entertainment for Vast Horizons."

"Hmmm" was the only response that Desi gave.

"It's perfect timing, too," he continued. "Tomorrow we've got a few meetings to tie up things. We're talking with some network executives to hammer out our position for next year's season."

"Oh, really? So by tomorrow you should know what network we'll be on?"

Randall scratched his ear as a nervous reflex, realizing that he was now moving in dangerous waters, especially since Sharon and Desi were friends. Sharon would be at the meetings. It was possible she might talk about what went on. There was also the possibility she might not, though, seeing as she hadn't even called Desi and told her about being hired by the company.

"I don't think we'll have the answer by tomorrow," he said. "But at least we'll have a better idea about which network feels like the best fit."

"Do you have a preference?"

"Ahhh. Yes, and no. I'd rather not say."

Desi found his response a bit strange.

"Has my contract been put together yet?"

"Yes, it has. It'll be sent over to your agent's office first thing tomorrow morning, unless you want it sent somewhere else."

"No, that's fine. He'll get it over to me. I'm really anxious to get started on things."

"So am I," he said.

Desi clicked off the TV. Nothing was on but religious programming and national news shows. Her thoughts were turning.

"Well, Randall," she began, "I appreciate you calling to check on me and tell me about Sharon. I'm excited about it. I trust her. Your company will be in safe hands."

"I know it will. She's my homegirl, and she really knows her stuff."

His mind was turning as well.

"I'm going to get up and get my day started," Desi said, about to make her exit.

"Great. I'm going to get back to writing," he replied, just as eager to hang up. "Remember, Desi, if there's anything you need, for any reason, feel free to give me a call. You have all my numbers, right?"

"I've got them all right here."

"Terrific. Alright then, have a good one."

"Thanks, Randall. You have a good one, too."

The cordless phone rang twice.

Sharon was sitting on the floor of her living room, between the sofa and the coffee table. She picked up the phone and clicked it on.

"Hello?"

"Sharon?"

"Yeah. What's up, Randall?"

Randall's legs were no longer propped on his desk. Now he was in serious mode, upright in his office chair, his legs perpendicular to the floor.

"I didn't wake you, did I?"

"No, but it is kind of early."

"Yeah," he replied, doodling nervously on his desk calendar. "I apologize about that."

"What's up?"

"Look, I wanted to talk to you about . . ."

"Hold on, Randall," she said. "This is crazy. My other line just beeped."

Randall knew who it was before she clicked over.

"Hello?"

"Sharon?"

"Yo, Dez, what's up? I got Randall on the other line."

"Oh, really?" Desi asked, her brows raised. "What's he want?"

"Don't know yet," Sharon replied. "He called right before you did."

Desi smirked.

"Do me a favor, Sharon."

"What's that?"

"Call me as soon as you get off the phone with him. Something strange is going on. I don't know what it is, but I can feel it."

"Strange like what?" Sharon asked.

"If I knew, I wouldn't be asking you to call me back, now would I?"

"Yeah . . . well. Alright, I'll call you back."

"Bye."

Sharon clicked back over.

"Yo."

"Hey, Sharon," Randall said. "Is everything alright?"

"What makes you think there's something wrong, Randall? All I did was click over the phone."

"You were gone for a while. I just thought that something might be up."

Sharon pushed herself up from the floor and began walking towards the kitchen.

"Alright . . . talk to me," she said. "What's going on this morning? What is it that you really want?"

Randall's doodling was fierce. A large section of the calendar was black from where he had scribbled Sanskrit characters over and over as he waited for her to click back to him.

"Jet talked to you about those meetings tomorrow, right?"

"Yes, he did," she replied as she walked into the kitchen. She opened one of the cabinets over the sink and reached for a juice glass.

"Did he tell you what kind of meetings they were?" Randall's voice was hesitant.

"They're pitch meetings, Randall," she said, opening the refrigerator and taking out a carton of orange juice. "Cold pitch meetings, from what I understand."

"Yes," he answered, "that's exactly what they are."

Sharon poured the juice into her glass, drank all of it while standing at the counter, then refilled it again.

"So why did you tell Desi that you guys practically had your show locked up in terms of network placement? She thinks you're way beyond the pitch phase, and on the verge of committing to a network."

Caught, with nothing to say to refute it, he sighed.

Sharon walked into the living room with the juice, leaving the carton on the kitchen counter.

"Hello? Hello? Are you still on the line?"

"I'm here, Sharon."

"You know it's fucked up that you didn't tell her the truth, right?" She sat on the edge of the couch. "There wasn't any point in gassing her up. Dez is cool people, and she wants a chance to make it, just like you."

"She wouldn't have been down if I didn't massage things a little, and you know it."

"You guys are paying her a hundred g just to sign, right?"

"Yes."

"That's free and clear money for her, regardless of whether you have a network or not, right?"

"Yes."

"Then why wouldn't she have signed? You could have just said having her name and Jet's name attached gave the project more selling power. That, and a hundred-thousand-dollar check, would have been all the gassing she needed."

Randall's doodling was out of control. His pen had run dry. He reached for another.

"Shit, Randall, you and Steve have Emmys. You're tested as a writing team. You know you're gonna get picked up by somebody. There was no need for you to tell the girl a lie."

He doodled on, trying to decide how to pose the question.

Sharon drank her juice, waiting for him to ask it.

"Do you think it's possible," he began, "friend to friend, old friends at that, for you to not let her know that I lied to her?"

Sharon shook her head, disgusted with him and all men.

"And you have the nerve to throw up the fact that you and I are old friends. How busted is *that*, Randall?"

"Sharon . . . this is an excellent project. You know it. I know Jet told you all about it, and I know that Desi has, too. We believe in it. Steve and I *are* great writers, just as you say, and once the networks are put on to *Ambitions*, you know there's going to be a fight over who's going to get it."

"If you believed all that, then why did you lie?"

Randall threw the pen down on his desk.

"Dammit, Sharon, I'll do anything to make sure this project has a chance!" he exclaimed. "I wanted Desi for it, and I was willing to do whatever I had to to make sure I got her. The role was written just for her. I know I should have stepped to her straight up about everything, but I didn't. I wasn't being sheisty. I was just making sure the show had a chance."

"I'm not gonna lie for you," Sharon said. "I've had my fill of having the backs of men that have their own agendas going on."

"I'm not asking you to lie. And I'm not just some man, so save whatever beef it is you have with us as a species for the one you really mean it for. I'm an old friend. You know my intentions are good."

Sharon set the empty juice glass on the coffee table.

"No I don't, Randall. I don't know whose intentions are what anymore."

Neither of them said anything. Sharon's other line beeped.

"Hold on," she said, "I've gotta get that."

"Hello?"

"Sharon, it's me. Are you still on the phone?"

"Yeah. Give me a minute. I'll call you right back."

"Okay, but make sure you call me," Desi insisted.

"Yeah, yeah, I will."

Sharon clicked back over.

"That was Desi, wasn't it?" Randall asked.

"You know, Randall," she replied, "I *do* have a life, and the two of you are *not* in the center of it."

"So that wasn't Desi?"

Sharon didn't answer.

"Are you going to tell her the truth?" he asked. "Just do me this one nice, Sharon. I made a mistake. I'll admit that to you. But it's important to me to have Desi believe in me. If you tell her I lied, if you tell her that now, this early in the game, she's never going to believe anything I ever say again."

"You should have thought about that, Randall."

"I am thinking about it," he said with a sigh. "I want to prove to her that I can produce a vehicle that will put her on the top. I want her to know that she can trust me. My ends have good intentions, Sharon, even if the means seem a little fucked up."

Sharon picked up the glass again and drained it dry of the dregs.

"I've gotta go," she said.

"Alright, Sharon. But just do this for me . . . please. My lie didn't hurt anybody. And I truly believe the show is going to be picked up."

"Like I said," she replied, "I've gotta go."

"Bet," he said. "I'm not going to beg you. I'll see you tomorrow."

"You'll see me tomorrow. Peace."

She clicked off.

Randall hung up the phone and stared ahead at the top of the tree outside his office window. The wind was unusually high for a late September Sunday morning, and the branches and leaves swayed and rustled before him.

He wasn't sure what was going to happen or what Sharon would decide to do. It was important to him to not have Desi mistrust him.

Whatever he was going to do, he knew he had to do it soon.

"So what's the deal?"

"In reference to what?" Sharon asked.

Desi was in her paisley silk robe, sitting at her kitchen table, eating a piece of dry wheat toast.

"What did Randall call you for? He was barely off the phone with me before he dialed you up."

"Oh," Sharon replied, "he just had some concerns about tomorrow."

Desi sipped from a glass of pineapple juice.

"Things don't look good, do they?" she asked. "This show really isn't going to be on next season. Come on, you can tell me. I should have known that this was too good to be true."

Sharon let out a short laugh.

"I can't believe this is coming from you," she said. "What happened to all that confidence and faith you were just lecturing to me about the other day? Now here it is, Sunday morning . . . a day that I would imagine your faith would be at its strongest . . . and you're saying things like 'I should have known.'"

Desi picked at her toast.

"Well?" Sharon pressed. "What happened to that immaculate, immutable faith of yours?"

"It's just being tested," Desi said in a small voice. "I never said I was perfect. I still have fear. I just do my best to try to overcome it."

Sharon was stretched out on the couch.

"You don't know from fear. Try living with it every day, having it sit on the back of your neck, constantly slapping you around, pulling your hair and shit, reminding you that it rules you, and not the other way around. I couldn't take it anymore. I found a way to kill my fear. Faith wasn't coming fast enough, so I helped it out a little."

"What are you talking about, Sharon?"

"What do you think?"

Desi stopped picking at her toast.

"You didn't have an abortion, did you?"

"If you mean did I abort the baby? No. If you're asking if I aborted Glen? Well, yes, I'll have to say that's true."

Desi gasped.

"*Sharon!* What happened? Did he ask you to get rid of the baby?"

"No."

"Did he say he didn't want anything to do with you?"

"No, he didn't."

"Well," she said, fishing for possibilities, "did he hit you?"

"Now, come on," Sharon replied. "Who do I look like?"

"I just thought I'd ask," Desi said. "So what happened? What did he do?"

"Nothing," Sharon replied, launching into a tirade. "He came over here with a stupid bouquet of flowers. As long as things are good and just the way he wants it, he shows me all kinds of affection. But the minute his little ecology is thrown slightly out of balance, that's when brothers like him bail."

"So he said he couldn't deal after you told him you were pregnant."

"No. I didn't give him a chance to say anything. I showed him the test results, and then I threw him out."

Desi stared into her pineapple juice, stunned by Sharon's words.

"Is that what you wanted?"

"I don't need him, Dez. I'm a little too ghetto for him in the first place."

"What?! Since when did you become ghetto? You're about as ghetto as I am."

"It doesn't matter. He's gone. Who needs him? Me and my baby will get along just fine."

Sharon kicked at a pillow on the sofa that was right near her feet.

"So you are going to keep the baby?"

"What else would I do with it?"

Desi sipped her juice.

"Glen hasn't tried to call you?" she asked.

"Call me for what? He's not going to call. He's not trying to deal with me anymore now that he knows I'm about to be a burden."

Sharon's eyes misted over in anger.

"Let's stop talking about him," she said. "He's gone, that's it. The end. Back to the lecture at hand."

"Are you sure you're okay?" Desi asked.

"You wanted to know what was up with Randall and the show, am I right?"

"Yes, I did."

"Well," Sharon replied, kicking the pillow off the couch, "everything is going to be fine. We have meetings scheduled for tomorrow, and we're gonna make sure this thing gets done."

"You're not just saying that to placate me, are you?"

Tears were streaking down Sharon's face.

"Do I seem like I care about placating anybody right now?" she asked.

"No."

"Exactly. So leave me alone and concentrate on getting your faith back right. Stop being so quick to get scared again."

Desi smiled.

"Thanks, Sharon. Hey, Sharon."

"What?"

"Why didn't you give Glen a chance to talk?"

Sharon laughed bitterly.

"Talk about what? He's got nothing he can say to me. It's over. And now so am I. Peace out, Dez."

"Okay . . . I'll talk to you later."

Desi clicked her phone off, worried about Sharon.

Sharon leaned down and grabbed the pillow she had kicked off the couch. She clutched it closely to her breast, and burst into tears.

The ringing phone woke her up.

She had been asleep on the couch, still clutching the pillow, for more than three hours.

"Hello?"

"Hello."

"Who is this?" she asked.

"Who do you think?"

"Why do you sound like that?"

"How do you expect me to sound?"

Neither of them said anything.

"Well . . . what do you want?"

"An explanation. You owe me that much at least. You might not think so, but you do. You owe me that."

Sharon sat up, wiping away the moisture that had gathered on the side of her face while she slept.

"I can't do it right now," she answered curtly.

"Then when is a good time?"

"Tomorrow. After six."

"Alright. I'll call you then."

The sound of a dial tone filled Sharon's ear, disturbing her almost as much as the call itself. She clicked off the phone and laid it on the table. She made a move to get up from the couch. The room instantly began to spin.

Sharon gripped the cushions on the couch for balance. She

laid, facedown, burrowing into the cream-colored cloth. Her stomach began to lurch, and an excruciating pain shot through her abdomen.

Terrified, she tried to remain still, hoping the feeling would quickly pass away. The sharp pain intensified, like a bolt of fire inside her loins. Sharon balled up on the couch, bringing her knees close to her chest. The pain continued.

Her knees shook erratically on their own, in a desperate attempt to minimize what she was feeling. When she glanced down and saw the blood between her legs and on the cushion, she picked up the phone and dialed.

"Hello?"

"I need help! Please get over here, I'm bleeding!"

"You're bleeding where? Sharon, where are you bleeding?"

"Between my legs, Dez, between my legs!"

"Oh, God! I'm afraid I won't get over there fast enough. I'm going to call 911 and have them send over an ambulance."

Sharon was openly crying, the pain ripping through her in spasms.

"Just do something, *please!* I'm losing my baby, Dez, aren't I? Tell me, am I losing my baby?"

"Just calm down, Sharon," Desi said. "I'm going to click over and get 911 on the other line."

Sharon squeezed her legs together, trying to blot out the pain. She could feel the blood squishing between her thighs as she rocked to keep the sharp bolts at bay.

"*God forgive me, God forgive me, God forgive me,*" she prayed through tears. "*I know I don't deserve a baby. I know I don't. That's why you're taking this one away.*"

Desi clicked back on the line.

"They're on the way, Sharon," she said. "I'm going to stay on the phone until they get there. Is the bolt locked on your front door?"

"Yes. And it hurts too much for me to get up."

"Well, they're just going to have to break in to get you."

"I don't care. Dez, I think I'm losing my baby."

"You don't know that, Sharon," Desi said. "Things like this happen during pregnancies all the time."

"I did it. I smoked too much weed. I drank wine. I didn't care. I hurt my baby. I killed it, I know."

She rocked on the couch, the blood beneath her soaking deep into the cushion.

"I've fucked up so many times in my life, Dez," she sobbed. "It's like I can't do anything right. Maybe I was trying to kill it the whole time."

"*Ssssshhhh,*" Desi whispered. "Listen to my voice and try to be calm. Everything's going to be just fine, Sharon. Everything's going to be just fine."

When Sharon awoke in the hospital bed, Glen was sitting in a chair beside her. He was wearing a gray sweatsuit. A large welt streaked across his face. He was fast asleep.

She blinked her eyes a few times, looking around for a clock. There was a large white one on the wall before her. It was 7:08 P.M.

"I'm going to miss *60 Minutes,*" she mumbled.

Glen's eyes opened.

He leaned forward, taking her hand. Sharon drew it away.

"You shouldn't have come here."

"Where else would I be?" he asked, his brows knitted in anger. "Don't be stupid, Sharon. You act like this wasn't my baby, too!"

"*Wasn't?*" she whispered, and then began to cry. She turned her face away so that he couldn't see.

Glen, stricken, came around to the other side of the bed. He sat on the edge of the mattress and pulled her into his arms, rocking her gently.

"Honey, I am so sorry that this happened. I am so very sorry."

Sharon was sobbing quietly, her body shaking with every breath and tear.

"Why did you leave me then?" she cried.

Glen's face, above hers, contorted in surprise.

"I never *left* you! You *told* me to leave! You're the one who put me off!"

"I know how you feel about ghetto girls and baby's mamas," she said, her arms hanging limply around his back. "I wasn't about to have you throw that in my face and make me feel worse than I already did."

"I am truly sorry, Sharon," he replied. "I would never do that to you. Sometimes I just talk shit without even realizing what I'm saying."

"You weren't talking shit," she said. "You have a definite opinion about unmarried pregnant women who live under poor conditions."

"Alright," he agreed. "I guess I do, and I know it's wrong. But when I saw those pregnancy tests, Sharon, I was actually happy."

She stopped crying and pushed back from him.

"What do you mean, you were happy? I thought you didn't want any kids."

Glen wiped the tears away from her face.

"I *don't* want kids. At least, I don't *think* I do. Not right now. But when I figured out that you were having mine, something about that made me happy. I don't know. Something about it made me proud."

Sharon turned away, the tears welling up again. She thought about Jackson and his expression in the photograph.

"Sharon . . . Sharon . . ." He pulled her face towards his. "I'm not saying I'm ready for marriage. I don't know yet. That's something I want to be sure about. I'm not saying I want to be a daddy. Before Friday, I would have never even entertained the thought."

Sharon's lip quivered as she watched him speak.

"All I know is that I was happy to know you had something of mine growing inside of you. I don't know if that means I've got a huge ego, or if it means that you're my soulmate. All I know is that it made me happy. That is, until you hit me in the back and gashed me across the face."

Sharon giggled, still sniffling, as she reached up and traced the outline of the welt cutting across his cheek.

"I'm sorry," she whispered. "I was mad."

"Well," he said, pulling her close to him, "now I know to get as far out of the way as possible the next time you're angry. You almost put my eyes out with those pretty pink flowers."

"I'm sorry," she said with a laugh.

"Apology accepted," he replied.

He rubbed her back, part of which was exposed through the flimsy hospital gown. She rested her head against his shoulder, wrapping her arms tightly around his waist.

"I love you, Glen," she whispered, not caring that she said it first.

"I love you, too, Sharon," he answered, his voice just as soft. "Don't scare me like this anymore. You and I, we can get through anything. I don't care what it is. Just don't count me out like that, or decide what it is that I want or that I might do."

"Okay."

"Promise me," he said.

"Alright, I promise."

"Good. We're gonna do this just like we said before. One day at a time."

He kissed her forehead and rubbed her back.

"What *is* this, anyway?" he asked, feeling the small nodule along her lower spine. "I've always felt it, but I've never known exactly what it was."

Sharon didn't answer, the sound of his words fading as she gazed absently over his shoulder, past the doorway, and into the hall.

• • •

"Randall, Sharon's not going to make those meetings tomorrow."

"What do you mean, she can't make them?" he asked. "When I talked to her earlier today, she said she'd be there."

"She's in the hospital. There's no way that she'll be able to come."

Randall was watching *Dateline*. He put the sound on mute.

"What's she doing in the hospital?" he asked. "Is it something serious? Is she going to be alright?"

"She's going to be just fine. But she'll need about three days or so before she can get started with things."

"*Damn!*" Randall exclaimed, concerned for his friend, and also concerned for himself.

Desi was quiet. It had been a long day for her. After meeting Sharon at the hospital, she immediately called Glen. Once he arrived, she came home, changed clothes, and went for a run to clear her mind. She lay across her bed now, fresh from a hot shower. Her nerves were finally relaxed, and she didn't feel like doing or saying anything that would upset them again.

Randall didn't know how to interpret her silence. He wasn't sure if Sharon had told her about his lie. He was too afraid to ask.

"Would you like me to come to the meetings tomorrow?" she asked.

Randall froze.

If he said yes, it might not necessarily be a bad thing. They could bring her to the meetings to show that she had truly signed on. But then she would know that this was the first meeting they were having with the networks.

If he said no, she might be offended. She was new to television, and might not understand what was going on. Randall had been in meetings before where naïve first-timers made egregious mistakes.

"Deal squashers," he called them. He had no idea if Desi was a deal maker, or a deal squasher. He had no idea of how to find out, either, short of letting her participate.

There was far too much for her to have to be briefed on. The more he considered it, the more he saw that it wouldn't work.

"We should be fine, Desi," he said. "Your contract will be coming tomorrow, so I expected you to be tied up with your legal counsel, reviewing it. What I'll do is update you immediately after things occur. Is that alright?"

"Sounds fine," she said.

Inside, he heaved a sigh, relieved that she had apparently not learned anything from Sharon. He debated for a moment whether he should still confess.

When he heard a yawn coming from her end of the phone, he decided not to.

"Do you think it's okay if I send Sharon some flowers?" he asked.

"Sure. That would be nice. She's at the UCLA Medical Center."

Desi yawned again, exhausted.

"Okay. Well, you sound like you need to get some sleep."

"I'm pretty tired," she said.

"Well, I'm going to knock out too, once I take care of a few things. Tomorrow's a big day for all of us."

"Just keep me in the loop."

"I'll do just that, Desi," Randall said. "Have a good night."

"Yeah," Desi said. "You guys better come out of there with a deal tomorrow. Remember, you promised to make me a star!"

"We're giving it one thousand percent."

"That's all I need to hear," she replied. "Goodnight."

Desi clicked off her cordless phone and laid it on the bed beside her. She only intended to lay there for a few moments.

Seconds later, she was in a deep sleep.

ASK, AND YE SHALL DECEIVE

Meredith lay in her sumptuous California king–size bed, with its rich chocolate sheets, chocolate velvet duvet cover, and chocolate shams and pillowcases.

She had been in that very bed with Wade, what seemed like at least a thousand times during their fourteen-year affair, rolling and romping without a thought other than the moment. Now she lay in it alone, nothing to soothe her save the enchanting aroma of the melon candle burning on her nightstand.

And the satisfaction of knowing tomorrow would be the beginning of the end of Anna Weldon.

The phone rang twice, then stopped. Meredith continued to languish, having become accustomed to erratic phones her entire murky life.

She had sent over the proposal for *Native Suns*, which was actually an identical copy of *Ambitions*, untweaked, except that she changed the names of the characters and the restaurant. Had she been the one to present it to NBC, she would have tweaked it considerably, making the issue of idea infringement just a shadow of a question that no one could actually cling to.

But since Anna *insisted* the presentation of the show be left to her and Wade, Meredith decided she'd make it fun. Make it worth Anna's while.

She also sent over the action plan for *Stickies* and *Westwood*, as requested, essentially making Anna's job much easier, yet not being able to take any of the credit for the work.

She rolled around on the sheets, thrilled at the possibilities of the following day. All she wore was a smile, and a big one at that.

"Take *that*, Wade Massey!" she said to the air. "Let's see if your precious little wife can keep you afloat while she's trying to save herself."

MIDLOGUE #3

Alicia sat in the library, surfing the Net.

She searched a superengine called Dogpile, and it gave her several options for looking up phone numbers, personal files, and addresses.

She clicked the one called Bigfoot.

When the page opened up, she typed in her mother's name. The system claimed to be able to locate anybody. It did.

Under her mother's name, there was only one listing. It gave an address, an e-mail address, and a phone number. The phone number was the same as the one Alicia already had.

She jotted down the information, forgetting, in her haste, that she could select Print *from the file option menu, and just as easily have a hard copy of the information.*

That didn't matter much to Alicia. She was so focused on the task ahead that all she could think about was getting to the next step.

She brought up the Web site for MapQuest. Once she punched in her mother's address, MapQuest would give her exact directions, from her door to her mother's, and all the turns in between.

Now all she needed to do was wait.

If things didn't go well by six o'clock the next day, Alicia was determined to take the matter on herself.

Part Four

Decisions

NET NOIR

Devin had a program on his computer called InterPeek, something he had ordered from the Net for $39.95. It claimed to be able to cull from the Web even the most buried information on a person's life. His brother in Brooklyn had forwarded an e-mail advertising the product, and when he read the flashing e-mail script, it piqued his curiosity.

Discover deep dark SECRETS about your relatives, friends, enemies, employers—even your lover or spouse! The NEW InterPeek has it all!!

Devin couldn't resist. He was always curious about his clients and the people he did business with, from their liquidity to their backgrounds. He immediately ordered it, and found it a useful tool when trying to negotiate. It was like having a map to a person's Achilles' heel.

Now the software had a different value. With it, nothing was sacred. It located addresses from just a name, unlisted phone numbers, license plates, driving records, and social security numbers, and allowed for anonymous, untraceable e-mails, criminal background searches, and education verification.

He had already punched in Bettina, but didn't find much of interest with her, other than a few changes of residence. There was nothing drastic, which surprised him. He had expected plenty of secrets, perhaps a criminal record or two, but found none of that.

He'd spent way too much time obsessing over her, he knew, but she'd hurt him, and hurt him bad. It was late, and his wife was already in bed asleep. He didn't want to go to bed, not with her. His longing for Bettina was much too great. He didn't even want to pretend with his wife anymore.

Devin was in love. He knew it. And while he had turned vindictive and cost Bettina her job, he didn't really mean to hurt her. He just wanted her to know how bad she made him feel.

Bored, determined, grasping for any kind of connecting straw, he punched in name after name, all the names he could remember her telling him about as they lay in her bed and talked about their lives.

The query on Randall James produced an interesting dossier, with his double degrees and an annulled marriage that occurred right after high school.

He punched in Dawson Jonas. Jet's record was most impressive. Devin still found it incredible how much information InterPeek provided. Jet had an awful driving record, including two DUIs that had never been made public.

He typed in Steve Karst, first spelling the name Carst, but coming up with someone in Iowa. When he used the letter K, and changed the Steve to Steven, he found him, address, unlisted phone number, and all. He lived on Wilshire in Beverly Hills. He was a white man with blond hair.

Devin wondered if that was who Bettina had gone out with.

Devin had the license plate number of the white man's car, the result of tailing them a good ways down Sepulveda until they turned on Imperial and got on the 105. He crossed-checked the information. It came up as Steven Karst. According to his driving information, he was listed as a white male with blond hair. It was definitely him.

Steve had an incredible listing of assets: properties in London, Prague, Vail, Vancouver, and some twenty-seven others.

There was a Gulfstream parked in a hangar in Denver. There were four other license plate listings for his four other California vehicles, which included a 911, an 850i, a Testarossa, and a Diablo.

Steve obviously had a thing for fast cars and fast women.

Steve was obviously *paid*.

Now he knew why Bettina had bounced. Mr. Karst had much loot, and Devin was beginning to pale in comparison.

The quarter-million-dollar commission he had told her about was now a reality. It was delivered to him on Friday by day's end, via a wire into his private bank account—the result of the deal having been closed that morning. *After* Bettina kicked him out. The reason he originally told her about it was because it was so close at hand. He wanted her to know how liquid he would soon be.

He was not a poor man. He had never been poor. With that money, he had planned to give Bettina the world. But she had ruined it. If she had just waited a few more hours, she would have known that.

Timing was everything.

Devin picked up the phone and dialed Steve's number, not knowing what he would say to him or why he was even making the call. He dialed *67 first, so his number couldn't be displayed if Steve had caller ID. He waited and waited, but no one ever picked up. When it rolled over to voice mail, Devin terminated the call.

Well, at least I have the number, he thought.

He was going to tell Steve about Bettina. How she used men, especially men like him, for money and gain. Steve would leave her alone then. And she could come back to him.

He dialed *67, then punched in Bettina's number.

She answered on the first ring. He immediately hung up.

Perhaps he's there with her.

Devin's mind raced wildly as he imagined what Bettina must be doing with Steve at that moment. He remembered the red satin scarves and the way he used to tie her up to the bed. He had done so just five days earlier, and she had loved it. When he spanked her with the cat-o'-nine-tails, she cried out for more lashings, more pain.

When he imagined her red nails digging deep into Steve's white back, he thought he would go insane.

He got up from the computer, pacing the room. He couldn't leave. It was after midnight, and he would have no explanation to give his wife. He didn't care at this point, but it didn't make any sense to go anywhere when there was nowhere for him to go.

He couldn't go to Bettina's. She had secured parking and controlled access. He would have just ended up spending the night in front of her building, which served no purpose, either, other than to make him seem like a stalker or a trespasser.

He sat down at the computer again, needing something to do with his nervous energy.

InterPeek was still up on his screen.

Out of restlessness, he typed in another name.

Meredith Reynolds.

The screen churned and changed, bringing up a series of linked pages of information. Devin scrolled through them, quickly at first, then slowing down as more things fascinated him.

Somehow, he backed into a different name. Hazel Atkins. Curious, he dug some more.

He kept probing and probing.

The night began to fade into gray.

Bettina's phone rang first thing Monday morning at six.

"Hello?"

There was silence.

"Goodbye," she said.

"*Bettina!*" a voice whispered. "Don't hang up! I really need to talk to you!"

She couldn't believe he had the nerve.

"What do you want, Devin? Or didn't you ruin things enough? I can't believe you have the audacity to call me, after what you did."

"You started it, Bettina. I was in love with you."

"You were in love with the sex. I doubt if you ever even noticed my face. I'm hanging up."

She clicked off the phone.

He called right back.

"Don't *do* this!" he pleaded. "I was, am still, in love with you, and you have no right to say it was all about sex!"

"Devin, you humiliated me in front of everyone at Massey-Weldon. I shared with you confidential information during an intimate moment, and you turned around and used it against me because I decided to break things off."

"I'm sorry. Really . . . I am."

"Too late for sorry. The die is cast."

"What if I have a way for you to humiliate Massey-Weldon back?" he offered.

"Save your bullshit for the next fool. I'm finished."

"Bettina . . . I found out some stuff about Meredith. Some ugly stuff. She once killed a guy."

Bettina was now sitting up in bed. She rubbed her eyes and yawned.

"Devin, you're reaching. Enough is enough. You fucked me over. There's no turning back."

"I have the proof right here. I swear it. I have this software called InterPeek . . . it's what private detectives use to do searches on people. I was bored last night and just started punching in names. Meredith's produced the wildest shit I've ever seen."

Now Bettina was listening.

"How do you know it's Meredith at Massey-Weldon?"

"Because it told me her address, phone number, and current place of employment first. She lives in Hollywood Hills, right?"

"Yeah . . . she does."

Devin realized that he had her attention.

"From there, I just kept digging and digging and digging. She changed her name almost twenty years ago. She used to be Hazel Atkins, from Boston. She has a long-ass juvenile rap sheet. Teen prostitution, petty larceny, grand theft auto."

Bettina's mouth was wide open.

"*Get outta here!*" she whispered. "Are you kidding me? This isn't some ploy just to get back at me some more, is it? Because, if it is, Devin, I'm letting you know right now—"

"No, Bettina. That's what I'm trying to tell you. Last time she was seen as Hazel, her name was on a lease in Hawthorne with an older man. He was, like, thirty years older than her. Some guy named Emerson Cody. Next thing you know, her name was changed. She even got a new social security number."

"Then how can you say she killed somebody?"

"Because, I looked up info on Emerson Cody," Devin said excitedly. "I went all into back issues of newspapers and stuff, and I found this blurb about him being hit over the head with a bottle, and hemorrhaging to death. His car was stolen, and his live-in girlfriend was missing. But I guess he was just some poor white-trash-looking guy who had a drinking problem, so the police never cared to dig into it too deep, and just kind of left it alone."

"Okay, so what makes you say she did it?" Bettina asked.

"With InterPeek, I can pull up information on people living and deceased. I punched in Emerson Cody's name and got his old license plate number from the state of Massachusetts. Then I checked activity on it in California, and found that three months after Emerson's death, the car was bought by a Meredith Reynolds. Two months after that, she sold the car to someone else."

"When did she do her name change?"

"Three months after Emerson's death."

"Oh my God!" Bettina exclaimed.

"I know," Devin replied, happy to have done something to draw her in. "Isn't it wild?"

Bettina had her knees raised. The comforter was pulled up to her chin. She checked the time. It was 6:20 A.M. Soon she'd have to be up and ready for her first day at work. Her feelings were mixed. She expected to be more excited than she was.

"Do you want to use this?" he asked. "I mean, I know it's my fault that you got fired, but I'm sure she probably embarrassed you pretty badly in the process."

"Don't remind me, Devin. That was some low-down shit you pulled."

"I know, Bettina, but I'm crazy about you."

She grew quiet, her lips pressed together.

"You know that, right?" he kept on. "I've never been this way about any woman in my life. Any woman. It's like you've got my soul on lock, or something."

He was so Brooklyn. In a few short days, Bettina had almost forgotten just how Brooklyn he was.

"None of that is relevant now," she responded.

"I finally got my commission," he said.

"Good," she replied. "You should be really happy."

"I'm not happy without you to share it with me."

Bettina leaned her chin against her knees.

"Let me make it up to you for ruining your job."

"How's that?" she said. "There's no way you can ever make up for that."

"Can't we just talk about it? All I think about is you, Bettina. I don't want anything else, if I can't be with you."

She took in a deep breath and stretched out her legs.

"Let's take care of this Meredith thing first," she said. "I want to do to that bitch just what she did to me."

"It's on. You know I'm down for whatever. I can take off work today, if you want."

"Yeah, I want. Give me about three hours. Once I find out she's in the office, I'm going to give her a call."

"Bet," he said, "do you want me to bring the papers I printed out over?"

She thought about it briefly, considering if Devin might actually try to hurt her. She honestly didn't believe he would.

"Alright, you can bring them. Don't come until around eight-thirty. That will give me some time to get up, get dressed, and maybe eat a little something."

"You starting your new job today?" he asked.

"Yeah, I'm supposed to."

"Okay. I'll be there at eight-thirty sharp. I'll bring you some breakfast, that way you won't have to cook."

"Whatever," Bettina said. "And, Devin . . . I'm warning you. Don't try anything stupid when you get over here. This is about Meredith, and that's it."

"Fine," he replied. "Whatever you want."

She hung up the phone, a smile creeping across her face. She finally had her chance to get back at Meredith. Now that bitch would know what it felt like for Bettina to be slighted by her for so many years.

She got up and went to her dresser. She had bought lingerie on Sunday. Not much, just enough to have options and a sufficient amount to get through the week.

She reached in and took out a pair of pink lace panties and a pink lace bra, and headed to the shower.

Devin sat in his office at home, printing out a second set of the data he had gathered on Meredith. His pulse was electric. He couldn't believe that he had gotten Bettina to listen, let alone stay on the phone as long as she did. And now he was actually going over to her house. He walked quietly down the hall, to his bedroom. He tiptoed into the room, trying not to disturb his wife.

She was already awake.

"Where are you going?"

"To take a shower," he mumbled.

She glanced over at the clock beside the bed.

"It's six-thirty. Why are you taking a shower at this hour?"

He stopped walking and stood in front of the bed.

"Because it's Monday morning," he said in a firm tone, "and I have some business to take care of. Do you mind?"

She was silent.

He moved away from the bed, towards the bathroom.

"I'm not stupid, you know." She was angry. "I'm tired of always being left by myself. I may as well be that way for real. It's not like you're ever really here for me and the children."

Devin was already inside, running the shower.

He scrubbed away, humming a melodyless tune. He was so excited about seeing Bettina again. She was even going to let him come into her home.

That InterPeek had been well worth the price. He felt like a real detective. One of those Philip Marlowe, film noir types.

He soaped and rinsed, and rinsed and soaped, thinking of ways to kill the time until he could head to Santa Monica.

Devin walked in with a bag filled with Styrofoam containers of food in one hand, and a folder filled with papers in the other.

Bettina closed the door behind him.

It was the first time they had been in each other's presence since Friday morning. Bettina thought she would loathe him when she saw him. It surprised her to find that she didn't.

Devin wanted to hug her, but he knew his place. He put the bag on the kitchen counter.

"I brought pancakes and sausages. I know how much you love sausage for breakfast."

"Thanks," she said.

She was dressed for work, wearing an ice-blue minisuit.

"You look great," Devin said cautiously.

"Thanks" was again all she replied.

Bettina pulled the containers out of the bag. She opened the lid on the first one. It had pancakes and sausage, just like he said. She put it to the side. She opened the second one. It had grits, eggs, bacon, and biscuits.

"Is this one yours?"

"I got it for both of us. I thought we could share it all."

Bettina opened a kitchen drawer and pulled out two forks. She handed one to him.

"Thanks," he said.

This minimal exchange went on for a few more moments, until Bettina and Devin were sitting beside each other on bar stools at the kitchen counter, eating the food.

He opened the folder, showing her all he'd found.

They lingered for a long time over breakfast and the print-outs, laughing and scheming as they plotted Meredith's undoing.

By the time Bettina checked the clock, it was nine-thirty. She was late for her first day of work. She hadn't even called in. By the time she drove there, it would be something after ten. Her gut instinct told her not to bother going in at all that day. She could call later and tell them something. Then, tomorrow, she could start fresh again.

"I'm not going in," she told Devin.

"Good," he said. "Then let's give ol' girl a call, and get this thing rolling."

Meredith sat listening on the phone as Bettina and Devin ran down their litany of demands.

It had taken Bettina a few moments to track her down. When she was told that Meredith wasn't in the office, Bettina pulled out her Day-Timer, where she kept the numbers of all of Massey-Weldon's people-that-mattered, and called her at home.

Meredith had found their demands funny at first. That is, until Bettina said the name Hazel Atkins. After that, Meredith listened, trying to figure out which way to proceed for her best interests.

"I want at least five months' severance," Bettina said. "One month for every year that I spent with the company. And I want it given to me in a lump sum, not some biweekly disbursement that I've got to wait for in the mail."

"But I'm not due back at the office until tomorrow," Meredith protested.

"You can make a phone call to Human Resources and Payroll right now. They'll approve the severance just on your verbal request. I've seen it done before. Besides, you're the damn head of Entertainment and Development."

They made her put them on hold while she made the call. Meredith wasn't even sure if she could do it. She didn't know if Anna had done anything yet to impact her authority.

Bettina and Devin waited. She came back to them, saying it had been approved.

"I want them to send the check over today," Bettina added.

"Well, why didn't you tell me that when I first spoke to them," Meredith spat. "I don't know if they can cut it that fast."

"Call them back and make it happen," Devin said.

Meredith unhappily obliged.

"The check will be delivered to your residence no later than three o'clock," she said glumly when she clicked back over to them.

"Act like you're happy about it," Bettina said. "Come on . . . show me some enthusiasm!"

"*Your check will be delivered by no later than three, Bettina!*" Meredith said in a singsongy voice.

She wondered how she had gotten to this moment in her life. She'd known it was bound to come up, sooner or later, but she certainly didn't expect it in the form of the foolishness she was enduring now.

"Meredith, what kind of credit card do you have?" Devin asked.

"I beg your pardon?" she returned.

"You heard me," he said. "What kind of credit card do you have?"

She huffed.

"I have more than one. I mainly use my platinum card."

"I have one of those," he said. "The limit on it is stupid, right?"

"Excuse me?"

Bettina laughed.

"Don't worry about it," he replied. "This is what we want you to do. We want you to take out two billboards. One on La Cienega somewhere between Manchester and Wilshire, and another one on Wilshire between Doheny and La Brea. Charge them to your platinum card. You can do it right now on the phone."

"You two are *nuts!*" she screamed. "This whole thing has gone way too far!"

"Fine," Devin said. "I'll just call up my boy in the LAPD, get these papers over to him, and start things rolling. Nice talking to you, Meredith."

"*Wait!*" she exclaimed, wanting to get their demands over with. She had her own drama to create shortly after two o'clock. "What do you want me to put on the billboards?"

"That's more like it," Devin said. "Well, they both should read: 'I'm so sorry for the lies that I told. Bettina, you were the best employee I ever worked with. Love, Meredith Reynolds.' "

"I'm not going to put my last name!" she hissed. "My reputation in this town will be *over!*"

"It will be over one way or another," Bettina replied. "Either by criminal procedure or public acknowledgment of what you did to me. Both are humiliating, but I think you'll find one a little bit more drastic than the other."

Meredith sighed.

"Give me the number," she said.

"Make sure you call them while we're still on the phone," Devin said. He read the phone number to her. "We'll be right here waiting when you click back."

Meredith pulled out her wallet, which was beside the bed where she was sitting. She removed the platinum card and clicked over to the other line.

As she dialed, it occurred to her how rapidly her world was crumbling around her. After this was over, she would have to do something.

Quick.

"That was fun," Devin said, smiling.

"Yes, it was."

Bettina was sitting on her couch, fingering the severance check that had been delivered just moments before.

"Did I make up for getting you fired?" he asked, still sitting at the kitchen counter.

Bettina studied the dollar amount of the check. Twelve thousand five hundred dollars. More than enough to completely replenish her lingerie supply and replace her bed with a new one.

"You did alright," she said.

Devin grinned, thinking he'd finally gotten to her.

Bettina leaned back against the couch.

"I think you'd better be going now," she said.

Devin frowned.

"What's that? I thought we were going to talk."

She glanced over at him. Her left brow was raised.

"Talk about what? There's nothing left for us to talk about. Devin, I'm not changing my mind. Sure, I was wrong in how I handled you Friday morning. I apologize for that. But I made some personal decisions that I'm sticking to. There's no way I'm going to turn back now."

Devin felt his blood begin to churn. He'd done all this for her, and *still* it wasn't enough.

Forget it, he thought. *Ain't no bitch worth being sweated like this.*

Bettina saw the fire in his eyes.

"Remember . . . ," she said, "you told me you wouldn't come over here and start no mess."

He got up from the stool and walked towards the door.

"I'm not about to," he replied sharply. "I just wish I'd known you were gonna pull a stunt like this."

He grabbed the door handle.

"I would have just stayed my ass at home."

He opened the door and slammed it behind him.

"Well," Bettina said, kissing the check, "on behalf of me and this money, we thank your ass . . . most graciously!"

She threw her head back and kicked her feet in the air, giddy with glee.

PITCHING A FIT

"And she has already committed to the show?"

"Yes, she has. If you look through the packet, you will see a signed letter from her stating such."

Randall was speaking now, after Steve had been holding court for more than ten minutes.

They were at the NBC offices in Burbank.

The two executives, Chase Carmichael and Vivian Starks, flipped through the proposal for *Ambitions*. Steve, Randall, and Jet sat patiently, in wait for any further questions.

"This is pretty impressive," said Chase, a twenty-something wunderkind whom Randall knew from his earlier days at the network. Chase was the one who shepherded *Westwood* through when Massey-Weldon originally pitched it, so he was already familiar with Randall and Steve as award-winning writers. "A show like this has the potential to straddle lines and garner several different demographics. It could also give our lineup another dimension. Viewers are open. Look at what happened with *Providence*."

"I agree," Vivian said, studying a page. She was a thirty-three-year-old, tall, intense redhead with a hard-line approach. "It's great you did so much homework on this and addressed it all in your proposal. It makes it that much easier when we take it to the top." She flipped another page. "Out of curiosity," she probed, "why didn't Massey-Weldon get behind this project? I'm assuming you approached them with it."

"We talked to Meredith about it, but she couldn't see its viability," Steve replied. "That was one of the reasons for our departure."

"I see," Vivian said.

"We really believe in this show," Jet said in his booming voice in an attempt to move the dialogue in the room back to a positive note. "And you know these guys. Their writing has already proven itself."

"Oh, I don't question that in the slightest," Chase remarked. "*Westwood* has dominated the Nielsens for two straight years. I don't know what's going to happen to it now that you two have walked."

"You can bet that Wade and Anna are putting together a new team as we speak," Randall said.

Chase stood up, walking around the room. He took a deep breath, then let it out.

"This is where the dilemma arises," he said. "You know you've put us in a precarious position, right?"

Randall said nothing. Jet crossed his legs.

"They're not happy at the top about you guys walking off *Westwood*," Vivian said. "Not happy at all."

"But that's an internal thing," Steve said. "It directly relates to how Massey-Weldon treated us as a writing team."

"But it also affects *this* company's bottom line," Vivian replied. "What was going on over there is really, when you get down to it, of no relevance to us. As a production company, Massey-Weldon provides us with high-quality product, according to the deal we negotiate. We expect them to keep providing that same high-quality product. There was no notice of a change in writers. There was no action plan. It's the new fall season, and there are more episodes that have to be written. We can't afford to lose ratings on a show as popular as *Westwood*."

"Then it's up to Massey-Weldon to maintain that high quality," Jet interjected. "We have our own production company now, and you know from experience that we can provide the high-quality material you've come to expect."

The atmosphere in the room had become thick. Tense.

"So how do we resolve this?" Randall asked. "We're not going back to Massey-Weldon, so that's pretty much the same as saying we'll never write for *Westwood* again."

Chase cleared his throat.

"You can't be so black-and-white about this, Randall," Chase said.

"I don't get what you mean," he replied.

"He means you have to be open," Vivian said. "Is there no way you can work out some kind of deal with Massey-Weldon where they can commission you to write a few more episodes? It would be easier, if new writers are going to come on, for it to happen *after* hiatus, not at the start of the season with just a few episodes in the can. It gives us more time to work out the transition."

"Something like that would come at a serious premium," Steve said.

"Which could only be to your advantage, don't you think?" Chase returned.

"Are you talking about enough episodes for the rest of the year?" Randall asked.

"That would be ideal," Vivian said.

Randall and Steve searched each other's eyes.

"It's not our decision," Steve finally said. "Wade and Anna might not want us anywhere near the project anymore."

"But we have to know that you're at least willing to come to the table," Chase said. "That makes it easier for us to take *Ambitions* in and sell it to the boss. It's better than me and Vivian going in there trying to sell the company on doing a deal with two high-strung Emmy-winning writers who just walked off one of our top-rated shows, leaving us sucking wind."

"It doesn't sound good when you put it like that," Jet commented.

"And we're not high-strung, Chase," Randall said, "and you know it."

"Exactly," Chase replied. "It's all in how we're able to couch it. You see, it's a whole other ball game when we go in there and say, 'Look, Boss. These guys were getting screwed over at Massey-Weldon, but they've got a great work ethic, and they're good guys. They're willing to finish out the season with *Westwood* and give us the rest of the episodes, if Anna and Wade let them. On another note, they've formed their own production company, and they've got this great new show that we want to talk to you about for next year's lineup.'"

"Sounds much better, don't you think?" Vivian commented.

Steve, Randall, and Jet couldn't help but agree.

"So what you're saying is, you're willing to take this project on?" Randall asked, leaning forward in his chair. "You see its viability."

"We definitely see it," Vivian replied.

"And we're willing to go to the top with it," Chase added. "But there's a certain amount of compromise that has to come with it. This can work for you and for us."

"Makes sense," Jet said.

"Good." Chase smiled. "Then we're all in agreement?"

Everyone affirmed.

"Alright. Vivian and I have a meeting at one-thirty with the boss. We're going to talk to him about it. I'm going to spend the next couple of hours reviewing everything in this packet. It's my intention to give him the hard sell."

"Actually," Vivian said to Chase, "Anna and Wade are coming in at two. That would be a good time for us to feel out their position on *Westwood*."

"Good idea," he said. He clapped his hands together. "Alright, guys!" Chase got up from his chair. So did the others. "We'll take this thing to the next level. We'll give it a good fight."

"That's what we want to hear," Randall replied.

"This is making the rounds, right?" Vivian asked.

"Yes," Jet answered. "We have three other meetings scheduled after this one."

"But we're the first." This came from Chase.

It was a rhetorical statement.

"You're the first," Steve replied.

"And if you had your druthers . . . ?" Vivian asked.

"You're good, Vivian," Jet said with a laugh. "We're not crazy enough to answer that question."

They all laughed.

"Alright, guys," Chase said. "Give us until late this afternoon. We'll have some feedback for you, one way or another."

"Great," Jet replied. "We're look forward to hearing from you."

Everyone shook hands. Steve, Randall, and Jet walked out of the room.

They were halfway down the hall before any of them spoke.

"And if you had your druthers?" Steve asked.

"I'd *ruther* be here, wouldn't you?" Randall replied.

Jet put his arms around their shoulders, and they wended their way out of the building.

"And that's the storyline for *Native Suns*."

Anna smiled as she closed the proposal. She had studied it thoroughly the night before, and delivered it with aplomb. She was prim and poised in a red business suit, her lipstick and nails an exact match.

Chase, Vivian, the head of Programming, the Entertainment president, and the president of the company, each with a proposal in front of them, looked on in horror.

"What's wrong?" Anna smiled, observing the uniformity of their expressions.

"Anna," the president demanded, "what's going on here?!"

Wade interrupted.

"This is a new show. We think it'd be great for the network. We're working out the situation with *Westwood*, and we also wanted to talk about this."

The president angrily pounded the table.

"This show was just pitched to me a half an hour ago," he said, flipping through the proposal. "Only it was under a different name. *Ambitions*. It came from your former employees, Randall James and Steve Karst, and their new production company. It's the exact . . . same . . . show. So would somebody *please* tell me what the *hell* is going on?!"

Anna's face flushed to nearly the color of her suit. She stood before them, her lips pressed tight.

"I'm waiting for an explanation," he reiterated.

Anna's pager vibrated. She usually kept it in her purse, but today it was on her hip, in anticipation of a response about new writers.

"Excuse me," she said, and nervously checked it.

Feel stupid yet? was the message she saw.

Anna's fingers trembled as she held the pager in her hand. Wade could tell there was something seriously wrong.

"I think there's been a big mistake," she muttered.

"What we want to know is," Chase said, "does this proposal really belong to you? Randall and Steve said they pitched it to Meredith, but that she turned it down."

"Can I make a quick phone call?" Anna asked, mortified.

"Make it quick," the president said. He turned to Wade. "Now, what are we going to do about this mess with *Westwood?*"

Anna stepped into the hall. She dialed Meredith's number.

"How does it feel to be humiliated, you *bitch,*" Meredith said when she answered the phone.

"How could you *do* this!" Anna demanded. "You made me and Wade look like *idiots* in there!"

"You wanted to present the idea. See what happens when you get what you want?"

"You know you're fired, right?"

"Doesn't matter. I've had my fill of your company, *and* your husband. You're welcome to have both of them back."

She clicked off the phone in Anna's ear.

Anna stood in the hall, so angry she couldn't stop trembling.

The limousine made its way down Pico, back towards the building in Century City.

"So we pay them to write the remaining episodes," Wade said. "There's no way around it. That's the only way that we can save face."

Anna sat beside him, seething.

"What's your take on this, honey?" he pressed.

Anna exhaled sharply.

"You allowed me to put myself in a situation that challenged my entire integrity," she said with gritted teeth. "My integrity, my ethic, that's all I had left."

"Anna, I had no idea that Meredith—"

She slapped him. Hard. The blow sent his face slamming into the seat back behind him.

"If you *ever* utter her name to me again . . . ," she began.

Wade's left cheek bore a visible handprint. He stared at his wife.

"I've endured fourteen years of you fucking her, taking her away on trips, padding her salary, and me turning a blind eye to it," she snarled. "I've borne the brunt of this town's scuttlebutt and ridicule, and smiled in the face of it, supporting you. I will *not* endure a moment more."

"What are you saying, Anna?" Wade asked nervously. "We can work this out."

"There's nothing to work out," she replied flatly. "I want a divorce."

The three of them were riding in Jet's limousine, on their way back to Vast Horizon's offices, when Randall's cell phone rang.

It was Chase.

"What's the good word?" Randall asked.

"Looks like we have a go," Chase said. "Even better. The boss wants to talk about a development deal."

"You're shitting me, right?"

"I shit you not," he replied. "Can you guys be here for a meeting tomorrow morning at ten?"

"We'll be there first thing." Randall grinned. "Good looking out, Chase."

"Good writing, Randall. Keep it up. We'll be expecting it for quite some time. Come ready to talk about more ideas."

"Yeah. You got it. See you tomorrow."

Randall pressed *End* and dropped his jaw.

"What just happened?" Steve asked.

"Yeah," Jet boomed, "what's the skinny?"

"They're talking development deal. They want us back in their offices tomorrow morning at ten o'clock."

"Oh *shit!*" Jet bellowed. He high-fived Steve.

Randall dialed a number on his cell phone.

"Who are you calling?" Steve asked.

"Desi. I told her I would give her an update on things."

Desi sat beside Sharon's hospital bed. She was holding three copies of her contract with Vast Horizons in her lap. Glen, who was sitting in a chair on the other side of Sharon's bed, had already reviewed them.

"So everything looks good," Sharon croaked sleepily.

"I think it's really happening, Sharon," Desi said, beaming. "I'm so excited. I could just jump out of my skin!"

"Goodness," Sharon chuckled, "please, don't do that! I've had enough drama, don't you think?"

"Ha, ha, very funny."

"Funny hell. I'm just not in the mood to see no skin being jumped out of, that's all I'm saying."

"Randall says they have another meeting scheduled tomorrow morning. NBC is talking a development deal. Can you believe that?"

"You know what, Dez?" Sharon commented. "I'm getting to the point where I can believe anything."

Glen snickered. Sharon rolled her eyes at him.

"Did Randall call you at all?" Desi asked.

"No," she said, "but he sent me those flowers yesterday."

She pointed at a large bouquet near the door. Desi smiled.

"He's a nice guy, isn't he?"

"Yeah," Sharon replied. "He's straight." She paused, then said it. "Did he ever come straight with you?"

Desi's brows knitted.

"Come straight with me about what?"

"Did you tell Dez the news?" Glen asked, interrupting. Sharon turned towards him. He cut his eyes at her. Sharon got the message.

"She's only been here for five minutes, Glen. Give me a chance to open my mouth."

"What news?" Desi asked.

Sharon clucked her tongue.

"He just wants you to know that he's moving in with me," she replied with mock annoyance.

"Oh, Glen, that's great!"

Sharon snickered.

"You say that, but you're not the one who's going to be living with him."

Desi shook her head, chuckling.

"Glen, don't mind her. She's probably so happy about this, she can't stand herself. That's what's wrong with her, you know. She can't ever admit when something really makes her happy."

"I know," Glen said. "I'm going to break her out of that."

"You're not breaking me out of anything," Sharon grunted. "I know how to say when I'm happy."

Desi and Glen stared at her, waiting for the words.

"So I'm happy, alright?!" she snapped. "Damn! A person can't even enjoy feeling good without people fucking it up."

Desi laughed.

"Help her, Glen," she said.

"I'll do my best," he replied, his eyes meeting Sharon's.

• • •

Desi was back at home, sitting in her burnished leather armchair.

"Is there something you need to come clean with me about?"

"What do you mean?" Randall asked, sitting on the couch across from her.

The contracts were spread out on the coffee table in front of him.

"Sharon mentioned something about you needing to come clean."

Randall's eyes widened. Desi hadn't signed the contracts yet. He hesitated.

"Aw, *fuck* it." He sighed. "I'm tired of dancing around this thing. If I don't tell you now, it'll be hanging over me forever."

"Tell me what?" she asked with concern.

Randall leaned back against the burnished leather couch, his hands on his head. He took a deep breath, closed his eyes, opened them, then leaned forward, looking her straight in the face.

"I lied to you, Desi," he announced. "I made you think we already had networks on the hook about *Ambitions*. Today was the first day we ever talked to anybody. I can sit here and tell you a million reasons about why I lied, but it doesn't matter. If you don't want to sign, I'll understand."

When he finished, his shoulders slumped, as if a huge burden had been lifted.

Desi was frowning.

"Would you have told me if I hadn't asked?"

"I don't know," he replied honestly. "I had a couple of moments when I almost told you, but I think it was because I was afraid that Sharon would tell you first, not because my conscience was bothering me."

Desi laughed angrily, shaking her head.

"This town is all about the get-over, isn't it?" she said. "Just once, *once*, I would like to meet somebody who wasn't all about pulling a fast one on me."

Randall stared at the floor, then the contracts, then her.

"I wasn't trying to get over on you," he whispered.

"I'll never really know that now, will I?" she replied.

Randall wrestled with his conscience a little more.

As long as I'm in the confessing mode, he thought, *I may as well come clean with it all.*

"There's something else . . . ," he said.

"What?" Desi replied, her voice thick with sarcasm. "You mean there's even more to this little deception of yours?"

Randall sighed heavily.

"Yeah, and it's something that I know is really going to piss you off. Just know that my heart was in the right place, and my intentions were good."

"Cut the bull, Randall," she said, waving her hand, "and just spit it out."

He bit his bottom lip.

"I knew about the job at Neiman Marcus. A friend told me they were about to hire you. I called you the same day because I knew you'd be more open to taking my offer, rather than submitting to theirs."

Desi's eyes instantly welled up as embarrassment washed over her.

"Desi," he said haltingly, "look . . . it's nothing to be ashamed of. We all gotta do what we gotta do to survive."

She stared down at the floor, afraid to bring her hands up to her face, for fear they would ignite a free-flow of tears.

"Desi," he pleaded. "Desi, I . . . I never would have done it if I didn't believe . . ."

Desi sat in the leather chair, burning a blurry hole into the floor. Randall sat across from her on the sofa, unsure of what to do.

"Hand me the contracts," she finally said.

He looked up at her.

"Give them to me," she repeated. "I'm still going to sign them. I want to be a part of this."

"Thank you, Desi," he said with relief.

"Save it, Randall."

He handed her the contracts and a pen.

She took them, flipped to the back page, and put down her signature. She did it two more times. She slid the contracts and pen back in his direction.

"You know, I thought you were one of the good ones," she said.

He looked down, ashamed.

"I always thought so, too," he said in a small voice. "I guess I would have never noticed if it hadn't been for you. I suddenly feel like an enormous ass."

"Well, you should!" she shouted, surprising herself. "Go, Randall."

He gathered up the contracts and put them into his briefcase. He slid the pen into his inside coat pocket. He stood up from the couch.

"I'm really sorry I disappointed you, Desi. I think I've disappointed myself even more."

She said nothing, not even making eye contact with him.

Randall walked towards the door.

"In time, I will show you that I'm not as shallow as you, or I, believe I am." He ran his fingers over the doorknob, his words barely audible. "I'm going to do everything in my power to make this up to you. I am. I always believed in you. That's the truth. I've got you on a pedestal so high . . ."

His words trailed off. Desi allowed herself to look at him. Randall cleared his throat.

"I'll call you after the meeting tomorrow," he said, opening the door.

Desi didn't respond.

As he closed the door behind him, he could see tears streaking down her cheeks.

JUST WHEN YOU THOUGHT IT WAS SAFE

Meredith stood in line at the counter for Northwest. Her ticket was first class, one-way, straight to Seattle.

The bogus résumés had already been printed. The new ID was all set to go.

She glanced down at the ID in her hand on top of her ticket. Elise McRierdon. It had a really nice ring.

She was all set to go. The software industry was booming, and needed good executives. She was a whiz at it already, having personally been in charge of Massey-Weldon's invasion of the Internet.

She ran her left hand across her closely cropped chestnut hair, then checked her watch.

It was 7:28 P.M.

As the line moved forward, Meredith wondered how easy it would be to adjust to all that rain.

She was in the middle of an extensive article in *Macworld* about next-generation servers. She had been underlining text and scribbling furiously in the margins, girding herself up for interview questions to come.

"Hi, Mom," a voice above her said.

Meredith looked up, annoyed.

There stood a tall, dark-haired girl, dressed in baggy overalls and an oversized jean jacket with FUBU emblazoned on the front. Her right eyebrow was pierced, and her hair was a series of short, bedraggled, unraveling twisties peeking from beneath a knitted cap.

She stared down at Meredith with deep, penetrating, hypnotic eyes. Familiar eyes. Where had she seen eyes like that before?

"Excuse me?" Meredith said.

"You heard me, Mom," the girl repeated, the left corner of her mouth raised in a half smirk. When she spoke, Meredith noticed the tongue stud.

She closed her magazine.

"I'm afraid you have me confused with someone else," she replied, glancing nervously about the gate area. Perhaps this was some trick of Anna's. Or that wench Bettina. She'd pulled her share of stunts already.

Meredith shrugged and raised her upturned palms in a gesture of helplessness.

"I'm sorry . . . I can't help you."

To Meredith's alarm, the girl sat in the empty seat beside her.

"Okay . . . I guess it's too soon for the mom thing to work," the girl replied with a sigh, her dark eyes dancing and twinkling. "Maybe we should start on a first-name basis."

The girl held out her hand.

"Hi, Hazel. My name is Alicia. What a pleasure it is to finally meet you . . . *again!* You're a hard person to follow, you know. Especially in this crazy LA traffic. *Whoooooo!*"

Meredith's throat was thick with a chunk of something that felt as big as a brick. She couldn't breathe.

"Now, I *know* you're not just gonna leave my hand hanging like that!" Alicia said in a loud voice.

Heads turned in their direction.

Hesistant, almost afraid, Meredith shook Alicia's hand.

She looked into the eyes.

Tommy Dennis's eyes.

As the Northwest employee began to call for early boarding, all Meredith could hear was the deafening roar of her own blood percolating wildly beneath the surface of her skin.

Bettina dialed Steve's cell phone.

"Hello?" he answered. He sounded as if he were in moving traffic.

"Hi."

"Well, *hey* there!" he replied, pleased to hear her voice.

Bettina, caught off guard by his enthusiasm, began to smile.

"Look . . . ," she began, "I just want to apologize for not making it in today. I don't want you guys to get the idea that I'm not going to take my job at Vast Horizons seriously."

"Apology accepted. Nobody thought that anyway."

"Thank you," she said.

"Guess what, though?" Steve piped. "We had a banner day today. Things went really well, and we've got a meeting tomorrow that might mean big things, Miss Hayes, big things! You'd better be ready to write!"

"Oh, I'm ready," she replied. "I've been waiting for this for what seems like my whole life."

"Good! Then that means you should have a lifetime worth of ideas bottled up and ready to go!"

Bettina chuckled. Steve's effervescence was too contagious for her to resist.

There was a pregnant moment.

She could hear Steve breathing.

"*About the other night* . . . ," they both began.

Bettina laughed. So did Steve.

"You first," he said.

"No, you," she insisted.

"You sure?"

"Positive."

She ran her hand across her curls, waiting for his words.

He took a breath first.

"Look . . . I'm sorry I was so aggressive. I had no business prying into your personal life the way I did."

"*No, no . . .* ," she countered, "I'm just as much to blame. I way overreacted to what you said. I assumed you were being possessive, and I treated you coldly as a result. That was wrong. I had no right to assume you were acting that way." She paused. "You weren't, were you?"

"No," he answered softly. "I merely wanted to know if that guy was serious competition. There I was, enjoying getting to know you, and, all of a sudden, there's another guy in the picture. I needed to know if I should even get my hopes up."

Bettina blushed.

"There's no guy in the picture."

"Good," he replied. "Wait! I'm a guy."

"You're not in the picture yet," she answered, her voice filled with mischief.

"Well . . . ," he coaxed, "is there at least a possibility that I can somehow burst through the frame and work myself in?"

Bettina laughed out loud.

"I think we're getting way ahead of ourselves. Why don't we do this a minute at a time."

Steve chuckled.

"That slow, huh?"

"If I'm not mistaken, Steve Karst, your exact words to me were that you *wanted* to take it slow. You said you'd been hurt a lot in your life, and you weren't having it anymore."

"I did say that, didn't I," he muttered.

"Yes, you did." She laughed.

There was a pause. Bettina could hear the roaring of cars in Steve's background as they whizzed by.

"How do you feel about waffles?" Steve asked.

"Love 'em," Bettina replied.

"Well . . . ," he began, "I haven't had dinner yet, but I was thinking maybe we could hop over to—"

"You've *got* to be kidding!" She laughed, realizing where he was headed. "You want Roscoe's *again?!* Steve, this is ridiculous!"

"Look," he said, "I told you Saturday was my day of rest. It's Monday now, and I want my bird!"

They were both laughing. The sound was a liberating tune that made them both feel free.

"You game?" he asked.

Bettina snickered.

"Yeah . . . I guess I could go for a waffle, some wings, and some greens."

"Great. I'll pick you up in fifteen minutes. I'm not that far away."

Bettina smiled.

"Alright. I'll see you in fifteen minutes."

She was about to click off the phone when she heard his voice calling out.

"Yeah?" she asked.

"Thank you," he said.

"For what?"

"I don't know. Maybe one of these days, together, we'll figure it out."

EPILOGUE

Desi was at home, in her living room, pacing, listening, as the nominations for the Primetime Emmy Awards were being announced on the E! Entertainment channel, live, from the Leonard H. Goldenson Theatre in North Hollywood.

Her entire body was trembling. They had just begun announcing the category of Outstanding Lead Actress in a Drama Series.

"Lorraine Bracco as Dr. Jennifer Melfi in *The Sopranos*, Desi Sheridan as Raquel Easmon in *Ambitions* . . ."

Desi screamed, drowning out the other names that followed.

Her phone immediately began to ring. She snatched it up.

"*I heard it, I heard it!*" she squealed into whoever's ear it was on the other end of the receiver.

"*You heard it?!*" Sharon shouted. "Girl! Can you *believe* this shit! This is some un-*freaking*-believable shit!"

Desi froze in place.

"Are you saying you didn't believe in me? That I shouldn't have gotten the nomination?"

"No, *fool!*" Sharon exclaimed, clutching her tremendous belly. "You know that's not what I'm saying!"

Desi laughed, cutting her eyes at Randall, who was sitting on the couch, catatonic. He'd been that way since somewhere around *Ambitions'* third nomination. The one for Desi made it nomination number six.

The show had already been nominated for Outstanding Drama

Series, Outstanding Writing for a Drama Series (for the "Foolish Hearts" episode, which had been conceived and mostly written by Bettina), Outstanding Directing for a Drama Series, Outstanding Art Direction for a Series (for the "Two-Ton Turkey" Thanksgiving episode), and Outstanding Sound Mixing for a Drama Series (the "Stranded" episode, where Desi's character was stuck in the desert for two days).

"I know that's not what you're saying," Desi squealed with giddy delight. "I'm just teasing. But, Sharon, isn't this incredible?"

"This needs to stop," Sharon said, "before I mess around and deliver this baby. The Oscars were bad enough!"

"Yeah," Desi said, brimming with nervous energy. "I thought I was gonna pop that night. And look at all the scripts and offers that have been coming my way since then. Imagine if I'd won? Imagine how it's going to be with *this* thrown into the mix? I never knew a nomination could be such a powerful thing!"

"You're sitting pretty, Desi Sheridan," Sharon replied. "You're hot property these days."

"God is good," Desi returned. "But don't act like He's not taking good care of you."

Sharon smiled, thinking of her work on Jackson Bennett's film. Everyone wanted to work with her now. The film had experienced critical and commercial success, finally netting Jackson his elusive Oscars: two—one for Directing and one for Screenplay Based on Material Previously Produced or Published—much to Sharon's combined glee and despair. Now that he'd been made official by the recognition of Hollywood gentry, his mouth shot off at ten times its normal rate.

"Being hot property's a serious thing," Sharon said to Desi. "People expect you to be a role model all of a sudden. It's bad enough I can't smoke weed the way I used to anymore."

"You're crazy," Desi replied, "you know that? And you *are* a role model, whether you like it or not. If not for the rest of the world, at least for that baby you got baking in the oven."

"Yeah, yeah," Sharon submitted. "Role model, schmole model.

I'm too old to be having a baby anyway. My baby's gonna come out covered with dust."

Desi broke into laughter.

"*Sharon!* Stop it! You know darn well that you're not old. There are tons of women having their first babies in their thirties and forties. Don't act like this is news. Didn't your friend Rhonda just have a baby? She's thirty-nine."

"Yeah, well . . . ," Sharon muttered. "Her baby came out fine. But Rhonda looks like she's twelve to begin with. I'm forty."

"And you look like you're all of fourteen!" Desi chided. "Stop acting like you're not as happy as everybody knows you are. You're not fooling anybody."

Sharon grinned.

"Yeah . . . I'm happy. But this role model business is going a bit too far. My man's working triple time, trying to be a role model."

"Your man is chief counsel for Vast Horizons," Desi replied. "He can't help but work triple time. And you ought to be happy he's acting like a role model. Isn't that what you want from a husband-to-be?"

Desi glanced over at Randall, who was still catatonic.

"At least your man can form words," she added. "Mine has been in a stupor for the last half hour."

Sharon smiled, rubbing her belly. The almost-vulgar large ring on her left hand glinted with the shift of her fingers.

"Randall did good, Desi. You gotta give him that. Just think, two years ago, we were just getting started with all this. Scared to death about how things were gonna turn out."

Desi was still pacing. Her adrenaline was far too high for her to keep still.

"Actually," she nervously corrected, "two years ago, we weren't even talking about it. All that stuff happened in September. Now here it is, July, *less* than two years, and we've got Emmy nominations up the wazoo. Can you believe it?"

"Yes," Sharon said confidently. "I definitely can."

Desi chuckled.

"Looks like somebody picked themselves up an extra dose of faith since that fateful September."

"Looks like somebody preached it to me long enough that it damn near osmosed itself from her body to mine."

They both laughed.

Desi's phone beeped.

"Hold on, Sharon. This is probably for Randall."

She clicked over.

"Hello?"

"Hey there! Congratulations!"

Desi beamed.

"Congratulations to you, too! How does it feel to finally have your writing acknowledged, and at such a high level, no less?"

Bettina grinned.

"That episode got nominated because you guys acted your butts off," she said.

"Can't have good acting without good writing. I'm glad Randall and Steve have you as a part of the writing team."

"I know. It's like a dream come true. Next stop . . . producing!"

"This has been a dream for us all, Bettina," Desi replied. "Hey, where's Steve?"

"He's right here. Is Randall in the same kind of daze that Steve is?"

"Yeah. He's been slack-jawed and wide-eyed for a good little while."

"You'd think they'd never won Emmys before," Bettina said.

"Wouldn't you? Oh," Desi remembered, "I've got Sharon on the other line."

"Okay, I'll make this quick. Steve wanted me to find out if you guys wanted to meet over at Roscoe's later."

Desi scrunched up her nose.

"I'm more of an M & M's girl, myself."

Desi heard Bettina say something to Steve in the background. She heard Steve mutter something back. Bettina laughed and said something else in return.

"He wants to know if they have fried chicken," she said to Desi. "I told him yes. Is he not the blackest nonblack surfer boy you ever met in your life?"

Desi smiled into the phone.

"We don't mind going to M & M's," Bettina said. "Ask Sharon if she and Glen will meet us there, okay?"

"Sure. I know she'll be down. What time is good?"

"How about . . . say, seven? At the one on Manchester."

"Fine, and seven is perfect," Desi agreed. "We'll see you then."

She clicked back over to Sharon.

"My daughter told me to tell you hi," Sharon droned. "I just blew the dust off of her, now she's headed off to college."

"I'm sorry to keep you on hold so long," Desi chuckled. "That was Bettina. She and Steve want us all to meet them at the M & M's on Manchester."

"What time?"

"Seven. You down?"

"Yeah," Sharon said. "I'll see if I can pull my man away from his role modeling long enough to eat."

"You think Jet and Jackson might want to come?" Desi asked.

"Jet might be hard to track down. I spoke to him last night, and he was supposed to be flying to Chicago this morning. He wanted me to keep him updated on the nominations, so I've been sending him pages and e-mails."

"What about Jackson?"

"He's in Zimbabwe."

"Oh. Well, I guess it's just us chickens eating chicken."

"Fine by me," Sharon said.

"Alright then. See you at seven?"

"With a big ol' belly in front of me, you will."

"Here's to doing something this town didn't think we could!"

Randall had his glass of lemonade iced tea raised in a toast. The food had just arrived, and they had already said grace.

"We jumped in the game," he continued, "and, in our first season, ended up with *six* nominations!"

Sharon, Glen, Bettina, Steve, and Desi all raised their glasses.

"Doesn't matter if we win," Randall said, "although, don't get me wrong, that would be right nice . . ."

Everyone laughed.

"What matters most is that we're in the game, and we're in it *fierce*."

"*Here, here!*" Glen chimed.

"And we're sticking together, thick and thin, through it all," Desi added.

"*Here, here!*" Sharon mimicked, taking a sip of tea.

"And this is just the beginning for Vast Horizons," Bettina said. "Our next goal . . . *world domination!*"

"*Here, here!*" they all agreed.

All eyes fixed on Steve, who was aggressively digging into his macaroni and cheese. They waited for him to offer up a toast.

Steve felt the burning eyes and glanced up from his food.

"Hey . . . how come nobody ever told me about this place?" he asked, his cheeks stuffed full of macaroni.

The table erupted in laughter.

"Come on, Steve," Bettina said, nudging him. "Be serious for a minute. You're not even supposed to be eating just yet."

"Alright, alright," he managed, swallowing. He lifted his glass of lemonade.

"To a job well done. There's no better formula for success than a lot of faith, and a little ambition."

"Amen!" Desi and Sharon piped.

"Now," Steve continued, "let's dispense with all this chitter-chatter. There's a bird on this plate that's been calling my name."

Randall clapped him on the back, as everyone dove into their food and the eating began.

ACKNOWLEDGMENTS

I give all glory to God, for loving me, ever changing me for the better, and having the patience to walk with me, and often carry me, as I make my journey through this maze of life. Without Him, I would be lost. Through Him, I am becoming all that I could, and should, be.

Extra Special Thanks to:

My wonderful, amazing mother, *Lillie B. Files,* who has evolved into so many things for me—my counselor, my sounding board, my inspiration, my friend.

My brother, *Arthur James Files, Jr.,* for teaching me so much so early in my life.

Michael Cory Davis, my confidante, my soldier, my friend. Thank you for walking with me and fighting for me. I appreciate all that you have done, and all that we have gone through together. As a result of knowing you, my life has been forever changed. You have a magnificent spirit, and I know that you are destined for many things positive and great.

Victoria Christopher Murray, my dear, dear sister-in-spirit and friend. You are a reminder to me that God is real and has purpose in all that He does. Your presence in my life is a miracle. Vickilita, I thank Him for you every day.

Eric Jerome Dickey. What would I do without you? You are one of the kindest people I have ever met in my life. Your generosity of spirit would fill up a stadium. You make me laugh, you listen, you encourage, and you refuse to watch me settle for less in anything that I do. Thank you for challenging me, harassing me to write, and being a blessing to my world with every breath that you take.

R. M. Johnson. You are, indeed, the most incredible person and THE kindest man—so calm, so centered, so considerate. You are Peace in Pants. To borrow from Billy Joel, *"he comes to me when I'm feeling down . . . inspires me, without a sound."* Meeting you was something bigger than I could have ever imagined.

Jacquatte Rolle. Amazing how we always reconnect, isn't it? That's because our souls are bound, my sister. My love for you is infinite.

Courtney Rolle. You will see me very soon. I may seem absent, but you are very much present in my heart.

Bryan Keith Ayer. For just being Beav.

The Brackett Family—Eric, Sharlyn Simon, Charles, Ted, Jim, Bobby (Percy), Sallye Cooper Brackett, Shunda, Cheric, and Charleston (P-nut) Brackett, Charla and Chauncey Shines, Curtis and Debra Cooper and kids, Daetrick Brackett, Wanda in Orlando. The Files Family—Louis and family, Charlestine (Dot) and Sam Carter and family, Ella Mae, Betty Jean and family, Rural (Bumpsy) Files and family, Lura (Niney) and family, Inez Files and family, Cleveland (Benny) in Natchez, the Files clan in Birmingham, Alabama, and any other Files (there are far too many to mention) that I may have forgotten, you are remembered in spirit.

The Davis family from Brooklyn—Chez (what a warm and beautiful spirit you are!), Seabert, Kishane and Trish, Nicole, and the great and wonderful Doris Rattigan.

Shirley Ann Mausby and family, Douglas White (you and Lynn and I will hang out eventually, I promise!), Mary and Willie Davis in Atlanta, Willie Mae Baltimore, Annie Pearl Nixon and family, Shara, Walter, and Alicia (Nikki) Dickerson and the rest of the May family, Shirley Brackett and John, Harry C. Douglas, Jr., Rachel Douglas, Pamela O. Douglas, and Willie Mae Douglas and Harry Douglas, Sr., the Capers, Prince, and Fenderson families, my newfound family in Southern California (Patsy Davis and the rest of the families), my Boston family the Essexes (Dawn, Petey, Sandra, Michelle, Addie Belle, Bo, and everybody), all branches of the Rolle family, Lisa "Brownie" Brown and her sister Kim and family, Suzette Webb and family, R. Malcolm Jones and family, Shonda Cheekes and family, Yvette Hayward and family, Karla Greene, Dominique Dickey, Pat Houser and family, Brenda Alexander and family, Brenda Williams and family, Frank Jenkins and family, Sherlina Washington and family, the Brown family in Hollywood, Florida, Rhonda Ware and family, Mommy German and Ed, Vernette and the rest of the Mayweather family, Bernadette Andrews and family (wherever you are), Andrea and Patrick and all the old crew, Bruce McCrear and all my peeps in Birmingham, Keith and JoAnn Davis and family, Eric Warmack and family, Andy and Mary Gregory and family, all my old friends from the Kinder-Care days, Blake and Terry and the crew in L.A., Carol Ozemhoya, Kim Bondy, Bo Griffin, Olive Salih, and Alison Tomlinson, Pamela Crockett and family, Leroy Baylor, Michel Marriott, David Aronberg, Kevin Cowan, Abdul Giwa, Jr., M.D., and family, Louis Oliver, Bryonn Rolly Bains (we MUST see each other soon, this is ridiculous!), my live twin, Theresa Coffer and Antoine Coffer of Afrocentric Books, (I luh y'all . . . it's time we got together again and did something crazy and fun), Troy, Rejeana, and Jalen Kobe Mathis, Eric Saunders, Lee Eric Smith, Rod Crouther, Dana, Kristi, Madison and Shelby Lee, Rodney Lee and family, Cyndi, Dionne, Darryl Ranard Nobles, Marty and Monique Berg and Dinky (Eliane), Linda Ferguson in L.A., and Lance Powell in New York.

All my friends who weather the entertainment industry (books, film, TV, music) with panache and aplomb: Shaun Robinson (girl, the glazed walnut prawns at Eurochow! My goodness!), Sherri Sneed (thank you for all the wisdom and knowledge you have so willingly shared with me), Dawnn Lewis (you have truly been a blessing in my life), LaJoyce Brookshire (love ya much) and family, Kimberla Lawson Roby (my sister-in-spirit) and family, E. Lynn Harris (thank you for making this walk so much easier for all of us), Sheneska Jackson (can't wait to hang out with you now that I'm in Cali), Van Whitfield (the phantom—I don't get to talk to you nearly enough), Colin Channer (I cannot say enough about you . . . you are a mind-reader, a side-splitter, an anecdote-teller without parallel, and I'm so happy to say that I can call you my family), Timm McCann (we go way back, don't we?), Omar Tyree, Yolanda Joe, Franklin White, Blair S. Walker, Steven Barnes and Tananarive Due, Patrice Gaines, Tawanna Butler, Kiki Henson in St. Louis, David Haynes, Lisa Saxton, Sharony Andrews, Christine Saunders, Jackie Jacobs, all my old friends over at Warner Books (Taura, Doris, Cheryl, Michelle, and Cassandra), Caryn Karmatz-Rudy and Anita Diggs (you are both two truly kind individuals), Larry Kirshbaum (for being one of the first people to believe in me), Dr. Joseph Marshall, Jr., Jill Tracey, B.J. Barry, Raj, Nanci Thomas, and all the other authors, artists, and creative spirits out there striving to make it through.

A special shout-out to my renewed friendship with Alton "Butter"

McLean, music exec extraordinaire. While the means in which we met were somewhat shady (haha), now there's nothing but bright light shining through. I know in you I have a friend indeed. We now truly know the meaning of "keeping it real"!

To all the bookstores who've had my back: The Florida Connection—Janet at Tenaj, Jackie at Montsho, Felecia at Books for Thought, Naseem at Nefertiti, D.C. at Afro-n-Books-n-Things, and Akbar at Pyramid; Shondalon and Sundyata at RaMin Books in New Jersey, Desiree at Afrocentric in Chicago, Shelly and David Jones of Mirror Images Books and Toys in Charleston, S.C., Jim at Zahra's in L.A., James at Eso Won in L.A., Faye and Cassandra at Sisterspace in D.C., and anyone else I forgot to mention.

Much thanks to the Sorors of Alpha Kappa Alpha Sorority, Inc., and all the organizations and book clubs that have shown me so much support.

Thanks to my editor Dominick Anfuso, to Catherine Hurst for all her support, and to Dawn Daniels and Imar Hutchins.

To Shannon Jackson, for making my life so much easier.

To my four-footed furry joys—my boopies, the Reco-Fivises (my dogs)—Milo, Lola, and Brooklyn (and Telly in Florida). If only you could talk, type, and take dictation. What a wonderful world this would be!

If I forgot anybody, please forgive me. It's because my brain is too jumbled, but know that you are present and acknowledged in spirit.

And to the readers, none of this would be possible without you. Love infinite.